'I'm dead serious. We're going to handle the takeover of General Motors.'

'Holy shit!' Lee put his hot dog down on the grass and stood up.

'Before we go any further, let me tell you guys that I had full discretion in picking anybody I wanted. This is going to take an enormous amount of work and time. You both will have available just about twenty-four hours a day, and you can forget about any private social life for a while. But since you're both bachelors, I figured you won't mind the hours and that you'd like to be in on this caper. If either of you wants out, you're free to say so right now.'

Dave Hill was shaking his head slowly. 'Are you kidding? This will be the hottest thing in the business, not to mention the most fun.'

Peter Tanous
&
Paul Rubinstein

THE PETRODOLLAR TAKEOVER

Arrow Books

Arrow Books Limited
3 Fitzroy Square, London W1

An imprint of the Hutchinson Publishing Group

London Melbourne Sydney Auckland
Wellington Johannesburg and agencies
throughout the world

First published by André Deutsch Ltd in 1976
Arrow edition 1977
Reprinted 1978
© P. Tanous and P. Rubinstein 1975

Made and printed in Great Britain
by The Anchor Press Ltd
Tiptree, Essex

ISBN 0 09 915150 2

FOR OUR GANG:
Joy, Ann, Chris, Helene
Jason, Kim and Willy

Acknowledgments

WE would like to express our thanks for his invaluable assistance, enormous patience, moral support, pithy suggestions, and charming company to Theron Raines. Without him we never could have done it.

We also extend heartfelt thanks for the cordial and prompt help we received from Faisal Al-Sowayel, Saud Al-Sowayel, Edmund J. Desmond, George A. Francis, Michele Hoffmann, Adam Holender, Leila Jolly, Phoebe Loftus, Ruth Quinn, Harold G. Reise, and George A. Saks.

A special tribute to Stefanie Xenakis whose extraordinary typing skills and incisive comments were of particular value to us.

Prologue

COLONEL MOHAMMED FALEH, commander of the 2nd Armored Battalion, Royal Saudi Arabian Army, opened the hatch of his French-made AMX-30 tank and stood up, adjusting his binoculars to see beyond the dust and smoke immediately in front of his position. The tank was parallel to the beach, but parked on the lee side of a dune that concealed it from the enemy. He knew after one sweep of his glasses that the coordinated attack he had mounted in high hopes of driving the Iranian invaders into the Persian Gulf had once again failed.

Although the Iranian detachment was small in number, it was equipped with the new General Motors M-85 main battle tanks, well dug-in within a perimeter that allowed them enough room to obtain supplies and reinforcements every night under the cover of darkness. The perimeter, which was expanding by a few hundred yards daily, was beginning to look more and more dangerous to Faleh.

As he reached wearily down for the radio mike to give the order to retire, he saw one of his tanks, obviously damaged, lurch between two dunes about fifty yards to his right, heading away from the enemy position. The engine was making an unnatural whine, the hatch was open, and he could see the commander's head sticking up in front of the hatch cover. Two Iranian M-85's hove into view in hot pursuit. The Saudi tank stopped, its gun traversing and firing, and Faleh distinctly saw the shell bounce off the heavy armor of the M-85 just as the Iranian's gun roared in reply. In the next instant, the tank commander's upper torso, two arms, a head, and a trunk hurtled into the air and landed, twitching, twenty yards away. Then a bright orange sheet of flame erupted from the Saudi tank, the M-85's turned away and clanked back down the hill, and Faleh heard the muffled explosion of the unused ammunition in the burning tank.

The skirmish was in its second week. Iranian forces had crossed the Persian Gulf and landed in the Saudi Arabian desert near the town of Al Jubayl. Saudi forces had been lax about their state of combat readiness since the peaceful resolution of the Arab-Israeli conflict some years before. The Iranians were only at battalion strength, and the dispute did not appear serious at the outset. Iran and Saudi Arabia could not agree on drilling rights in the Gulf, and when the Saudis massed troops and armament along the coast near Al Jubayl, the brash young Shah of Iran determined that this was a hostile act. Al Jubayl's small population contained a number of Iranian fishermen, and using this as a pretext, the Iranians launched a small "protection force."

"Get the military command in Riyadh on the radio," Faleh shouted. The connection was made instantly. "Ahmed, this is Faleh. We have just lost another tank."

"That is the fourth today."

"I do not need to be reminded of that," Faleh snapped. "You know as well as I do that our tanks are inferior."

"I know, I know, Faleh," sighed the voice from Riyadh. "I will speak with the Minister of Defense."

"Hurry."

"I will. He knows. He will understand."

"Inshalla."

"Inshalla."

Abdulaziz Khalif finished assembling the papers he would need for his appointment with the Prime Minister. As Saudi Arabia's Minister of Defense, he did not need to be reminded of the Iranian forces' superior equipment. For weeks, the daily casualty reports and requisitions for armor replacements had been flooding across his desk. He glanced at his solid gold Rolex watch. He had a half hour to spare. None of the tension left his body as he sat back in the heavy armchair behind his desk. The military situation that confronted him had worn down his nerves too far for any relaxation. His eyes fell on one of the framed photographs at the corner of a nearby table. It was a picture of himself taken at his graduation from the Royal Military College at Sandhurst, the famous military school that produces Britain's finest army officers. He smiled as he recalled the grudging reactions of his British classmates and instructors when young Khalif, whose dark skin contrasted noticeably with the pallid complexions of his peers, was graduated at the head of his class, with an overall academic achievement ranking third in Sandhurst's history since its founding in 1802.

But that had been twenty years ago, and Khalif's present problem was unlike any of those he had so deftly mastered at the Royal Military College. Although not particularly religious, he repeated to himself his favorite quotation from the Koran:

"God obligeth no man to more than he hath given him the ability to perform."

God had given Abdulaziz Khalif a great deal of ability, so much that he had been named Minister of Defense at the age of thirty-seven. But now he needed tanks, far better tanks than those he had, or all his foregoing success could be brought to ruin.

A short while later, Khalif entered the ornate offices of the aging Prime Minister, who had held his post since his appointment during the last year of the reign of the late King Faisal. The twenty-five-foot ceilings, Louis XV furniture, and gold-finished woodwork were more reminiscent of Versailles than Riyadh and reflected the tastes of an old man who had become accustomed to the finest European art and design of the last five centuries and who could

11

afford to indulge his tastes. The Prime Minister, draped in a long, white *mishlah* finished in gold braid, sat behind his antique desk in the long, wide room. Every inch of the floor was covered with Oriental rugs, mostly Isfahans and Nains whose uniquely beautiful intricate patterns made the Prime Minister willing to ignore their Iranian origin. Khalif took a seat in one of the armchairs facing the Prime Minister's desk, but at a distance of nearly twenty feet from it. He was also wearing a *mishlah*, the preferred dress for men in Saudi Arabia, although he often went to work at the ministry in his general's uniform.

The coffee server appeared, armed with a long beaked, brass coffee pot and several small cups without handles. He poured a half cup for the Prime Minister and silently handed it to him. As the Prime Minister drank, the server approached Khalif and poured another cup. The aroma of the light-brown mixture of coffee and spicy cardamon filled Khalif's nostrils, and he drank the liquid down in one gulp. He handed the cup back to the server, shaking it in the traditional manner to indicate that he wanted no more.

The Prime Minister looked up from the papers on his desk. *"Na'am."*

"Your Excellency, we have lost another four tanks today." Khalif spoke calmly, just above a whisper.

"Go on, Khalif," the Prime Minister said sympathetically.

"Our men are brave and well trained. But our equipment is no match for the Iranians! The American tanks are far superior."

"The Iranians are testing us, Khalif. They wish to see if they can hope to win a war against us."

"I agree, Your Excellency. And there is more bad news. According to our intelligence, the M-85 tanks, which the Iranians currently use, will be superseded by a new model, the M-90, at the end of this year. That is barely nine months away."

12

"I am also aware of that."

"Then you know, sir, that we cannot buy these tanks. The Iranians negotiated an exclusive supply deal with the American manufacturer two years ago. We did not care at the time, as the arrangement was similar to the arms-for-oil deal we made with the French. But our French tanks' armor and firepower have proven inadequate."

The sweat trickled down Khalif's forehead. He wondered how many more of his men had died while he calmly explained the problem to the Prime Minister. And did this man fully comprehend the enormity of what Khalif was saying?

"You are worried, Khalif."

"I am, sir. I fear the Iranians may start an unrestricted war with us when they have the new tanks. My men do not have a chance. They are dying . . ."

"Khalif!" The Prime Minister raised his voice to remind the younger man that he was becoming unnecessarily emotional. Then he gave him a look of sympathy and understanding. "I know you are concerned for your men and for your country."

"That is my only concern."

Both men sat silently for a few seconds. Then the Prime Minister looked at Khalif and spoke: "I will now reveal a secret to you which you will repeat to no one."

Abdulaziz Khalif understood the meaning and the consequence of a breach of trust.

"Abdulaziz," the Prime Minister spoke, as if to a son. "Are you aware of who manufactures the tanks and military equipment the enemy uses?"

Khalif thought for a moment, a little puzzled by the question. "They are supplied from many countries, but the manufacturer of those deadly tanks is General Motors."

"That is correct, my son," the Prime Minister said, "and by the end of this year, Saudi Arabia will own General Motors."

Chapter 1

JOHN HADDAD put down the report he had been reading and picked up the phone on the first buzz. His secretary informed him that Marwan Suwadi, of the Saudi Arabian Consulate in New York, was on the line. Marwan had been a classmate of John's at Harvard.

"John, Marwan here."

Marwan's usually high-pitched voice sounded strained, as though he were under pressure. They had been more than acquaintances but less than close friends at college, primarily because John was unable to take Marwan seriously. A practical joker, Marwan was incessantly in search of diversion and entertainment, always willing to pick up the check. It was not that he liked to throw his money around, but Marwan coveted social acceptance by his American friends, and if it had to be bought, he could afford the price.

Over the past few weeks, Marwan had been inviting John to various diplomatic functions at the Consulate, and although each occasion seemed to have some official purpose, John felt that he was being paraded around for review. Marwan had pointedly introduced him to various functionaries, but no reason was ever given for the unusual attention.

"Hello, Marwan, have you recovered from the other night?"

"No . . . I mean, yes, but I must see you tonight. Are you free for dinner?"

"Listen, I'm really not up to another one of those receptions . . ."

Marwan interrupted. "No, no, just the two of us. It's something important, serious. Can you make it?"

"Well, if it's urgent, I'll make it."

"Good! You won't regret it, I promise. Are you planning to see Charlotte soon? Don't forget to give her my best."

"Yeah, I'm planning a weekend with her in Washington."

John was going to Washington Friday evening to spend the weekend with Charlotte Grogan as he had many times before. He did have one social commitment there—to meet Congressman Samuel Jennings of Michigan, the Chairman of the House Foreign Affairs Committee, who was an old friend of Charlotte and her father.

"Is Gertrude's OK with you for tonight?"

"It's fine if you're paying! I can walk there from my apartment. How about seven thirty?"

"Perfect, John. I'll see you then."

Marwan sounded really serious, and John knew him well enough to know that he was not serious unless he absolutely had to be. The Suwadi family were members of one of the leading Saudi Arabian tribes. Sunnite Moslems, as were most Saudi Arabians, they were also Wahabis, descendants of the founders of the puritanical movement of the eighteenth century. The Suwadis were distantly related to the Saud family of the Nejd, the vast plateau region of Central Arabia. Ibn Saud, the great Wahabi leader, had conquered the Nejd from the Turks in the early part of the twentieth century, and there had been many Suwadis at his side during the battles that gave birth to modern Saudi Arabia. This historical background lodged the Suwadis unshakably among the first families in the kingdom, both in wealth and in political influence.

Despite his frivolous antics, Marwan's behavior belied a strong urge to succeed in his own right. He didn't mind being rich, but inherited wealth did not command the respect for personal achievement that Marwan longed to earn for himself. Until he found the right opportunity, and himself in the process, he worked at the Saudi Arabian Consulate in New York, a job that was largely honorific, and like so much else in Marwan's life, it had been given to him because of his family connections. His serious ambitions were known to no one but himself, while in the eyes of his friends, he remained an amiable, generous playboy.

15

Back at Harvard there had been an incident when Marwan, who had kept a string of polo ponies in Cambridge, galloped down tiny, narrow Copperthwaite Street and into the main Dunster House courtyard, his Arab robes flowing behind him, ullulating the high-pitched desert Arab war cry. It still took some adjustment on John's part to believe that Marwan might have some serious business to discuss. Well, he would find out soon enough. Besides, Gertrude's was a terrific French restaurant, despite the name, and it was always fun to eat there. In the meantime, there was work to be done, and John went back to the business of a young executive in the corporate finance department of Thompson, Caldwell and Company.

John walked out of the Fidelity Building into a blinding late afternoon sun. He reached into an inside pocket for his sunglasses and put them on. The Fidelity Building, in midtown Manhattan, was an unusual place for a stockbroker's main offices to be located. But then more of the traditional, old-line investment firms were moving away from Wall Street these days. "We'd rather be nearer to our clients than to our competitors" was the phrase used by the humorless senior partner in response to a *Wall Street Journal* reporter's question about the move.

The rush-hour traffic was at a standstill as John continued the easy stroll to his East Sixty-seventh Street apartment. He walked home every day, weather permitting, and was thankful that he could avoid the uncertain and unsettling ride in the filthy Lexington Avenue Subway from Wall Street. How many New Yorkers were lucky enough to be able to walk to work?

It was a slow week. The kind where minutes seem like hours and Wednesday feels as if it ought to be Friday. John recalled other times when he had left the office exhausted, his work still unfinished. Back at home, he would collapse into a comfortable armchair and mentally retrace all of the day's events and decisions, taking pleasure from the

16

thoughts of what he had accomplished. He enjoyed hard work and thrived on pressure, but there had been little work and no pressure lately.

At thirty-two, John Haddad was trim and physically fit. Although not handsome, he had an undeniable charm, or so he had been told by several female friends whose opinions meant something to him. He stood just under six feet tall, and his dark hair and complexion reflected his grandparents' Syrian origin.

John's grandparents on his father's side had emigrated to the United States from Syria some fifty years earlier while his father was still a boy. They established themselves in Brooklyn, near Atlantic Avenue, where a large Arab colony still existed. John's grandfather was a merchant, and with some borrowed money from generous relatives, he opened a small shoe store. The business was profitable enough to sustain them without luxury, but the Haddads could not provide an expensive education for their son, Michael. The latter, lacking any special motivation for higher learning, dropped out of New York University after two years, and joined the family business. He soon married Helen Maloof, the beautiful daughter of a Lebanese merchant, who had prospered in the wholesale fabrics business. The wedding took place in the Maronite Catholic church in Brooklyn Heights and was a heralded event in the local community. Michael Haddad had a flair for business, and used it to manage the shoe store for his aging father. Helen, whose talents were more intellectual and artistic, remained at home.

By the time John Haddad was born, there were three shoe stores in Brooklyn bearing the Haddad name. But there were never any more than three, and John felt his father's disappointment, even as a child. Michael Haddad was not at all ashamed of the fact that he wanted to be rich. But he failed.

As John grew older, he developed his father's merchant instincts and was influenced by his mother's intellect and sensitivity. He was an only child, and his father nurtured a deep conviction that John would fulfill his own missed ambitions. To this end, money was set aside to assure that he would have a good education, prep school, college, even graduate school. That was the way it was in America, especially on the East Coast. John had joined Thompson, Caldwell seven years earlier, upon graduation with honors from Georgetown Law School and, having completed the traditional training program, began to work in the firm's Corporate Finance Department.

At the end of the summer following his second year of law school, John decided that he would rather be an investment banker than a lawyer. He had worked the previous summer at Davis, Polk and Wardwell, one of the top Wall Street law firms. The second summer, he snared a job at the brokerage firm of Smith, Barney and Co. One of his first assignments, as a summer fill-in, was to assist the manager of the corporate finance department in concluding the last delicate steps of closing a pending deal. To John, investment bankers were a rare species, hailing from places like London or Zurich, who did some sort of mysterious trickery in finance for someone else's benefit. He was working at a stockbrokerage firm. But when he referred to himself—and the manager by implication—as a stockbroker, all hell broke loose.

"Young man," said the crusty old manager, "the *stock-brokers* are upstairs in the boardroom talking to their wives on the phone, pretending to do business, and shooting rubber bands at each other to pass the time. *We* are investment bankers negotiating a creative capital investment. Don't you ever forget that again!"

Now he knew. Investment bankers are people who work in the corporate finance departments of the brokerage firms, devising ways by which large and small companies can raise money.

Besides the obvious ways of borrowing from banks and floating issues of stock to the public, he soon discovered that there were myriad other avenues. The enormous pools of money that slosh around in the hands of giant insurance companies, union pension funds, company pension funds, private groups of large investors and others are always looking for a profitable home. At the same time, the capital requirements of industry and commerce are constantly expanding. John found that the investment bankers stood squarely between this enormous supply and this constant demand. They could guide the flow of money into the most promising enterprises. But their role was much more than that of guides. They sat as judges, hearing the pleas of supplicants for money mustering their arguments in favor of their projects. Invariably, as the screening process functioned, the investment bankers turned down many more than they accepted, and this was a manifestation of power not found in most professional fields. On the money supply side, John met some of the men who controlled the huge funds of large institutions, and learned how to deal with them. It was a taste of power far superior to the high influence promised by his mentors at law school as the reward for pursuing a legal career. To the investment bankers, lawyers were merely employees hired to do the detail work generated by their own successful combinations of new capital structures.

While being careful to cultivate the right people who might be helpful to him in the future, John found himself packaging new varieties of stocks, bonds, and warrants calculated to satisfy the needs and sometimes the egos of his investors and his entrepreneurs. When the summer had ended and he had to leave for the last year of law school, he knew he would be back to stay.

After he finished law school, John headed for New York, where he was interviewed by three firms: Morgan, Stanley; Smith, Barney; and Thompson, Caldwell. All three offered him jobs, but he chose Thompson, Caldwell, based on a hint of early responsibility and officership, as well as a salary that, at twenty-three thousand dollars a year to start, was three thousand better than the other two had offered.

He did have one concern. Unlike the other two firms he interviewed, Thompson, Caldwell had a whispered reputation for snobbery to the point of discrimination. John asked one of his interviewers if it were true that the firm preferred certain types of backgrounds, notably WASP's, over others. The executive, startled at John's naïve candor, replied indignantly that all employees of Thompson, Caldwell were evaluated on merit and any rumor to the contrary was just malicious gossip.

The hint of rapid promotion was no small part of the attractiveness of Thompson, Caldwell's offer because, as John knew very well, the officers of Wall Street firms are given the opportunity to acquire stock in the firm at highly favorable terms. He saw this as a tangible way to build some capital for himself early in his career, something that his father had never been able to achieve. And, best of all, Thompson, Caldwell was one of a handful of Wall Street firms whose own shares were traded on the New York Stock Exchange. John felt that once he had become a stockholder, he would enjoy seeing the value of his holdings printed in the paper every morning.

Thompson, Caldwell was an old-line, well-respected New York investment banking and brokerage firm with an impressive list of corporate clients, an excellent research department that provided detailed investment information to large institutions such as banks, mutual funds, and insurance companies, advising them on stock purchases, and a one-hundred-twenty-year-old tradition in the business. John Haddad moved up quickly in the firm and was assigned to work with a vice-president in the mergers and acquisitions department. It was in this department that mergers between companies were dreamed up or a plan for a large company to take over a smaller one was devised and executed. He worked tirelessly on relatively boring statistical comparisons of different companies in the same industry, a task traditionally performed—and hated—by junior members of the corporate finance department. But John did his work with such willingness that he was quickly singled out for better jobs.

After only three three years at the firm, John Haddad was promoted to assistant vice-president, over the heads of a number of other young men. A year after that promotion, at the age of twenty-nine, he achieved brief prominence in the financial community. At that time, Thompson, Caldwell had been asked by a major client, the Pacific Petroleum Corporation, one of the largest oil companies in the country, to help it acquire another company, Siesta Inns of America. Siesta Inns, with thirteen hundred motels around the world, was second only to Holiday Inns as the largest hotel company in the world. PAPCO, a larger refiner and distributor of gasoline, needed an acquisition to diversify itself from the gasoline business. Ever since the devastating oil shortage brought on by the Israeli "Yom Kippur War" of 1973 and the Arab embargo that followed it, oil companies had suffered several years of erratic earnings. The Arabs were able to control crude oil prices at will, and they had taken full advantage of their position. What was needed, PAPCO management thought, was a major acquisition with a steady flow of profits that would have the effect of stabilizing PAPCO's earnings once the companies were merged.

Siesta Inns was a perfect acquisition for PAPCO; the idea of a lodging company combined with a gasoline company made a lot of sense. The president of PAPCO, a burly ex-oil rigger, had visions of a PAPCO gas station at every Siesta Inn, as well as a common credit card for payment of lodging and automotive services.

The only problem was that Siesta Inns did not particularly want to be acquired. The presidents of PAPCO and Siesta Inns had met, at PAPCO's instigation, and the early result of the meeting had been a mutual feeling of intense dislike between the two men. Since this only increased

PAPCO's resolve to buy the smaller company, the takeover would have to be done on an "unfriendly" basis. Takeovers required expert financial skills, so PAPCO called on Thompson, Caldwell.

The acquisition project was assigned to Charles "Chip" Clark, a Thompson, Caldwell senior vice-president, and John Haddad. There was little doubt from the start that a bloody business battle was about to be joined. PAPCO, using Thompson, Caldwell as brokers, began to accumulate shares of Siesta Inns on the New York Stock Exchange. The results were far too slow for PAPCO's aggressive president, but Clark warned him that any faster rate of purchase of Siesta shares would drive up the price and, more important, draw attention to the purchaser.

Although a broker on the Floor of the New York Stock Exchange does not have to reveal for whom he is buying or selling stock at any time, he must, according to the rules, give the name of his own firm as the seller or the buyer. This rule is absolutely necessary because without it, after a day in which twenty or thirty million shares are traded, no one would know who owed stock or money to whom. When one broker begins to consistently buy large quantities of the same stock, day after day, he tends not only to bid up the price too fast, but also to attract curiosity about the real identity of the buyer, his client. The Floor Specialist who supervises all trading in Siesta shares would be quick to notify the Siesta management, whose continuing approval of his handling of the stock is necessary to the specialist's keeping his lucrative position. Siesta, knowing Thompson, Caldwell to be PAPCO's investment bankers, would immediately realize for whose account their shares were being accumulated.

After several weeks of buying Siesta stock on the market, John Haddad recommended a public tender offer, and the recommendation was accepted by PAPCO. The papers were filed with the Securities and Exchange Commission in Washington, and a few days later, full-page advertisements appeared in the *Wall Street Journal* and the New York *Times*, announcing Pacific Petroleum Corporation's offer to purchase up to two million shares of the Siesta Inns of America common stock from whoever owned it at $20 per share, a handsome premium over the price of $12¼ at which Siesta Inns had closed on the New York Stock Exchange the day before.

The next day, the management of Siesta Inns held a press conference describing the tender offer as a "raid" and advising the Siesta Inns shareholders to reject it by not tendering their stock. John Haddad was prepared for this move and had drafted a press release describing the Siesta Inns management as "sleepy and self-satisfied." Thereafter, the fight entered a legal phase, when Siesta Inns sought an injunction against PAPCO on every conceivable ground that their lawyers could imagine.

As a lawyer himself, John welcomed the legal phase of the conflict. It allowed him to display a knowledge of the law that was rare among investment bankers. He held a press conference in Thompson, Caldwell's plush conference room and systematically refuted every charge Siesta Inns had made. In the process, he had used some extremely inelegant, but eminently quotable phrases, to describe Siesta. "The name of the company reflects its management's principal activity most afternoons after lunch."

Not long after the first press conference, John Haddad's name became widely known on the Street. The takeover battle lasted for months, and John continued to use his well-tested skills as an investment banker with his knowledge of the law to fight for his client. He ultimately won, and Siesta Inns negotiated an "amicable" takeover by PAPCO, whereby all of Siesta Inns' former executives were kept on the payroll, some at salary increases of up to twenty-five percent.

Besides the prominence it had afforded him, the Siesta Inns takeover was another milestone for John, this one more personal and even potentially dangerous. During the acquisition proceedings, he had, for the first time, violated a major securities law as well as the regulations of the New York Stock Exchange.

At the time, Michael Haddad, John's father, faced a financial crisis in his business. He desperately needed twenty thousand dollars to repay a bank loan, or he faced possible bankruptcy. Michael had hinted of this to his son, but he was far too proud to ask John for outright help. It didn't matter; John did not have the money. In spite of his adequate salary, John was only clearing about fifteen thousand a year after taxes and deductions. The expense of living in mid-Manhattan had never permitted him to accumulate any significant savings. But for days John was tormented with guilt. For the first time, his parents needed his help, and he could not provide it.

John later thought of a way to help his father, but rejected the idea at once. As the same thought recurred, he relented until finally, conscious of the risk it would entail, he decided to give in. He borrowed twenty thousand dollars from Marwan Suwadi, his only friend who could come up with that much money on short notice. Marwan asked no questions about the purpose of the loan, and they agreed that it would be repaid within a month. John lent the money to his father and told him to buy shares of Siesta Inns. Michael Haddad was not to open a brokerage account himself but was to use the account of a trusted friend. The result would be a sure profit for Michael Haddad because his son would launch a tender offer for Siesta Inns at a much higher price. The original loan could then be repaid.

This decision was a particularly agonizing one for John. He had to violate the law and compromise his professional career. Although he was acting out of loyalty and not greed, he knew that the authorities would show little compassion if the incident were ever discovered.

John's apartment was in a solid old brownstone with high ceilings and spacious rooms. It appealed to him more

24

than the apartments he had seen in modern buildings whose paper-thin walls and sleazy fixtures still commanded astronomical rents. He had a large living room, a good-sized kitchen, and a decent bedroom, furnished with big comfortable pieces. There was ample space for a bachelor, even when John's girlfriend Charlotte came up from Washington to stay with him.

When he arrived home, John went straight into the kitchen, poured some Scotch over ice, and allowed as much water in the glass as could get in during a rapid pass under a trickling faucet. Then he settled comfortably on the living room couch, propped his feet up on the coffee table, and switched the TV on to watch the news. The announcer's familiar voice faded, then the scene changed to taped coverage of a New York City mayoral candidate showing how safe it was to walk in Harlem these days, especially with seven aides, three camera crews, and a platoon of police. John sipped his Scotch and allowed himself to be distracted from the television set.

Another uneventful day, save for Marwan's call. Why, John wondered, did he always feel more tired at the end of a slow day than after one filled with pressure, deadlines, and incessant phone calls? Besides, inactivity left time for thinking, and his thinking had recently led to doubts about the direction and timing of his career.

Investment banking was a peculiar business, characterized, more than any other professional field, by an "old boy" philosophy that had long disappeared in most American professions. At Thompson, Caldwell, the hiring practices were a model of openmindedness. There were blacks, Indians, Jews, and ethnic combinations of all sorts. But as the executive pyramid narrowed at the top, so did the variety of men found there. At the level of managing director, most of the firm had much in common: membership in the Knickerbocker Club, a New England prep school, one of the proper Ivy League colleges, and, of course, an impeccable Anglo-Saxon heritage.

John had never paid much attention to these inconspicuous prejudices. He had got along well with most of his colleagues and had never personally sensed any conscious discrimination. But one recent incident had surprised him and had raised chilling suspicions in his mind that perhaps the bias was getting closer to home—his home.

Every summer, the Investment Banking Industry Association held a two-day convention in Boston that was attended by Corporate Finance Department representatives from most of the major Wall Street firms. The theme varied from year to year, and this time the program would feature merger and acquisition procedures. When he first learned of the convention theme, John was certain that he would be tapped to participate; there were not more than three other executives at Thompson, Caldwell who had greater knowledge of corporate acquisitions than he had, and the firm would send a six-man delegation.

So John's surprise was genuine indeed when he was not invited to attend. Equally surprising to him was that another logical candidate, Anthony DiPaoli, who had engineered two successful mergers, was not selected either. The men who would go to Boston, all officers in Thompson, Caldwell's Corporate Finance Department, had Anglo-Saxon names that had appeared for generations on the rosters of several prominent investment banking firms.

At first John dispelled the idea that discrimination had been involved. Later, Tony DiPaoli made a crack to him about it. Tony had been with Thompson, Caldwell for fourteen years, and he told John that he never expected to be selected. "It's always like that around here," he said, "the perfect caste system." John was angry at first, then indignant at having been made to feel inferior to colleagues he had always considered his friends.

The TV weatherman pointed to a satellite photograph that didn't mean anything to anybody except other weathermen. His presence on the screen told John that it was almost seven, time to shower and get dressed for dinner with Marwan.

Chapter 2

A QUICK three-block walk brought John to Gertrude's, an East Side bistro that occupied the ground floor of a town house on a block between Lexington and Third Avenues much like his own—tall, leafy sycamore trees, tightly parked cars of every description, and quiet brownstones. Going down the three stairs at the entrance and through the outside door, John was immediately engulfed in the subdued but urgent hum of conversation punctuated by occasional clinks of glasses and rattles of cutlery. The artificial but not unpleasant odor of the air conditioning combined with rich whiffs of delicious foods in various stages of preparation emanating from the kitchen.

He spotted Marwan at the only corner table, where the banquette turned the corner of the main dining room. It was a typical New York restaurant, relying on noise and close quarters to create a privacy that could not be provided by wide separations between tables because of the prohibitive cost of every square foot of Manhattan space.

The bar that he had to push past to reach Marwan was three deep in thirsty bodies. One girl sat on a barstool, obviously on her second drink, watching the door. Her black, shiny hair was cut short, with bangs across her forehead, and John saw her expression change from hope to disappointment as she squinted at him, too vain to pick up and put on her glasses lying on the bar next to her bag. She was oblivious of the crowd hemming her in, and, to them, she did not exist. The people to her left and right were each facing away from her, and she was all alone. What a shame Marwan was waiting; this could have been interesting.

John drew a breath, and plunging past the thin fashion models and prosperous-looking young executives crowding the bar, he squeezed through to Marwan. In one smooth motion he slid his knees under the table and sat down on the banquette cushion.

"I have run the gauntlet for you, and I'm ready to listen."
John smiled, shaking hands with his friend.

After they had ordered their dinner from the harried waiter, Marwan began his explanation.

"John, I've been working on a project for my government for the past six months. The project involves you, to a very great extent. Let me tell you about it from the beginning."

Marwan explained how, last October, the consulate had received, through the Saudi Embassy in Washington, an unusual request from the Ministry of Petroleum and Mineral Resources, commonly known as the Ministry of Oil. The request was to provide a list of names of Americans who met a specific set of qualifications, including Arab heritage, good education, and a thorough familiarity with American financial practices. No reason had been given for the inquiry, and the consulate had been cautioned to maintain the strictest secrecy about it.

The waiter interrupted Marwan's narrative by bringing the vichyssoise. Marwan watched him impatiently, then continued talking as soon as the waiter had straightened up and taken a step away.

"About a month later, we were able to submit a list of one hundred and thirty-two names, all of whom met the ministry's requirements. You were, of course, on the list."

John opened his mouth, about to ask a question, but Marwan held up his hand, palm out.

"Wait," he said, "let me give you the whole story step by step." John subsided, willing himself to control his curiosity, which was growing fast. He could see that Marwan was enjoying occupying center stage and that it would be unkind to cut him short. Marwan continued.

"We did not hear any more after we sent the first list, and the whole matter was soon forgotten by the people at the embassy in Washington and here at the consulate. Then in the middle of December we received new orders."

He was forced to pause again as the waiter cleared the soup plates and replaced them with steaming dishes of the *plat du jour,* a sliced filet of beef with mushroom sauce, garnished with tiny roast potato balls and fresh buttered string beans. Marwan went on with his story. The new message from the Ministry of Oil had informed them that the original list of one hundred and thirty-two had been narrowed down to twenty names. Marwan half-joked about there having been eighteen women on the first list, but none on the second. In any case, he did not know what criteria had been used to arrive at the twenty men. John Haddad was on this final list.

The accompanying instructions were further to reduce the selection to five names. This time an elaborate set of criteria had been furnished, but Marwan said he was not at liberty to reveal them. Outside investigative agencies had been used extensively for two purposes: to enable the consulate to assign small parts of the job to each investigator so that no single man would understand the full scope of what he was looking into and also simultaneously to ask for information totally irrelevant to what the Saudis were after, to confuse anyone who tried to piece it all together.

Three months time and more than three hundred pages of data had finally yielded the five names demanded by the Saudis. Marwan stopped talking to bolt down some of his food and catch up with John, who had already finished and was looking around for the waiter, to order some coffee.

"As you have undoubtedly guessed by now, John, you were one of the five."

John's curiosity was at a peak, but he resigned himself to waiting it out. He had frequently been required to keep a poker face in his investment banking activities, and had learned the value of maintaining his outward composure. The waiter sidled up to the table with an expectant expression, which changed to disappointment as John and Marwan waved away all suggestions for dessert and asked for only coffee.

Marwan resumed his narrative. "Day before yesterday, we received an order signed by the Minister of Oil, Sheikh

Anwar El-Bahar, telling us to contact you. Frankly, the Consul General would have done it himself, but since he knows we're friends, he asked me to see you." He tasted the coffee, which had just been served, and continued.

"We are asking you to fly to Beirut to meet with senior officials of the Ministry of Oil of Saudi Arabia. For some reasons of discretion, they prefer Beirut to Riyadh, where foreigners still attract attention. John, I know this is important to them. You were chosen out of one hundred and thirty-two original candidates. If for some reason you decide not to go, I am to ask an alternate, number two on the list. Incidentally, we are to pay you five thousand dollars plus your expenses for making this trip, regardless of the outcome."

At last John had an opening to ask some questions.

"Marwan, what the hell do they want?"

"I honestly don't know. Why don't you go and find out? You can wangle a few days off."

"How long would I have to be there, and when would they expect me?"

"You would be expected in Beirut next Tuesday, and remain there two days. You should allow a day on each end for travel time, though. Another thing, your employer is not to know of this trip."

The last condition puzzled John. As he thought about the proposal, he felt that his employers might enthusiastically endorse his going to the Middle East at the request of the Saudi Arabian government. After all, investment bankers always want to be where the money is, and Saudi Arabia had more liquid assets, figuratively and literally, than any other country in the world.

John debated with himself for a moment, but he knew he would go. There was nothing to lose, and although he earned a good salary, the five thousand would be welcome. He did not even formally accept Marwan's offer. The rest of the conversation took for granted that four days hence, on Sunday, April 21, John Haddad would be on Pan Am's new

30

nonstop flight 110 to Beirut. Flight 110 had recently received a good deal of publicity because it was the first regular commercial run of the new, supersonic Boeing 808's. After the cancellations of both the American and the Anglo-French designs of a few years earlier and the tragic crash of the Soviet supersonic plane at the Paris air show in 1973, the world's aviation industry had decided that faster-than-sound passenger planes were too costly to operate profitably. But then the emerging Arab financial power had made itself felt. The Arab leaders wanted to be able to zip around the world at those speeds, and they didn't care what it cost or whether it was profitable to the airlines. The airlines had to buy fuel from them, and it was in their interests to humor the Arabs. So a consortium of Arab banks had financed the design and construction of the 808's, and, of course, had insisted that the plane be used to service their part of the world. The service had been operational now for about two months, and John was already looking forward to the experience.

Chapter 3

THE airplane ticket, hotel reservation voucher, and traveler's checks were delivered to John Haddad at his office in a sealed envelope the following day. He examined the items carefully. Five hundred dollars in traveler's checks for two days' expenses. Not bad, and there would be five thousand dollars more for him when he returned. There was even some Lebanese money for the tips and taxi from the airport. The rules of the New York Stock Exchange, of which Thompson, Caldwell was a member, required him to report the payment he would receive. He thought about that, but quickly decided not to mention it.

John also noticed with satisfaction that the airline ticket was first class, a luxury he seldom enjoyed when traveling on business for his employer. Thompson, Caldwell's clearly articulated expense policy was that first-class air fare was permitted only to senior vice-presidents and above. The return trip coupon was "open" so that he could choose the date and time of his return.

Earlier in the day, John had spoken with Tom Richardson, the head of Thompson, Caldwell's Corporate Finance Department. Pleading fatigue and staleness, he told him he would like to take the next week off. Richardson was somewhat puzzled, since the financing business had been slow for months, and if some of his subordinates were suffering from anything, it was probably boredom. But he had never really understood John Haddad; he was different from the rest of Richardson's "boys." With a shrug, he told John he could have the time off.

Richardson had been on his feet during the conversation with John, for he was late for a luncheon meeting with Chip Clark, the supervisor of the PAPCO acquisition. Although Tom was Chip's boss, they were close friends and Chip could always be counted on for a pulse reading of the department.

While they were lunching at the Union League Club, Richardson mentioned that John Haddad had asked for some time off, claiming, of all things, that he was "tired." Chip Clark had also been thinking about John Haddad that morning.

"It's funny you mentioned him, Tom. I spoke to Haddad a couple of days ago, and I've got a strong feeling that he resents not being asked to the Boston convention."

"Did he say that?"

"Not in so many words. I just got the feeling, that's all."

Richardson detected the concern in Clark's voice, so he decided to pursue the point. "Well, we did *consider* him, didn't we?"

"Oh sure, but . . ." Clark fidgeted with his form. "Well,

32

the fact is he *did* deserve to go, but I just couldn't pick him."

"Look, Chip, I understand that." Richardson's nasal twang had a plaintive tone. "We have to send a delegation to Boston that is representative of the history and character of this firm. Now we can't put every detail of our tradition in the employee manuals."

"I know, I know," Clark replied, sounding very sorry he had brought it up.

"There's a nice bond dealers convention in Miami Beach next month," Richardson added. "Why not send Haddad and that Italian fellow in the department? That should set them straight."

That evening John Haddad sat in a full Eastern Airlines shuttle plane at La Guardia Airport waiting in line for a takeoff to Washington. Charlotte expected him to come down this weekend, and there was no reason not to, since he was not scheduled to leave for Beirut until Sunday night.

They had spoken the previous evening, and John had told Charlotte about the Beirut trip, although he had given her no details on the phone. He knew that the minute he stepped off the plane she would be brimming with questions.

Three years ago, when John had first met her, Charlotte Grogan was twenty-three years old. She looked like a typical bewildered American as she sat waiting for her lost suitcase at the Vienna airport. Charlotte had first attracted John's attention on the flight from Frankfurt. He had been at the front of the line when he boarded the plane, and he was already in his seat reading a magazine when most of the rest of the passengers got on. The magazine slipped from his lap as he adjusted his seat belt, and it fell in the aisle. As he leaned over to retrieve it, his head just missed bumping into the prettiest legs he had ever seen. He raised his head, inhaling a rich scent of perfume, and saw an amused little smile playing at the corners of a superbly formed, wide mouth that reminded him of Lauren Bacall. Thick auburn hair reaching the shoulders framed an oval face with high cheekbones, widely spaced blue eyes, and a perfect complexion. She murmured, "I'm sorry," and walked on to the seat diagonally across from him. She was tall, about five feet seven, with a well-proportioned figure that accentuated her attractiveness.

The luggage conveyor went round and round as passengers collected their suitcases and filed out of the terminal through the perfunctory customs check. John had his bag, but lingered, wanting a last good look at the young woman and perhaps an opportunity to talk to her. She was searching for some help, sure now that the last two pieces of luggage going around for the third time were not hers. Then a blue-overalled porter reached over and changed the arriving flight number on the sign suspended over the conveyor, retrieved the two unclaimed pieces, and walked away.

John offered assistance, and she gratefully accepted. After they filled out the lost luggage forms, they shared a taxi into town. She was staying at the Tyrol on Mariahilferstrasse, which was considerably more modest than the Sacher, where John had a reservation. The Sacher, best known for its famous Viennese pastry, the Sacher torte, was an old hotel rich in the traditions of the Hapsburgs whose life-style it so elegantly preserved.

That night they walked through narrow cobblestone streets to the Kursalon in Stadtpark, where manicured lawns and well-kept flower beds adorned winding paths leading to statues of Vienna's great composers. The Kursalon was an imposing restaurant, beautifully maintained in the romantic nineteenth-century tradition of the proud Viennese. The balmy July night made it perfect weather for outdoor dining. They sat on a vast terrace overlooking the dance floor, which was encircled by flickering candlelight from the surrounding tables. In front of them, a raised bandstand was the center of attention. The musicians, formally attired, played only waltzes from this, the very loca-

34

tion where Johann Strauss had often conducted his own orchestra. The preponderance of tourists in the summer crowd did not have the usual dampening effect on John. Even the waltzes, which he had always dreaded, seemed beautifully appropriate and easy to dance to.

They were comfortable and happy in each other's company, and John, who was used to casual romantic encounters, felt different this time. Normally, under these circumstances, he would be plotting his strategy to get the girl back to his hotel. But that night he enjoyed every minute they were together, appreciating both her intellect and her uninhibited sense of humor and enthusiasm. He questioned her at length about her background and her life and felt no pressure to become physically aggressive.

He learned that she came from Lake Harbor, Michigan, a well-to-do suburb of Detroit, but not in the class of Grosse Pointe, home of America's motor aristocracy. She was an only child, and after the death of her mother when she was thirteen, her father had accepted a transfer by his advertising agency to their Washington, D.C., office. She knew he had done it as much to get away from haunting memories of her mother in the comfortable frame house on Brentwood Road as he had to move ahead in his professional career.

Charlotte had wanted to be a teacher, and after graduation from a small Eastern Catholic girl's college, she went on to earn a master's degree in education at the American University in Washington. By the time she finished, there was a surplus of teachers, and desirable teaching jobs became impossible to find.

With the help of her father's friend, Representative Samuel Jennings of the Fourteenth District in Michigan, Charlotte Grogan got a job with WTOP-TV, the Washington CBS affiliate, in the news department. She adjusted quickly to the hectic routine, becoming well liked by her colleagues and superiors at the station and respected for her unflappable ability to cope with the daily crises of the news business. She had just received her first real break when the short-handed CBS Network Washington Bureau borrowed her from the local affiliate for an assignment to Vienna to cover the ongoing Strategic Arms Limitation Talks, dubbed "the SALT talks" by the press. She would be joined in Vienna by the bureau chief, and file daily reports on the activities surrounding the conference for use on the air.

John walked Charlotte back to her hotel, sorry that he would be in Vienna only that one night. He had two appointments the following morning in connection with a Eurodollar bond issue his firm was managing, and he would be flying to London in the afternoon. A suggestion that they might prolong the evening at his hotel was not taken up by Charlotte Grogan, although she did not resist a tentative kiss in front of her hotel. John promised to call her in Washington when he returned to New York, and he had no doubt that the promise would be kept.

John and Charlotte met again in Washington several months later, and again in New York. Shortly thereafter they became lovers, seeing each other at least twice a month. Within a year, each of them had excluded all but the most casual relationships with other members of the opposite sex, and their commitment to each other became firm and binding. They discussed marriage in terms of couples they knew or in generalities, but neither was fully ready. Charlotte had by now been made assistant news editor at the station. She might have given it up to marry John and move to New York, but he did not ask her to, and Charlotte had not become disenchanted enough with the world of the career girl to press him.

John suspected that the chances of meeting a more ideal girl were slim, but he did not feel comfortable contemplating the responsibilities of marriage and all that it would entail. He wanted much more than just the illusory security most people settle for when they get married. He was sure he would marry Charlotte someday, and, more important, he was reasonably sure she would wait.

But even Charlotte didn't know the true extent of John

Haddad's hopes and dreams for the future. John had always taken the "American Dream" literally, and he saw no reason why he shouldn't aspire to reach its upper limits. He wanted wealth, but not the ordinary, mortgaged kind, dependent on a continuing high salary to maintain his standard of living at the level he desired.

The wealth John sought was the kind that bought true freedom and time. Freedom from the petty and annoying daily decisions based on price—the infuriating worry about whether he could afford something. Freedom to invest in any industry or business he chose to run, or not to run any enterprise, but to be able to enter politics or diplomacy without asking for financial support.

And time, the only irreplaceable commodity. Time to think, time to plan, time to spend with his children some day, the way his father had never been able to do with him. The absence of being accountable to others for his time. This was the kind of wealth John wanted, and he knew that it might take millions to turn his dreams into realities.

The landing of the DC-9 in Washington jolted him out of his reverie. John joined the line of people filing out of the aircraft and soon spotted Charlotte's slim figure in the bustling Friday night crowd in the terminal. Despite the fact that they had met at this spot countless times, Charlotte beamed a broad smile at the sight of him, as if this were their first airport reunion.

She was wearing a white linen dress with a scoop neck and a single strand of pearls, a light-green silk sash around her waist accentuating the crisp whiteness of the dress. She looked relaxed but very elegant, and her straight light-auburn hair fell to her shoulders with only one gold-colored clasp holding it back on the right side opposite the part.

As he walked up to her, John put down his Lark carry-on case and gave her a long bear hug.

"Hi, sweetheart!" Charlotte said as she returned his embrace and kissed him on the cheek.

He let her go, saying, "Boy, I'm glad to see you . . . you look sensational! Good thing my plane was on time or one of these lecherous commuters would have tried to steal you away."

"As a matter of fact, I've had to turn down a couple of interesting propositions since I've been standing here," she said with a deadpan expression.

She started off in the direction of the luggage counter, but John grabbed her arm. "No, it's OK. This is all I'm taking to Beirut."

"Great, let's get out of here. I'm dressed for candlelight, not for fluorescent airports! We have a reservation at Billy Martin's Carriage House in Georgetown, and you'll have to pass up a shower before dinner. If I'd made it any later, we would have had to wait till nine for a table."

They walked up the stairs of the terminal, John's free arm around her waist, through the American Airlines area and out of the building to the parking lot. As they reached Charlotte's little Mustang, she automatically handed the keys to John. He always drove at night when they were together.

John headed out of National Airport along the Potomac to the turnoff for Key Bridge. Once over it, he was in Georgetown and made his way to Wisconsin Avenue where Billy Martin's Carriage House was located. He pulled the car into the parking lot across the street.

When they arrived at the restaurant, John asked for a table in the cozy barroom, and soon they found themselves sitting side by side in the flickering candlelight, feeling a pleasant anticipation of catching up with each other.

Their tall, cool drinks arrived, and Charlotte turning to John, folded her arms across her chest and said, "All right, Mr. Bond, you better talk now, or there will be trouble in your life . . . like I'll kick over this nice table! I've waited long enough to hear your cloak and dagger story."

He told her everything, including the details of his dinner meeting with Marwan Suwadi, and he even showed her the documents, Lebanese currency and traveler's checks he had received.

38

"Then you really have no idea why they want to see you?" she asked.

"They're being super-cagey, so I know damn well I won't learn the nuts and bolts of it until I get there. But I can make some broad educated guesses."

"Like what?"

"Marwan said that the three initial requirements were Arab origin, a good education, and a knowledge of finance. Obviously they don't want me to design a highway in the desert or build a fertilizer plant! Remember—as if we could forget—that Saudi Arabia has huge oil revenues and must invest the money someplace. My credentials in investment banking tie in well with that, and the Arab origin probably gives them extra confidence. I guess they want me for some investment project, maybe as an adviser of some sort."

"So far so good," she said. "Any clues as to what kind of project this might be?"

"No idea," John replied, "but I'll find out soon enough. I figure I have nothing to lose and at least the money they're paying me to gain."

"You've always wanted to be rich, haven't you?"

"Yes."

"Maybe this will be your chance."

"I hope so. But it's not just the money."

"What else then?"

John drew a deep breath and sat back in his chair. "There's security, of course, but I guess I just love to put business deals together. Did I ever tell you about my first successful business venture?"

"No, honey, I don't think you have." Charlotte was interested and did not want to lose this rare moment of reminiscing on John's part.

"When I was in high school, I sold balloons in Central Park. Fifty cents each. Business was lousy, even though there were zillions of kids in the park with their parents. I just couldn't get them to buy the balloons."

"What did you do?"

"I tried several things. I lowered the price. Nothing. I

39

dressed in funny clothes. They laughed a lot, but didn't buy. Then I got an idea. Still interested? Or am I rambling?"

"I love to hear stories about your past, and this one sounds fascinating."

"I got my girlfriend—you wouldn't have liked her—I got her to come to the park with me and give away ten cheap balloons to different kids, just when crowds were at a peak."

Charlotte wondered if she had missed something. "She gave ten balloons away?"

"Right. And my business soared. I sold out of balloons within the hour."

"Boy, am I confused."

"Think about it, sweetheart." John smiled, recalling his early business acumen. "We made ten kids very happy. But there were dozens of other kids watching who *didn't* get a free balloon. Those kids cried to their parents about not getting one."

"I think I get it."

"I think you do, too. The parents whose kids didn't get a free balloon felt guilty, so they bought one from me. But I raised the price of my balloons to sixty cents, which more than made up for the ones I gave away."

Charlotte threw back her head and laughed. "Darling, you're too much."

"I don't know about that, but I am hungry. Let's order."

They enjoyed a truly fine meal. First, wedges of pale orange-pink Persian melon, with a squeeze of lime juice to contrast with the sweetness. Then, the broiled shrimps, with split tails, cooked in butter with a mild hint of garlic. John and Charlotte had long had a mutual pact about the sharing of garlic. The shrimps were followed by a beautiful Chateaubriand, sliced thin, red in the center, garnished with creamy Béarnaise sauce, and a tossed green salad of Bibb lettuce and watercress with lemon dressing. Accompanying the dinner were half a bottle of pale-gold Chablis with the shrimps and a full bottle of 1973 Mouton Cadet with the steak. Neither of them could face thinking about dessert, and the dinner ended after the waiter brought the two cups of espresso with a twist of lemon peel.

After dinner they drove to Charlotte's high-rise apartment in suburban Bethesda, an area she preferred to the more fashionable Georgetown. Here in Bethesda, her building offered a swimming pool, tennis courts, and nicely landscaped gardens. The setting was much more to Charlotte Grogan's taste than city chic. John parked in the resident's lot, retrieved his suitcase from the back seat, and they rode up to her fourteenth-floor apartment. Inside, he gave her a long kiss and felt her passion rise. They stopped kissing long enough to unzip and unbutton and help each other undress until all of their clothing was in a heap in the armchair. Within minutes they were in bed, discovering each other again. He loved her very much and marveled at how, after three years, their passion for each other remained so intense. Later, they talked and laughed together before going to sleep.

Saturday turned out to be a beautiful morning, and after breakfast Charlotte tried hard to deny John the dubious triumph of trouncing her in two sets of tennis. Although there were plenty of people she knew who would gladly have made a foursome for doubles, John and Charlotte always played singles, not wanting strangers to intrude on their time alone.

After lunch they went to an early movie near the apartment, then back to change for cocktails with Charlotte's father. Harry Grogan lived in the fashionable northwest section of Washington, occupying a large apartment on the second floor of a big, old house on F Street, near Eighteenth. His housekeeper, Mrs. Gallagher, had been with him since the move from Michigan, and although she was now aging, she was happy to run his household and see to his simple needs.

John was always willing to spend time with Harry Grogan, both because he found him a refreshing change from the New York people in his life and because he couldn't resist evaluating and observing him as a potential father-in-law.

Harry saw them drive up the wide driveway, and he stepped out on the second-floor balcony off the library to wave a welcome.

"It's about time, kids," he boomed. "Sam Jennings and I are on our second drink and you'll have to catch up!"

When they reached the cool confines of Harry Grogan's library, with the built-in wet bar behind one false wall of book spines, Harry walked John over to the congressman. "Sam, I'd like you to meet John Haddad . . . he's almost family."

"How do you do, sir," said John. "It's an honor to meet you after hearing so much about you."

"I hope it wasn't all bad, son," said Jennings with a grin as he shook hands. "Are you taking good care of my favorite girl?"

Jennings looked exactly like what he was, a union shop steward wearing a suit. He was in his eighth term in the House of Representatives, hailing from a labor district populated primarily by members of the United Auto Workers. Through sheer seniority provided by his regular reelection every two years, he had reached the chairmanship of the House Foreign Affairs Committee. He was fiercely protective of the jobs of his constituents. Although most international political nuances escaped his limited comprehension, God help the man who laid a piece of legislation on his desk that smacked of automation or exporting jobs! He was a master of legislative delay and pigeonholing; he manipulated the rules of House procedures with the innate skill of a brain surgeon doing a delicate and possibly fatal operation successfully. But as a friend of the Grogan family he was a delightful asset.

John Haddad had done his homework on Jennings and had great respect for the old man's shrewdness. He didn't even hint at any of his immediate plans. The afternoon passed pleasantly, and as the sun began to fade, he and Charlotte said their good-byes and drove back to the apartment, light-headed from the effect of several cocktails.

After dinner they sprawled on the couch, glasses of cognac in hand, and watched television. The liquor was getting to Charlotte and she could feel a silly spell coming on. The grin on her face confirmed it.

"John, darling. . . ." There was a trace of singsong in her voice.

"Uh-huh."

"Oh, I forgot. One does not disturb the master when the news is on." The eleven o'clock news held little interest for Charlotte, even when she was not feeling the effects of a cocktail-drenched afternoon combined with cognac. As a news professional, she knew that the late news was nothing more than a rehash of the early evening edition that they had both watched. Just about the only difference on a spring night would be the scores of the late ball games.

"Charlotte, please." John was always afraid that he might miss something important and then feel like a dummy when informed of it the next day by a friend or, worse yet, a client.

"Yes, master."

"C'mon, honey. You know one of the things I like to watch on the goddamn TV is the news!"

"Yes, darling, the news is a BFD. I forgot. Forgive me."

"I'll bite, what's a BFD?"

"Big Fucking Deal." Charlotte blurted it out and got up, laughing uncontrollably as she walked into the bedroom.

She thought about John as she lay in bed in the darkened room, knowing he would come in as soon as the news ended. He did have his moods, but that had no effect on her love for him. It was hard for her to describe her feelings about John Haddad without lapsing into trite expressions that seemed inadequate. She was devoted to this man. He was intelligent, moody, self-centered, and highly ambitious, but he was also tender, enthusiastic, and sympathetic to others. What an incredible combination of character traits; and thank God he seemed to love her as much as she loved him. More and more, she was able to picture herself chucking her television news career and hitching her dreams to his.

John tiptoed into the dark room.

"Charlotte? Are you asleep?"

"No, darling. I waited."

Early Sunday afternoon they prepared for the trip to the airport. As John packed, Charlotte was subdued, hating the prospect of their impending separation. She often felt this way when John was traveling abroad. She knew how to cope with their being apart when it was only the two hundred and twenty miles between New York and Washington, but distances beyond that made the separation feel different, more intense.

Later, they drove Charlotte's car to Dulles Airport where John would connect to Kennedy International in New York for the Pan Am supersonic flight to Beirut.

"What will you do tonight, Charlotte?" John asked.

"I'm going home for dinner," she responded matter-of-factly.

John smiled to himself. Charlotte had had her own apartment for four years, but she still referred to the place where her father lived as home.

Chapter 4

AS the dusty meterless taxi of uncertain vintage drew up to the Phoenicia Hotel, John gave silent thanks for a safe arrival. The noisy, jouncing ride had been a marked contrast to the silent glide across the Atlantic and the European continent in the supersonic jet. The Lebanese taxi drivers had much in common with their counterparts in Mexico, who drove primarily by using their horns and gas pedals and had little interest in the functions of brakes and springs. He intentionally overpaid the driver, thus depriving him of the pleasure of a protracted bargaining session over the fare. The doorman, dressed in a Hollywood-style Turkish outfit with balloon pants, white shirt, and red vest, opened the door and took his bag.

He rather liked the Phoenicia, having stayed there twice before. The hotel was operated by the Intercontinental chain and was designed to provide the services, comforts, and communications that were now demanded by the active international business and diplomatic community. The hotel had its local touches too, such as a splendid waiter carrying a tray of tiny cups of strong coffee and offering them to whoever occupied the big armchairs and couches scattered about the lobby. Rich Arabs in burnooses, oil workers from Texas and Oklahoma, crews of Air France, Lufthansa, Pan Am, and a dozen other airlines, and bankers from all over the world made up a large part of the Phoenicia's clientele.

After filling out his registration form, John passed by the message desk and identified himself to the clerk. The man's expression changed from disinterest to respect as he handed John the only item in the numbered cubbyhole. The heavy, cream-colored envelope was embossed in gold with the crossed swords and palm of the Saudi Arabian crest, and marked with John's name in Arabic script, beautifully traced in India ink with a fine-nibbed pen. Not wanting to open it until he was alone, John slipped the envelope into his jacket pocket and followed the bellboy who was carrying his luggage to the elevators.

They stepped off at the eleventh floor, the bellboy leading him to a large attractive room facing north. The air conditioning created a welcome chill as well as a faintly antiseptic odor that gave the reassuring impression that no human being had been allowed to sully the space before. The view was unobstructed, with the city and the harbor in the foreground and the mountains in the distance, still capped with late spring snow. Below the snow line on the mountainsides John could see clusters of small houses forming little villages, one of which was surely his mother's ancestral home. He had visited the nameless village once, and felt humbled in the presence of the modest whitewashed clay house where his maternal grandfather had been born. It was not quite the same feeling looking at the village from this distance, but he recalled vividly the almost surreal emotion of standing before the scene of his past.

The room itself was generous, with a double bed in one area and farther back, a sitting-room arrangement containing a sofa, and a low table, with an armchair on either side. John sat in an armchair and opened the envelope. Inside there was a single sheet of crested stationery, and the handwritten message:

Would you kindly call me at your convenience upon arrival.

Bader Mahmoun
Room 614.

Relieved at finally being in touch with the originators of his trip, John went to the phone and tried to decipher the instructions for dialing another room that were etched in the plastic, then gave up and dialed O, asking the operator to make the connection for him.

"Marhaba," said the voice at the other end. John knew a few words of Arabic and that was one of them. It meant "hello."

"Mr. Mahmoun? This is John Haddad."

"How do you do, Mr. Haddad!" The voice was unctuous and too loud for the excellent connection. John had to hold the receiver away from his ear. "I am most happy you are here. I know that you must be tired after such a long trip, but will you allow me to come up and see you for just a moment or two?"

46

"Certainly," John replied without hesitation. The sooner he learned what this was all about, the better he'd like it.

"Fine, Mr. Haddad. I'll be there directly." He rang off.

During the five minutes before the knock on the door, John quickly unpacked his suitcase and put his clothes away. He paid special attention to hanging up his dark-blue suit, tailor-made by Davies and Son in London. It fitted almost perfectly, and each of the four sleeve buttons had its own operable buttonhole. Three shirts and three sets of underwear, a toilet kit, and several ties and socks were all that he had packed.

"Hello, Mr. Haddad." The greeting came from a short man dressed in a dark suit. His voice had a sugary intonation and he spoke with a distinctly Arabic accent. John was reminded of a barber he once knew—smooth, big smile, but always pushing the hair tonic for seventy-five cents extra. "I am Bader Mahmoun of the Saudi Arabian Ministry of Oil."

"Do come in, Mr. Mahmoun. May I order you some coffee?" John knew he couldn't go wrong offering coffee to an Arab.

"You are too kind, but it is not necessary—I will only keep you a few minutes."

They sat down together and Mahmoun went on. "Mr. Haddad, I wish to inform you that His Excellency, Sheikh Anwar El-Bahar, our Minister of Oil, is here in Beirut and would like to have dinner with you tonight. He is here on an official visit. Your itinerary was arranged to coincide with his stay without attracting undue attention. His Excellency realizes that you are tired from your long air journey, and the dinner tonight will be essentially social."

"I would be happy to dine with His Excellency tonight," John said, not showing his surprise. He had been told in New York that he would meet with "senior officials" of the Ministry of Oil, but he had not expected seeing the minister himself. The domain ruled by John's prospective dinner host had grown into the largest unit in the Saudi Arabian government. More than seventeen hundred professional employees worked there, many with advanced foreign degrees, which were still a rarity in Saudi Arabia.

"That's fine," Mahmoun continued. "May I suggest that you go to the minister's suite on the fourteenth floor at eight o'clock. He will be expecting you. The room number is 1411."

"Very well, Mr. Mahmoun. I'll be there."

John knew from his own family experience that Arab hospitality was not a myth; it was ingrained into the character of the people. Arabs loved to entertain, the more guests the better. But why would this dinner tonight be mainly social? His curiosity about the Saudis' reasons for wanting to see him was active enough, but now that the Oil Minister himself was involved, the anticipation was unbearable. El-Bahar must want to look him over, under the pretext of an informal dinner. All right, the minister held all the cards and he was playing them in his own casino. John would play them as they fell.

By now it was ten in the morning, but even though he had slept on the plane, the accelerated jet lag had disoriented him. His body was insisting the night wasn't over and he should still be sleeping. He stripped to his shorts, drew the curtains, then collapsed into the inviting double bed. His eyes closed, but he couldn't sleep. Thoughts about his upcoming meeting with Sheikh Anwar El-Bahar crowded into his mind.

John reviewed what he knew about the Oil Minister. He was sorry now that he hadn't had time to do some real homework before leaving for Beirut. El-Bahar had been educated at Harvard, earning both an undergraduate degree and the coveted Master of Business Administration from the famous "B" School. His face and name were familiar to many Americans as a result of numerous television appearances on talks shows, including *Meet the Press, Face the Nation,* and many more. His rise to prominence had coincided with the dramatic increases in world oil prices decreed by the cartel of oil exporters, the biggest of whom was his own country, Saudi Arabia. El-Bahar somehow had managed to put himself across as a reasonable and realistic administrator in spite of the damage his country's demands was doing to the economies of the Western nations. He had an engaging personality, which, combined with his avowed enthusiasm for United States society, made him a rather popular figure. Some even called him "flashy."

But, in truth, there was nothing flashy about El-Bahar. He was one of those men who happen to turn up at the right moment to fill an existing need. Before the Arab oil embargo of 1973 and 1974, the Arabs, and especially the Saudis, had permitted the British, Dutch, and French oil company giants to extract billions of barrels of their oil, while maintaining a very low price structure. This flow of easily available cheap fuel not only encouraged the industrialists of Western Europe and the United States to make their plants and essential services dependent on it, but also served to atrophy American domestic oil exploration because the cost of extraction at home was so much higher than importing cheap Arab crude. The sudden cutoff of the flow by the Arabs in retaliation for Western support of Israel was a numbing shock. Even after deliveries were restored some months later, the palmy days of inexhaustible cheap energy for the West were over. First the Arabs raised the price by a hundred percent and more. Then they put in motion programs to eliminate, step by step, the ownership of their oil fields by foreign companies. Finally, they had repossessed it all, and the petroleum companies had been reduced to the status of mere distributors for the Arabs.

El-Bahar's entire orientation to the business world was nurtured in the midst of the growth of Arab economic power. He did not think of his nation as "underdeveloped," the condescending parlance of the West. He was taught by the rising class of technocrats in his own country to have confidence and by the professors of the Harvard Business School how to handle the details. The result was a deliberate, progressive mind, flexible enough to assimilate rapid change and with enough vision to take advantage of whatever crossed his path in the form of opportunity. He was wholly loyal to his country, he enjoyed the full support of the government he represented, and he wielded the largest budget of any of the ministers. He was frequently consulted first by the government, even on matters that should formally have been assigned to other departments of the cabinet. El-Bahar was clearly in line to succeed to the prime ministership, and he was fully aware of it.

In his own fiefdom, El-Bahar had absolute power. He was served by an army of devoted civil servants attuned to instant implementation of the minister's policies. Fortunately for them, he was not foolish enough to stifle initiative, but, rather, he encouraged it. El-Bahar's subordinates knew they could get a fair hearing and an intelligent evaluation of their proposals. He was careful to temper his unquestioned dominance with great personal concern for the people who worked for him. It was well known in the ministry that El-Bahar had once broken off an important conference, summoned his own airplane, and rushed to pick up Mahmoun's father, who had suffered a heart attack at a remote outpost of the pipeline he supervised. The old man, still in his working clothes, had been wheeled into the operating theater of a renowned Swiss heart surgeon in Zurich within hours of the attack. A life was saved, and Mahmoun's fervent loyalty cemented. Even as he repaid loyalty, the Oil Minister was quick to punish disobedience. There were black marks on a few dossiers in the ministry, representing permanent exclusion from any responsible positions for several dozen people.

This was the man who would be looking John over tonight at dinner, for some mysterious purpose not yet revealed. As he finally drifted off to sleep, John hoped that he would measure up.

John awoke several hours later, feeling better but in need of a shower and shave. His ablutions performed, dressed in his dark-blue suit with a light-blue monogrammed cotton broadcloth shirt and red Hermès tie, he saw that he still had four hours to kill before the appointed time for meeting the Oil Minister. He considered calling some of his friends in Beirut, but decided against it. He couldn't very well tell them why he was in town, and he really didn't have the time to see them anyway. One call, the invitations would begin, and he would be doing nothing but answering messages. Also, his paying hosts—five thousand dollars' worth—were entitled to his availability while he was here.

The afternoon was beautiful, with a warm breeze coming from the mountains just inland of the city, and the last rays of the sun were still hot and glaring. John decided to take a stroll to use up the rest of the afternoon. He walked out of the Phoenicia and headed for the St. Georges Hotel.

The St. Georges was in a different class from the hotel John had just left. It catered to the same people who would demand rooms at Claridge's in London, the Ritz in Paris, or the Carlyle in New York. These people didn't want phones with dials on them or bathtubs with plastic shower curtains and shower heads over the tub. They had no use for lobby airline counters, newsstands, or escalators. The guests of the St. Georges stayed there because nothing had changed since 1938, the last year before World War II. Messages were brought on silver trays by young apprentice bellboys, the concierge ruled his allotted portion of the lobby like some minor potentate, and no one was inclined to raise his voice. Tables, lamps, wall paneling, rugs—nothing was ever removed. It was simply kept sparkling clean or polished or vacuumed, and it aged gracefully.

The lunch hour on the ocean terrace at the St. Georges lasted from one o'clock until late in the afternoon. John heard the gay clatter of the boisterous luncheon crowd as he entered from the street side through the brass-trimmed mahogany doors. He turned right and walked through the narrow lobby to the bar. A *maître d'hôtel* in a white jacket asked if he would be lunching and looked at his watch wistfully as though he were hinting that the chef would be leaving the kitchen soon. John politely declined, which brought a look of relief to the expressive face and stillness to the wringing hands of the anxious majordomo. The bar looked out over the semicircular terrace where crowded tables were topped by red parasols fluttering in the breeze. Almost every seat was filled by a colorful and elegant group of people from all walks of Beirut society and their international guests. At one table, a debonair Lebanese cabinet member and his sleekly groomed wife entertained four well-dressed couples. At another, a rich old jewel merchant, an enormous diamond flashing on the little finger of his right hand, huddled closely with three stunning girls young enough to be his granddaughters, a loud giggle occasionally bursting from the group.

Most of the men were attired in conservative lounge suits, a very few wearing Arab dress. But the ladies shone in Diors, St. Laurents, and designs from the newest rage, a young couturier of questionable gender who called himself Asalan of Cairo. Lunch at the St. Georges was almost a daily ritual for the predominantly local crowd. There was laughter, gesticulation, table hopping, and the exchange of exaggerated busses in the air alongside both cheeks among friends who had not seen each other since the previous night's dinner party, accompanied by cries of "Darling!"

The low-hanging, reddening sun made dark glasses a necessity rather than a cosmetic ornament; John put his glasses on and stepped out on the terrace. The *maître d'hôtel* showed him to a small table beside the railing, from which he had an excellent view of the late sunbathers on the jetty and the occasional water-skier roaring by, throwing a white plume of water yards into the air. John liked the lazy ease of these supremely civilized people and their very French ability to create pleasure for the eye, the body, and the palate on the gilded terrace of the St. Georges.

Hans Sloman was engrossed in a conversation with his Saudi Arabian client and didn't even look up as John sat down, two tables away. Sloman felt uncomfortable talking business out in the open in this frivolous crowd. He preferred the atmosphere of his native Zurich, where conversations were held behind closed doors in absolute privacy.

Sloman's companion, Ahmed Sharif, was turning out to be a disappointment. Lured to Beirut by Sharif's vague hints about new deposits for his troubled bank, Sloman was learning that he had overestimated Sharif's assets. He should have known better. But how was a hard-working Swiss banker supposed to fathom these Arabs? He couldn't afford to miss some possibly lucrative deal by being unwilling to make a trip. Sharif held a high post in the Saudi Ministry of Oil and kept a healthy account in Zurich at Sloman's bank. He added to the account every few weeks and had not yet made a withdrawal in the four years he had been building up his nest egg. Sloman had never speculated on Sharif's source of funds, but from long experience with secret accounts he was quite sure that his client was doing something dishonest and probably illegal to acquire them. As Sharif spoke vaguely of the possibility of larger deposits in the future, Sloman became determined to extract something from him immediately to assist his ailing bank. In better times Sloman would never have considered doing such a thing, but now he was convinced that his own survival was at stake.

Ahmed Sharif sensed Sloman's disappointment and felt bad about it. He realized now that Sloman had expected a large new deposit of some kind, perhaps even some official business from the Oil Ministry, instead of merely his regular addition to his own account. Sharif had looked upon his trip to Beirut in the retinue of Sheikh El-Bahar as a chance to extend some hospitality to Sloman, never thinking that a trip to Lebanon from Zurich might be inconvenient for the banker.

Gambling on the credibility of the reputation of Swiss bankers for omniscience in money matters, Sloman launched his threat. "Ahmed, I have been watching your activities for some years now, and the concurrent growth of your account. You must know that we investigate our clients quite carefully. Even in Switzerland there are laws about the handling of, shall we say, 'hot' money. Now I find I must insist on something substantial from you to make it worthwhile continuing our arrangement."

Sharif's mouth turned down and a pang of fear suddenly struck his heart at this unexpected attack. He knew far better than Sloman the seriousness of the penalties he faced at home if he were discovered. His fear served to convince him that Sloman was well informed. In his panic, Sharif looked around, as though seeking help. His eye fell upon the face of John Haddad, sitting only a few feet away, and he immediately knew he had seen that face before. Of course, it was John Haddad, the young American they had investigated through the ministry. Haddad's dossier had contained a mass of reports and several photographs. Hoping to reinstate himself with Sloman and at the same time satisfy his demand, Sharif said, "Mr. Sloman, I'm very sorry the trip has not lived up to your expectations. I truly did not intend to mislead you, and I thought you would enjoy coming here for a day or two. But there is something I can tell you about which might be worthwhile."

Sloman looked up, interested. With that encouragement, Sharif continued. "That young American over there is involved in one of the biggest financial deals ever attempted, and he doesn't even know about it yet. Would you like to hear more?"

"Yes, yes, I'm always curious about such things." Sloman had learned long ago that it costs nothing to listen, and potential profit can always turn up from unexpected information.

"The American's name is John Haddad. He is an investment banker from New York. He must have just arrived here today. Haddad was chosen by my chief, the Oil Minister, to handle a takeover of an American company by Saudi Arabia. I know because I was involved in the processing of candidates. Before I tell you more, I must have your guarantee that you will not reveal the source of this story." Sharif had belatedly realized that in view of the risk he was taking it would be wise to emphasize the need for secrecy.

Sloman provided the reassurance Sharif sought. In a slightly offended tone, as though no threat had ever been made, he replied, "My dear Ahmed, you know our tradition of confidentiality. What passes between us will never be connected to you, rest assured."

Greatly relieved at having found something acceptable to the banker, Sharif outlined to Sloman the future plans of El-Bahar, John's role, and what he had gleaned about John's background.

Unaware that he was the subject of the intense conversation going on just a few feet away from him, John relaxed with a drink in the warm sunshine, savoring the atmosphere of his surroundings and wondering how many preliminaries he would have to go through before he would find out anything substantive to explain this mysterious trip to Beirut. He was nervous, hoping to make a good impression on the powerful minister, and wished he had a more confident knowledge of Arab customs and conventions.

John returned to the Phoenicia lobby just before the appointed time and went directly to the Oil Minister's floor. Bader Mahmoun admitted him to the suite and welcomed him. This obviously was a specially remodeled suite that occupied as much space as three ordinary ones. John found himself in a vast reception room with cream-colored marble floors partly covered with rich Persian rugs, each with a different intricate design but still a subtle match for its neighbor. At the far end of the room, a small area two steps higher contained a semicircular couch covered with bright-colored pillows.

Sheikh El-Bahar rose from the couch and approached John with his hand extended. He looked thinner than John had remembered from photographs, and his dark conservative suit looked odd against the background of an ancient tapestry hanging on the wall behind him.

"Good evening, Mr. Haddad. I am happy to meet you at last." Sheikh El-Bahar's English was flawless, with only a slight trace of accent.

"Good evening, Your Excellency. I am honored to be here."

"Come sit down. I hope you don't mind if I call you John."

"Of course not, sir." This did not mean he was being invited to call the Oil Minister "Anwar." Beside the couch a wheeled table was set with at least a dozen different bottles of various liquors, including twelve-year-old Scotch, Polish vodka, English gin, and even a fat dark-green bottle of Dom Pérignon champagne buried in a mound of crushed ice.

"Care for a drink, John?" El-Bahar's friendly tone put John at ease. He could readily understand why this man rated so high in diplomatic circles for charm and *savoir faire.*

"Frankly, Your Excellency, I do drink. But I would not want to offend anyone who, because of his religious beliefs, finds it objectionable."

El-Bahar was struck with John's poise. According to Moslem law, the consumption of any kind of alcohol was strictly forbidden. Even though Beirut, whose population was fifty percent Christian, had no such restrictions, John knew that in Saudi Arabia the sale, consumption, or dispensing of liquor was against the law. It was a wise precaution for him to let El-Bahar take the lead.

"Very thoughtful, John. But I must confess that I drink myself. Not in public and not in Saudi Arabia, of course!" El-Bahar laughed, then continued, "It's one of the bad habits I acquired at Harvard." The minister looked over at Mahmoun, who had remained standing. "I will have a Scotch and water. And you, John?"

"The same, please." John was smiling. El-Bahar had already succeeded in creating a feeling of camaraderie, that they were joined in friendly conspiracy against the established order. Mahmoun made the drinks, including one for himself, and joined the Oil Minister and his guest.

"Tonight we will go to a small restaurant outside of Beirut," El-Bahar said. "They serve remarkably good Lebanese food, which I happen to know you like, John, and this place has a lovely terrace on the sea. Also, I am not likely to be recognized there."

The three of them chatted for a while longer, El-Bahar guiding the conversation to subjects that gave John a chance to respond—the stock market, American sports, international trade—without once broaching the main reason for the meeting. The drinks finished, they proceeded down to the waiting unmarked limousine and were swiftly driven to the Al Pacha restaurant.

The owner stood at the door, obviously alerted to expect El-Bahar's party momentarily. Bowing respectfully, he escorted them to a well-situated table on the terrace. El-Bahar's request for privacy had been honored by making sure that all the tables immediately surrounding his were empty. The nearest occupied table was well out of earshot.

The Oil Minister ordered without looking at the menu, and soon countless plates were being served. The first course was the traditional *mezze,* the Lebanese *hors d'oeuvres,* for which a service of fifty dishes of varied delicacies was not uncommon.

Sheikh El-Bahar led the conversation and repeatedly mentioned things he knew about John and his past. John was aware that he had been investigated, from what Marwan had told him before asking him to make the trip, but the extent of the Oil Minister's knowledge of minute details about his life surprised him. He became more and more convinced that whatever was coming would be very important. Why else would such a man as El-Bahar give so much of his time to remembering such trivia? John had trouble reining in his imagination as the dinner progressed.

They were finishing the main dishes of *kibbe,* a Lebanese

57

equivalent of steak tartare using lamb instead of beef, and *tabbouleh,* a salad made of cooked cracked wheat and various vegetables, when El-Bahar asked, "John, do you consider yourself an Arab?"

Perhaps the Oil Minister expected a "yes" to that question. But John decided that he would be perfectly honest and candid. El-Bahar was too incisive and observant for John to try the old Madison Avenue game of getting the drift first, then going along with the current.

"Sheikh El-Bahar, I consider myself an American, but one who is proud of his Arab heritage, as I know other Americans feel, be they Italian, Chinese, Jewish, or any other nationality."

"I see," said El-Bahar. "Then let me ask you, do you think that as an American it would be objectionable to you if a foreigner, or several foreigners, owned and operated a major company or a business in the United States? Of course, I know that there are some foreign-owned firms in America, but most of them have either skillfully managed to keep this fact from the public, or else they are not sizable enough to cause anyone to be alarmed. I am curious to know how you feel about this."

"In principle, I see nothing at all wrong with foreign ownership of business in the United States," John replied with conviction. The world had become much too small and nations too interdependent to allow the petty nationalistic obstacles of small minds to stop the natural functioning of trade and commerce. "As long as the owners intend to operate the company in a way which protects all the stockholders and doesn't threaten the government. After all, American companies have billions of dollars of investments abroad, mostly in Europe and Canada. It would be difficult to assert that it's all right for us to own their companies but not vice versa. I guess there are some exceptions. In the United States a foreigner may not own a radio or television station. The idea is that if foreigners got hold of the electronic communications media they could subvert our country, or something like that. But that restriction applies even more stringently in virtually every other country too." John wondered what company they had in mind. At least he was beginning to get the drift of the Arab's planning; they were sounding him out about some sort of acquisition in the United States.

"Your friend, Charlotte Grogan, works in a television station in Washington, doesn't she?" El-Bahar asked.

"Yes, sir, she does. And I'm very impressed with both your intelligence reports and your personal ability to remember them in detail."

Sheikh El-Bahar laughed loudly. "Yes, indeed, my friend! We even learned some of that talent from your CIA. I think we have gone far enough for tonight; we can resume our conversation tomorrow at our next meeting. Now we shall return to the hotel and you can get some sleep."

El-Bahar turned to Mahmoun, who had said little all evening, and spoke rapidly to him in Arabic. Mahmoun nodded, accepting his instructions.

On the way back in the limousine, Mahmoun told John that he would be free the next day until three in the afternoon, at which time he would be called for at the Phoenicia and taken to the place of the next meeting with the minister. He cautioned John, should he see anyone he knew, not to disclose the reason for his being in Beirut or the fact that he had met with His Excellency. When they arrived at the Phoenicia, the two Arabs bade John good night at the elevator and went up to the suite.

"Mahmoun," El-Bahar said, "I feel he is the right man for our purpose."

"I'm sure you are making a good choice, Excellency."

"But meeting him was very important. The reports on him we received from America were just paper . . . black and white. We knew every detail of his past, but we did not know the man. Tonight Haddad's character was made known to us. He is extremely ambitious, I can tell that, and

59

I agree with it. He is also honest, which is indispensable. If he continues to satisfy me with his responses, tomorrow we will reveal our plan to him."

"Your Excellency, he is all that you say. I respectfully suggest that Mr. Haddad is also quite intelligent and capable of carrying out your plan."

The Oil Minister nodded. "Do you realize we are about to make financial history? I suspect the Americans will end up having a bit more respect for Arab business acumen after we have finished . . . perhaps we will even rate a case history in the texts of the Harvard Business School!"

Chapter 5

THE same limousine and driver were waiting for John that afternoon in front of the Phoenicia. He climbed into the rear and was soon speeding through downtown Beirut. The modern section of the city resembled the best of the French Riviera. White and pastel buildings, most with large balconies, lined wide streets with smart shops on the ground floors. Movie theaters, French-style sidewalk cafés, and big American cars crowding the curbs whipped past his peripheral vision.

By contrast, the old part of town through which they were now driving revealed the more traditional Middle Eastern setting. Crowded *souks,* shopping areas overflowing with screaming and gesticulating peddlers and hustling merchants, made driving dangerous. Youssef, the driver, seemed to steer through a sea of people totally oblivious of the noise of the car's horn. At times, the limousine would slow to a crawl, then stop, surrounded by countless pedestrians who walked in the street, occasionally allowing a car to pass.

During one of the stops, John could scarcely see around him, so dense was the crowd, when he heard a gentle tap on the closed car window. A small Arab boy, dressed in worn clothing, looked straight at him and held up a box of Chiclets gum. He was eight or nine, and his serene, pleading gaze masked the hardships that he had already endured in his young life.

Youssef gestured to the boy to go away, but John stopped him and reached into his pocket for some money. Suddenly, an older boy appeared and, in a swift motion, whacked the box out of the hands of the younger child, sending the gum sprawling over the sidewalk. The teenager laughed at his prank, while the boy, realizing that his entire merchant's inventory had been lost, burst into tears.

John got out of the car, his face flushed with anger. He slapped the older boy so hard that his hand hurt. Stunned, the vandal ran off, not wanting to risk being hit again. The little boy was on his knees, trying to salvage as much of the scattered merchandise as he could, and John went over to help him.

When they had finished, John smiled at his young friend and handed him a Lebanese ten-pound note, the equivalent of about four American dollars. The child took the money and looked up. He opened his mouth to speak, but his voice was drowned out by the cacophony of horns blasting angrily at the limousine that was blocking the tiny street. John hastily returned to the car, and as they drove off, he turned around and saw the little boy watching him, immobile, until he was engulfed by the crowd.

Later, as the car made its way through the narrow streets, Youssef broke the silence.

"If I may say so, sir, it was a most kind and generous thing you did."

"You know, Youssef," John replied, "I looked very much like that little boy when I was young. Who knows, if my grandparents had not emigrated to America, that boy could have been me."

61

Soon they were on a steep road climbing through the outskirts of the city. They rounded a bend, cutting off the view of the city through the rear window, and abruptly pulled off the road into a driveway. Youssef opened the rear door of the limousine and John was ushered into a modern pale yellow and white villa with thick stucco walls and tall narrow windows.

Sheikh El-Bahar, Mahmoun, and another man John had not yet met appeared and greeted him. This time the minister was wearing the traditional headdress and robes of the Saudi Arabians. His head was draped by the shoulder length, white linen *ghotra,* held securely in place by the black cords of the *igal,* which encircled his head and brow. Over the floor-length white *thobe* which looked like a monk's cassock, El Bahar wore a white *mishlah,* a long, robelike garment, open at the front. Along the sides and lower hem an intricate pattern was woven in gold filigree. The other two men were similarly, though less richly attired. Saudi men invariably felt more comfortable in their tribal attire, originally designed for the hot, dry climate of the desert. Here in the privacy of the villa, it was appropriate, whereas the previous night at the hotel and restaurant the robes would have been too conspicuous.

"Thank you for coming, John," the minister said. "You know Mahmoun, of course, and this is Mustafa Attifi of SAMA, the Saudi Arabian Monetary Agency. Mustafa has been kind enough to offer us the hospitality of his villa for our meeting." They shook hands all around. John made a conscious effort to conceal his impatience and proceed through the amenities at his hosts' leisurely pace. He was sure that his social behavior was being evaluated as well as his business acumen.

"Let us sit on the terrace," El-Bahar continued, leading them outside. "It is a lovely day and the view is splendid. There will be coffee served in a few minutes." The four men found seats around a glass-topped table.

As he lowered himself into the wrought-iron garden chair

with these cool, composed strangers who seemed to be smoothly proceeding from one phase to the next of a carefully planned exercise, John had a fluttery feeling in his stomach. It reminded him of the day at Cambridge when the dean had called him into his office. John had known the summons was for something important, but not whether it would be good news or bad. Then the dean had told him of his long-awaited acceptance by advance telephone notification from Georgetown Law, and the warm relief that flooded through his being was well worth the anxiety that went before.

The Oil Minister was finally ready to get down to business. "John, you have traveled a great distance and you have been patient. I will come right to the point. My country has a number of problems—some are well known, others are not. One problem, if it may be called that, is that we have a great deal of money to invest. Strange as it may sound, our deposits are no longer welcome in the major commercial banks all over the world."

El-Bahar went on to explain that once banks lend money out, it is usually on a long-term basis not subject to immediate repayment. The banks only keep sufficient cash on hand to meet the normal withdrawal needs of their many depositors. Moreover, the flow of new deposits coming in tends to counterbalance the withdrawals, so it often evens out. Thus, the banks can very accurately anticipate just how much cash turnover to expect from month to month, based on past experience. But what if a bank finds that one depositor could easily put the bank out of business just by writing a check for his total balance? No bank could afford to have as much as thirty percent of its deposits sitting around in cash not earning any income. So to prevent this kind of problem, the major banks had put a limit on the size of deposits acceptable from any single source.

"As you know," El-Bahar went on, "our enormous revenues of the past few years are still not invested in much of anything but bank deposits, but now we're wearing out our welcome very quickly. So we must find other channels of investment which will put to use a very large sum of money on a long-term basis. That is the first consideration."

The Oil Minister took a sip of his coffee, which had been unobtrusively served by a manservant while he was speaking. The three other men did not take their eyes off him as he continued, addressing himself to John.

"You are also undoubtedly aware that we have been engaged in a most troublesome and dangerous military confrontation with Iran. Now, despite the optimistic battle reports released daily by our Defense Ministry, we are losing badly. Oh, our soldiers are as good as theirs, but their American tanks are far superior to our French ones. Many of us in the government are seriously concerned that this conflict will be widened into an all-out war, particularly if the Iranians let their current success go to their heads. They have depleted their crude oil reserves much faster than we have used ours, they outnumber us substantially in population, and it is quite possible that they might try to repeat their conquests of two thousand years ago!

"In order to help solve these two problems in one stroke, we have decided to acquire a major American corporation."

El-Bahar paused, as much to rest his parched throat as for dramatic effect. John took the opportunity to answer.

"All that you have said makes perfect sense to me, Your Excellency. The whole world knows that your country has much money to invest, and I can now assume that you have in mind the acquisition of a company that manufactures some form of armament superior to your present suppliers'. But I'm sure you know that United States law prohibits foreign ownership of companies whose primary business is the manufacture of weapons." John reviewed in his mind the major American weapons companies—General Dynamics, Hughes Aircraft, McDonnell Douglas, Grumman—and couldn't guess which one the minister was hinting at.

"We are indeed aware of that, John."

"Have you decided on a specific company to acquire?"

"Oh, yes, John, we have, and we would like you to help us do it. We intend to acquire General Motors." El-Bahar had made up his mind about John and was willing to identify his goal.

John said nothing. He was stunned. Three pairs of Arab eyes fixed his unblinkingly in their gaze, gauging his reaction. He closed his eyes for a few seconds to escape their glare and organize his thoughts.

John was surprised by his own first reaction because it was emotional, and not at all cool-headed and pragmatic in the manner of an investment banker. Did these people, barely out of their goatskin tents on their barren deserts, really think they could take over the biggest industrial company in the Western world? Did they have the gall to think they could just *buy* America's largest and best-known corporate asset as though they were picking up some bauble across a jeweler's counter? In the next instant John recognized his thoughts for what they were, a defensive chauvinism in support of his parents' adopted country. Now it all fell into place. The oblique approach from Marwan, this mysterious trip to Beirut, last night's not so casual social evening with the penetrating questions. The Saudis were planning the financial coup of the century. They had thought it through and methodically gone about carrying it out. Their avenues had now converged on him. In effect he had been chosen as the purchasing agent in the largest purchase ever. But did they grasp the sheer size of General Motors?

"You did say 'General Motors,' Your Excellency—there's no mistake?"

The Oil Minister broke the tension by laughing. "Yes, my friend," he said with glee in his voice, "I do mean General Motors, and I fully understand your surprise."

"Your Excellency," John said, "do you know how much the company is worth? Let me see"—he paused—"there are about two hundred and eighty million shares of GM outstanding, so at the current price of about sixty dollars a share that means"—another pause as he looked up and calculated mentally—"that means General Motors has a current value in the stock market of almost seventeen-billion dollars!"

Sheikh El-Bahar was ready for the question, and his answer was at the tip of his tongue. "Are you aware of what Saudi Arabia's revenues were last year? Let me remind you. Last year we exported 4.38 billion barrels of oil at an average price of eleven dollars a barrel, for a total of 48.18 billion dollars. You see, all things are relative. We can afford to do what we want. The seventeen-billion-dollar figure you mentioned as General Motors' current value represents only about eighteen weeks' production of oil to us. As I said, we can easily afford it."

John realized that they weren't asking his advice—they were way ahead of him. He wouldn't volunteer any more self-evident estimates. The best thing to do was listen and learn more about the Arabs' plans. El-Bahar went on.

"There are other important reasons for our decision. Our country is in the midst of the biggest industrialization program in the history of the world. We are trying to bring Saudi Arabia into the twentieth century all in one jump. Hence, we have a great need for capital equipment of all kinds—trucks, power plants, locomotives, mining and petroleum drilling equipment, construction machinery, and more. General Motors manufactures much of what we need, so what better investment for us? The company's plants are located all over the world, so we will not be subject to the whims of any single government that might decide to embargo exports to us. We have used the embargo against the West. It is a nasty weapon, we know, and we want to be protected against it ourselves."

John Haddad was not about to dispute Sheikh El-Bahar's logic. General Motors was indeed a good investment, and it could also assure the Saudis their supply of military and industrial equipment, especially the tanks they needed to defeat the Iranians. He asked, "Have you thought about how you're going to proceed with the plan?"

"Only to a limited extent. You know that I have been to Harvard Business School and have some notion of how to acquire an American company. However, it is clear to me that we need highly professional help to do this job right, and we need someone we can trust, someone who will take complete charge of the operation for us. Do you understand?"

"I think I do, Your Excellency."

"Fine. Then you understand that you are the person we have chosen. You meet the qualifications we have set, including the fact that you have already successfully handled several corporate acquisitions in the United States."

"I'm very flattered and, frankly, somewhat overwhelmed." In reality, John felt he had reached firmer ground. This was what he knew all about, acquiring companies. The target was much bigger, to be sure, but still within the realm of his experience. He tried to put out of his mind the possible benefits that might accrue to him personally and focus on the immediate planning.

El-Bahar said, "That is not surprising. But don't worry, we don't expect a solution from you today."

"A couple of things do come to mind right away—you know that you only need to acquire a majority of the outstanding shares to control the company. Anything over fifty percent will do."

"Yes, of course, John. But we will expect your recommendation on this point."

"Another thing. What if political pressure is brought to bear on the U.S. government to forbid GM's falling under foreign control? I see now that you may have been thinking of this possibility when you asked me those questions about foreign ownership of American companies at dinner last night."

"Yes, we thought of that. We are not sure about it. We don't know whether it will happen and, if it does, from what quarter the pressure might come. That is one of the points you must also help us consider." El-Bahar had spent many hours trying to predict what the American govern-

67

ment might do, but had not succeeded to any satisfactory degree. This was a scheme that didn't permit the floating of trial balloons.

John decided not to venture an opinion now—he needed time to think it through. The Oil Minister finally posed the question.

"Before we proceed, John, I must know if you accept this assignment."

John's first impulse was to accept immediately, but he cautioned himself against jumping too fast. As the conversation had progressed, the role the Saudis had in mind for him had become more and more clear. But he wanted to know about the terms and conditions of the assignment before deciding.

"Your Excellency, I consider myself very fortunate to have been chosen by you and your associates for this job. I hope you won't think ill of me if I ask one or two questions before I respond . . . not about your own plans so much, but about how I would be expected to function if I took on this assignment."

"Go ahead and ask. I will answer, unless you touch upon certain topics which I am not free to discuss with outsiders."

"That's fair," John said, "I couldn't expect more. First I'd like to know how soon you would want me to complete the acquisition."

"The deadline is the end of this year, but we would prefer sooner."

"How many people actually know about it right now?"

"We four, Abdulaziz Khalif, our Defense Minister, the Prime Minister, our King, of course, and three senior officials of my ministry. Why do you ask that?"

"Because on Wall Street, news travels fast. I wanted to know if anyone in New York had any information. I still remember the day in the fall of 1974 when there was a rumor in New York that the Arabs were trying to buy IBM. Trading was suspended in the stock, then frantic buying ran it

68

up several points, even though the rumor was denied immediately. I would want to be able to control the release of information myself."

"Do you have any other questions, John?"

"What about the immense profits to the brokerage firm that handles this? Am I free to give this business to my own firm, Thompson, Caldwell, or have you chosen some other firm in advance?"

"Entirely up to you."

John could have gone on asking questions, but the essential ones had already been answered. They were willing to let him handle the whole thing and make the decisions. The story had not been leaked to the financial community. With those two advantages he felt sure he could succeed. He knew that he would never have another chance at something this big.

"Your Excellency, I would be honored to accept your assignment. I only have one more question, and this one is personal. How could you risk telling me so much of your plan before I agreed to join you? Wasn't it dangerous?"

"Perhaps," the Oil Minister replied, "but remember that we are thorough and careful people. We wanted you to know the full plan before accepting. That way we would be sure that you knew what you were committing yourself to accomplish. Also, keep in mind that we have investigated you quite deeply, and it is an uncontested fact of human life that no one is perfect. In your case, I am referring to an indiscretion you committed for your father's benefit at the time of the PAPCO-Siesta Inns merger."

Although El-Bahar's voice had not changed, John suddenly felt the ice-cold steel hand in the glove of conversational velvet. Until this moment he had thought the secret was quite safe. In helping his father, John had broken one of the basic tenets of law covering securities transactions, the "inside information" rule. For a hundred years the fundamental way of life in the stock market had been for the informed to prey upon the uninformed. The insiders, knowing what was happening before the public knew, had always contrived to sell before the bad news broke and buy before the good news reached the "little guy." The rule forbidding use of inside information had been on the books since 1942, but had never been enforced or ever interpreted by the courts. Then, in the 1960's, the scandal of the Texas Gulf Sulphur case broke. The geologist who had made a major new mineral find and a few of his immediate superiors had taken advantage of their knowledge to buy shares of Texas Gulf well in advance of public disclosure of the new discovery. Members of their families had passed on the word to some of their friends. A scandal broke, the long-dormant rule was finally enforced, and the inside traders were convicted. Ever since then, violation of the rule was no longer casually tolerated as before. John had risked being kicked out of the securities industry, being fined, and possibly being imprisoned. The Saudis' investigation must have turned up John's father's transaction. John saw that friendly as they were now, the Saudis were prepared to be as tough as necessary to protect their objectives. A brief chill went down his back, and he decided not to pursue the point.

El-Bahar went on "You are not to discuss this plan with anyone other than those who will be directly involved in the operation and the three of us here. Attifi will handle all monetary arrangements. He will see to it that the funds are transferred from our bank deposits worldwide to pay for the shares as you buy them. You should contact him on all financial matters. Get in touch with me personally or, if you cannot reach me, with Mahmoun, on anything pertaining to strategy or policy. '

"I will need a designated bank to hold the shares and arrange for payment," John said.

Attifi spoke for the first time. "We suggest you use Morgan Guaranty. We've been dealing with them for years and consider them reliable."

"I will probably want to deliver stock to the bank against payment. Who will advise the bank to accept the shares and pay out the money for them?"

"Whenever you wish funds remitted for share purchases, telex me in Jedda at SAMA. I will give you a set of test codes for transmittal verification and secrecy. Then I'll instruct Morgan to make payments on time."

John studied Attifi. His English was slightly accented in the manner of a German, but it was more likely learned in Zurich, the logical place to send such a man for financial training. John guessed his age to be about the same as his own, early thirties.

The Oil Minister spoke again. "Two final points. First, we will pay you personally five hundred thousand dollars for your services, payable in any currency and in any bank in the world, as you direct. And we will pay all other normal costs and fees involved in the purchase of the shares. Second, I will be in London on an official visit in two weeks. At that time I would like to review the overall strategy with you. Meanwhile, you understand that you are authorized to begin purchases of General Motors stock as of now. By the time we meet in London, I expect that you will have had a chancce to develop a program for the efficient acquisition of the company."

There was nothing more to add, and the meeting ended quietly. The three Arabs remained at the villa as Youssef drove John back to his hotel.

When the door to his room closed behind him, John was finally free to let loose his excitement. This was it! The one chance he had always hoped would come, and he would make the most of it. He felt a surge of elation as a kaleidoscope of pictures of the future flashed in microseconds through his brain. The look on the face of Elliott Grayson, Thompson, Caldwell's chairman, when he brought in *this* acquisition. The terms he would demand at Thompson,

Caldwell. He had the one in a million, the brass ring! General Motors executives, worried, rushing from Detroit to consult him. Should he start his own firm? An impressive plaque—J. HADDAD & CO., MEMBERS NEW YORK STOCK EXCHANGE AND OTHER PRINCIPAL EXCHANGES—at the front of Number 20 Wall Street. The Arabs were going to pay him half a million dollars. A huge fee, but he knew he could make much more out of this deal, and his options were many. He paced the room, unable to sit still, then, yielding to the impulse, decided to phone Charlotte in Washington. He gave the hotel operator the number of the television station, hoping he would catch her before she went out to lunch, for it was one o'clock there.

The call went through in about half an hour. After the endless operator talk, Charlotte was on the line. John spoke first.

"Hi, darling, it's me!"

"John, I didn't expect you to phone . . . are you all right?"

"Everything's fine, don't worry."

"I miss you, John, when are you coming home? I thought I'd take a day off and meet you at Kennedy and spend the night in New York."

"Sweetheart, I have a much better idea. Take the rest of the week off—it's only three working days—and meet me in Paris tomorrow. . . ."

She interrupted, "You've got to be kidding."

"No, no, I have to see you, and I desperately want some time together without anyone else around that we know."

"I can't just take off like that. . . ."

"Charlotte, please don't say no. Make up some excuse or ask for some vacation time, or anything. I promise I'll have you back in Washington on Sunday afternoon, and you can go back to work on Monday."

"Well, what should I pack . . . I don't know what to wear. . . ."

John knew her resistance was broken. "Pack what you'd pack for a few days in New York. The weather's the same. Charge the ticket on your American Express card, I'll pay you back. Take the Air France flight from Dulles to Paris tonight. It should get to Charles de Gaulle Airport at ten tomorrow morning . . . be careful not to accidentally book on a flight to Orly—there's still a few of those, you know. I'll get to De Gaulle about an hour after you on Middle East Airlines' morning flight from here, so wait for me at the airport. If anything goes wrong, I'll have a reservation at the Meurice and you can meet me there . . . oh yes, and go first class, we're rich!"

"You're really serious, aren't you? You want me to get on a plane tonight and come to Paris for the weekend, just like that. OK, you nut, I'm on my way."

"Great! Get going, don't drink too much champagne on the plane, and I'll see you in La Belle France tomorrow."

"Wait, John! You haven't told me what happened in Beirut."

"No way, kiddo, that's business . . . and what I am calling you about is pleasure!"

They each said good-bye three times, neither wishing to be the first to break the connection, and the conversation ended. John went down to the airlines desk in the lobby to exchange his plane tickets, discovering that he was profiting from the premium value of the supersonic flight's return fare, and to cable the Hotel Meurice in Paris to reserve a room for Monsieur et Madame Haddad of New York.

Shortly after John had left the cable operator, he was replaced at the counter by an amiable Hans Sloman, in whose hand was clutched a Lebanese note with a high number showing on the corner. At first the man shook his head, frowning angrily. But when Sloman added two more notes from his pocket to the one in his hand, the operator shrugged, bent low, and whispered in Sloman's ear as he slid the money across the counter and out of sight.

Chapter 6

CHARLES DE GAULLE Airport was opened to the public in March, 1974. At the time, the new facility was widely acclaimed to be the most modern and spectacular airport in the world. The satellite arrival and departure gates were connected to the main, circular terminal by a dazzling, futuristic group of cylindrical, glass-enclosed tubes equipped with moving walkways. These tubes converged and knotted themselves in Gordian twists at the terminal, much like the meeting of the maze of freeways in downtown Los Angeles, before disgorging their passengers onto solid ground. In spite of the visual impact, however, experienced air travelers had already formed their own opinions of the notoriously unreliable motorized paths.

When John debarked from the MEA jet at Satellite 3, he noticed the sign by the walkway that said EN DÉRANGEMENT—OUT OF ORDER, and he began the long trudge to the terminal on the sidewalk alongside the immobilized metal belt. He felt sorry for some of his fellow passengers who, unlike himself, were encumbered with heavy valises and unwieldy packages. There were not even any rolling luggage carts available to ease their loads.

In line for the passport control, John peered over the heads of the other passengers for a glimpse of Charlotte. She was there, on the other side of a low partition, waving energetically at the sight of him. The customs officer looked at his passport, then up at him, and handed it back to John without stamping it. A few more steps and he embraced Charlotte.

"Hello, darling! You don't look one bit like a girl who just spent the night on an airplane."

"I'm so excited being here! I still don't believe it." Charlotte was wearing a trim body shirt, cardigan sweater, and tailored slacks. She carried an Air France flight bag slung

74

over her shoulder. "Boy, first class is the way to travel. I could easily get spoiled by it."

John smiled. "A little luxury is good for you once in a while. Come on, let's get your suitcase and find a cab."

The Meurice Hotel on the Rue de Rivoli was one of the changeless old bastions of luxury in Paris. The lobby was small, designed to discourage the sort of heavy traffic that was all too frequent at the neighboring Intercontinental Hotel. The Meurice did not cater to tours, conventions, or airline crews. Once in its recent history, however, it had accommodated the most unwelcome organization ever to visit Paris. The Meurice was chosen by the fastidious officers of the Wehrmacht as headquarters for the German high command during the occupation of Paris in World War II. The hotel was one of the focal points of the fighting on the day of liberation, and the masonry on the outside still proudly bore a few of the bullet scars.

John registered himself and Charlotte as Mr. and Mrs. Haddad and presented his passport to the registration clerk. As was the custom in virtually every European hotel, his companion's passport was neither requested nor proffered.

They were given a superior room on the second floor, facing the beautiful Tuileries Gardens. The second floor, called *le premier étage* in French, is always the best location in any old French hotel. During the nineteenth century, this floor was called the *étage noble* because the proportions of the rooms and fixtures were more massive and imposing to satisfy the chosen few who were able to enjoy them. Besides, since there were no elevators then, the best paying clients had demanded the fewest stairs to climb.

John and Charlotte's room was furnished in Louis Seize, with a crystal chandelier hanging from the center of the lofty ceiling. There were two French windows draped with heavy gold curtains, and two double beds. After tipping the bellboy, John pulled closed the two massive French doors giving on the balcony, and suddenly the roar of the traffic outside on the Rue de Rivoli was hushed to a murmur. He drew the heavy gold silk curtains and transformed the room into a pitch-black hideaway, called down to the operator for a wakeup call at four in the afternoon, and beckoned Charlotte to bed.

Awakening from a refreshing sleep made sounder by the knowledge that no human being outside the hotel knew their whereabouts, John and Charlotte dressed for dinner, planning a nice long stroll through the fading afternoon sunlight. But John was unable to put the fantastic adventure he had just embarked on out of his mind. He couldn't adopt the passive and receptive attitude of a vacationing tourist. His brain was teeming with plans and possible strategies for pulling off the Saudis' coup. There was a chance he could pick up some stock here in Europe. Why not try?

He went to the telephone and called the concierge to have a reservation made for dinner at the Tour d'Argent, savoring the fun of being able to afford a very expensive three-star meal at the famous Paris landmark restaurant. It wasn't tourist season, so the chances were good that they would have a supremely undisturbed feast.

As he hung up the the telephone he glanced over and saw that Charlotte was still busy putting herself together for the evening. He couldn't resist. Speaking rapidly in French to the hotel operator and keeping his voice low, he placed a call to the International Department of Thompson, Caldwell in New York. Having learned what he needed to know, he then placed another call, this time to Bertrand et Companie in Geneva. After reaching the right partner of the Geneva bank and securing an appointment with him, he felt much better. Now some of the wheels would be in motion even before he returned to New York. Finally he called his own office at Thompson, Caldwell. Reaching Sue Anderson, his secretary, John promised he would be in Monday morning and would tackle the mountain of mail she told him was waiting on his blotter. Then, eagerly, he asked her

76

to give him the morning's opening prices of General Motors stock. He was just hanging up as Charlotte came back into the bedroom, dressed and ready.

Going out of the hotel and down the Rue de Rivoli, they stopped to look into the shop windows every few steps, Charlotte perfectly happy to be just looking, and John grateful that she was not a compulsive shopper like so many girls he had known. At the Rue Royale their route took them across the Place de la Concorde to the river, then along the right bank heading for Notre Dame, under the roof of branches of the massive trees along the embankment. They paid no attention to the heavy traffic of little cars roaring along the quai carrying homeward-bound Parisians like a swarm of gigantic, buzzing hornets.

John and Charlotte crossed the Seine at Notre Dame, just as the sun was setting, catching the old cathedral in its reddish glow. Seen from their table by the window in the restaurant, Paris had been transformed into an ocean of lights shining in front of the black velvet curtain of night.

After ordering cocktails, the *sole cardinale,* to be followed by the Tour d'Argent's famous duckling and a truly great Château Latour, John and Charlotte finally had a chance to talk at length. John traced everything that had happened to him from the moment he arrived in Beirut to his departure for Paris two days later. The narrative effort helped him organize his own thoughts and plans as he explained the massive size of the Arabs' endeavor to her. John went into considerable detail about the personality of El-Bahar, his commanding but at the same time warm attitude and his quick grasp of what was needed to accomplish the objectives. As he paused for a sip of wine, Charlotte broke in with a question John hadn't even considered.

"Can you trust them, John?" she asked. "What if they're using you just to test the water for this deal?"

John thought it was typical of her to think first of protecting him. "I'm pretty sure there's nothing like that to fear," he answered. "The Saudis will be forced to put up substantial money as soon as I start buying stock. If they fail to pay, I'll know in a few days. No, there wouldn't be any point in their leading me into a blind alley."

"What do you think the high mucka-mucks at Thompson, Caldwell will say to all this?"

"I really don't know. I'll be walking in the door with the biggest single financial transaction they've ever seen, and you'd think they would immediately offer me a partnership. But I have a feeling they're going to have a lot of trouble deciding how to handle me. Grayson has never had anyone outside of his coterie of favorites bring in a major deal."

"Then why don't you leave them and take it to one of the other good firms? Any one of them would let you write your own ticket for a thing this big."

"There are several reasons. First, I owe them some loyalty after all. They haven't openly mistreated me in any way, and they gave me my best offer when I was looking for a job. Then, too, I know the capabilities of the people in the firm, and whom to get to help me. It would be damn hard to handle in a new place with people I don't know well. I think I ought to try and stick with Thompson, Caldwell and make sure I get compensated properly. I can't imagine them actually trying to cheat me."

"OK, so you stick with Thompson, Caldwell for the time being. I have another question. Are you going to do anything about the deal while we're here in Paris?"

"I've been meaning to tell you . . . when I was making the dinner reservation I also called Geneva"—he flashed a guilty smile—"and I have an appointment with a banker there tomorrow to try to pick up some GM stock he's holding."

Hans Sloman's eyes darted from table to table as he stood in the entrance of the Tour d'Argent looking for John Haddad. After following him this far, Sloman hoped he would catch him alone and have a chance to talk. But the concierge at the Meurice had neglected to tell him that John had a female companion. When Sloman spotted John by the window, deeply engrossed in his conversation with Charlotte, he shrugged his shoulders, sighed, and motioned for the captain to show him to a table. He couldn't continue this strenuous detective work without a decent meal to give him strength.

Sloman's persistence was rooted in desperation. He had almost run out of options and his time was practically gone. His problems stemmed from his sincere generosity and observance of an old friendship. Ten years earlier, Sloman's closest friend, Günther Stahl, had been killed in an avalanche while skiing in the high Alps. The survivors were his wife, Greta, and his fifteen-year-old son, Kurt. Günther's life had been insufficiently insured, and Greta was fortunate to land a civil service job in the canton's central post office that paid barely enough to make ends meet. Kurt's education continued, largely financed by Sloman, who had promised Günther Stahl years before that he would take care of his son if anything ever happened to him. Sloman had hired young Kurt when he finished the university, and trained him as a currency trader at the bank. As the young man acquired more seniority, he also was permitted a certain amount of discretion in his trading, particularly when it came to positioning the bank's own funds. During one of the sudden runs on the U.S. dollar that had occurred the previous month while Sloman was away on a trip, Kurt had managed to put the bank in the position of holding an excessive supply of dollar futures on margin. The result was disastrous. The bank was forced to sell the contracts at the bottom of the slide, and the resulting deficit would soon be known. Sloman was determined not only to save the bank but also to save young Kurt from going to jail for mismanagement of funds, a very serious crime in Switzerland. Sloman needed an immediate infusion of money for the bank to cover the losses. There was no way he could get any kind of loan because the audit required would reveal the losses even sooner than they would come to light in the normal course of business. The information Sloman had extracted from Sharif in Beirut seemed to him the only solution. He had to find a way to turn his knowledge into money, and for that he had to approach John Haddad.

As John glanced up, watching the waiter deftly fillet the soles and transfer them to the warmed plates, he caught Sloman's eye for a fleeting moment. The man looked vaguely familiar, but John couldn't place him. Had he seen him in Beirut? Was he being followed? He decided to keep a sharp eye out from now on, and not to call Charlotte's attention to the man.

Charlotte had begun to think of some of the implications of the takeover. "Do you realize what a fantastic news story this is going to be? I could get a promotion out of this at CBS—maybe even a transfer to the national news staff in New York!"

John hated to dampen her enthusiasm, but he had to. "No way, darling. There won't be any scoops on this story. It has to be a secret until the official announcement, and then everyone will find out at the same time. I'm sorry."

"Well, what about an exclusive interview with El-Bahar? Can't you toss me a crumb or two?" Charlotte wasn't ready to give up so easily.

John admired her desire to succeed in the news business, but he couldn't afford any news leaks. As they continued with the dinner, he explained to her again that he had promised El-Bahar to keep it confidential and that he was relying on her to cooperate. Otherwise, there wouldn't be anything in it for him . . . the Arabs would take it away. John promised he would be away in Geneva for only a few hours the next day, and be back in time for dinner. Charlotte declared her intention of seeing the Impressionists at the Jeu de Paume museum. She had always rushed through on previous trips and would be delighted at the opportunity to take her time. She loved the small, sunny rooms of the little museum, made even brighter and warmer by the rich colors of the paintings, so different from the dark and venerable atmosphere of the Louvre. And she knew John was too keyed up to have the patience for browsing through an art museum with her.

Chapter 7

BERTRAND et Companie was one of the oldest and most respected private banks in Geneva, but no one would have guessed it from looking at the bank's office from the outside. It occupied an entire building on Rue de la Corraterie, in the heart of Geneva's banking district, where the most famous banks are those least distinguishable from ordinary one-hundred-year-old apartment buildings. You did not walk into Bertrand et Companie off the street, even if you knew what the small brass plaque on the door with only the inscription "B. ET CIE" stood for. Besides money, it took several recommendations to be considered, unless, of course, the prospective client was a world-renowned industrialist or a chief of state like so many others who banked there.

It was dark inside the bank when John walked in, but he saw the uniformed *huissier* rise quickly from behind a nearby table. The *huissiers* were a permanent fixture in European banks, generally elderly war veterans whose job was to escort visitors through the dark hallways into the appropriate offices. John told him he had an appointment with Monsieur Julien Bertrand, one of several partners in the firm who were direct descendants of the man who had founded the bank in 1824.

A phone call was made and John was ushered into a small, elegantly furnished sitting room. The *huissier* discreetly flicked a switch on his way out that lighted a small

81

sign outside indicating that the room was *occupé*. A minute later, John was joined by Julien Bertrand, a dapper man in his forties, somewhat more fashionably dressed than John had expected of a Swiss banker, with the red rosette of the French Légion d'honneur in his buttonhole.

"How do you do, Mr. Haddad. I do not believe we have met, but of course I know your firm well." Julien Bertrand spoke fluent English with authority and a bit of a British accent.

"Thank you for seeing me, Mr. Bertrand. As I mentioned to you on the phone from Paris, my activities at Thompson, Caldwell don't usually bring me into contact with institutional stock buyers, so I got your name from our International Department."

"I see."

"I'll get right to the point. I understand you have a rather sizable position in General Motors common stock."

"We do not normally divulge our securities holdings, Mr. Haddad, but since much of it was purchased through your firm, I suppose I can discuss it with you." Bertrand opened a leather file folder and pulled out an IBM computer runoff. He flipped through a few pages and stopped. "Here it is. General Motors . . . yes . . . we hold one hundred twelve thousand and two hundred shares for our clients. Do you have some news about the company?"

"No, I don't. The reason I'm here is that I represent another client who would like to buy the stock."

"But our stock is not for sale. We have no reason to sell it."

"I can't give you any fundamental reason to sell it, Mr. Bertrand, but I'm willing to buy your stock at a price above the current market." John looked at an antique clock on the fireplace. It was five P.M., which meant it was noon in New York, and the stock market had been open for two hours. "Would you be kind enough to tell me what General Motors is trading for today?" As John well knew, the Swiss banks were all equipped with the latest electronic quote

82

machines, which instantaneously gave every necessary bit of information on the U.S. stock market at the touch of a button.

Bertrand picked up a phone and dialed three digits.

"Charles, Bertrand ici. Donnez-moi le dernier cours de General Motors . . . bien merci. The last sale is fifty-nine and a half." He put the phone down.

"I am prepared to pay sixty-one and a half a share for your block." John studied the other man as the bid registered in his mind.

Bertrand did not say anything. He had to think fast. It was unusual to get a bid two points above the market price unless the stock was of a small company and traded very little. In that case, one could simply not acquire a large block of stock by buying it on the market without driving up the price. General Motors was another story. With so much stock outstanding, most large buyers just took their time and bought it on the New York Stock Exchange.

Bertrand had not mentioned to John Haddad that most of their stock had recently been purchased at about 57. Haddad probably knew that, though, since the stock had been bought through his firm. But he surely did not know that Bertrand et Companie was having some problems with its clients who had complained that their portfolios' performance in the U.S. stock market had been poor under Bertrand's management. Now here was a chance to make a quick profit that would please many clients and help restore the bank's reputation as a shrewd money manager. Julien Bertrand was tempted. But first he had to find out how much of his stock had been bought recently at 57. There was no point in selling stock that had been purchased long before at higher prices. He picked up the phone again and dialed.

"Charles, c'est encore moi. Dites-moi vite le nombre de titres de General Motors que nous avons acheté la semaine dernière à cinquante-sept." A pause. Bertrand's face was slightly flushed. *"D'accord. Merci.* Mr. Haddad, I would

be willing to sell you eighty-five thousand shares at sixty-one and a half. The remainder belongs to clients for whom we do not wish to sell. Is that satisfactory to you?"

"Yes, it is. May I call my office from here? We can probably do the trade right now."

"Fine. In fact, why not go to our trading room? We have a ticker display there and we can watch the transaction on the tape."

The two men rose and John followed Bertrand out. John's pulse had quickened, and he made a conscious effort to keep his excitement from showing.

The trading room was not the least bit in keeping with the somber and serious mood of the rest of the bank. It was a vast, neon-lit hall with all modern furniture. In the middle, a long semicircular desk accommodated six shirt-sleeved traders talking on the telephone. An array of flashing lights in front of them was nothing more than telephone lines to the major currency, gold, and stock markets in Europe. Overhead, on the wall along the wide side of the room, a display of electronic numbers showed all the trading data they needed. There was also a long, electronic board that showed prices of the transactions on the New York Stock Exchange, the American Stock Exchange, and the Over the Counter markets in lighted numbers and symbols that flashed by as fast as one could read them.

John Haddad and Julien Bertrand took seats at a table in the far corner of the room. Directly in front of them was a piece of equipment familiar to John; an electronic stock quotation machine that, at the press of a few buttons, displayed all of the current stock market information on the stock whose trading symbol had been punched into it. The machine was the same kind that was used in almost every brokerage office in the United States. John entered the letter G followed by the letter M on the keyboard. Then he pressed the larger button marked "FULL RECAP. Instantly, the television screen flashed numbers: LAST SALE 59½, BID 59¼; ASKED 59½, HIGH 59⅝, LOW 59½, VOLUME 12,500.

The machine gave all of the relevant information for the current day's trading as it was happening.

"If you wish, I will have the call put through now."

"Fine, thanks." John drew his attention away from the machine. "This is the number that goes right into our trading department in New York." He wrote it on a piece of paper.

A short while later, one of the phones in front of them rang and John picked it up.

"This is John Haddad. I'm calling from Geneva. Is Tony Cassetti there?" Cassetti was not the head of the Trading Department, but he had a reputation for being the most nimble stock trader around. "Tony, I need your help on a big transaction. I'm in the office of Bertrand et Companie in Geneva. I'm going to buy for a client eighty-five thousand shares of General Motors that Bertrand will sell to me. We've agreed on a price of sixty-one and a half. Can you handle it?"

"Sure, Johnny boy. Hey, that's a nice trade. I'll arrange a cross."

There were approximately 1,800 different stocks listed on the New York Stock Exchange. Brokerage firms that were Exchange members were required to trade listed stocks only on the floor of the New York Stock Exchange or on some other exchange, such as the small Pacific Coast Stock Exchange, where the same stock might also be listed.

Since the Exchange required its members to trade listed stocks on the floor of the Exchange, it meant that even when a single firm had a large buy and sell order in the same stock, the broker had to go down to the floor of the Exchange to consummate the trade. This type of transaction was referred to as a "cross," a trade in which a block of stock "crosses" from a buyer to a seller at a prearranged price without resorting to the auction procedures usually practiced on the Exchange floor.

Cassetti spoke into the phone: "Let's see. GM last sale fifty-nine and a half. You know we've gotta buy all the stock up to sixty-one and a half before we can cross it there. Do you want to deduct that from the eighty-five thou?"

Cassetti meant that to cross a block of stock on the New York Stock Exchange certain rules had to be followed in a pattern as rigid as an NASA countdown. First, in order to cross the block of stock at 61½, the stock price had to move from 59½ to 61½. Most of the Exchange's trading rules are based on fair play, so, in this case, if someone was willing to pay 61½ for some shares of General Motors, then those sellers who had already entered orders to sell their shares for 61½ or less, were entitled to be served first. This meant that Cassetti would have to start bidding on the floor of the Exchange for all GM stock, buying it at successively higher prices until the price reached 61½. Then he could sell Bertrand's block to himself at that price, effecting a cross. The sight of a broker standing near a trading post talking to himself out loud, fulfilling the requirement of transacting the trade openly, often startled a first-time visitor to the floor of the Exchange.

"Tony, I'll take all the stock you have to buy up to sixty-one and a half in addition to the eighty-five thousand." In most cases the buyer would deduct from the total amount of the cross the number of shares of stock he had to buy to move the stock up. This assured the buyer that he was not buying more stock than he had really wanted, and the seller invariably went along.

"Can you give me the account numbers for the trade, Johnny?"

John could hear the noise and shouting in the background of the trading room in New York and raised his voice to be sure that Cassetti heard him. "On the sell side, the account is Bertrand et Companie, Geneva. You can get the account number from the International Department." He lowered his voice and covered the mouthpiece with his hand so that the Swiss traders couldn't hear. "On the buy side, I need a new account opened in the name of Islam Investors Limited. The stock is to be delivered to Morgan

Guaranty against payment. Good luck, Tony. I'm going to leave this line open so we can talk, and we'll be watching your work on the tape."

John laid the phone down on the table. He and Bertrand fixed their attention to the electronic ticker tape on the wall, which was now moving rapidly. IBM 2s 425 ACY 54 GID 23 GM 59½ 4s 59⅝ 2,000 59¾.

"John, is that our stock on the tape?" Trading rooms were no place for formal forms of address. Bertrand was very alert, his eyes moving quickly with the flow of symbols and numbers across the board.

"I think it is. GM is moving up on volume. Let's wait a minute and see." John's hand was clutching the phone, but he did not put it up to his ear.

The tape continued to flash by. FED 3s 43¼ DOW 126 EAL 64⅛ GM 59¾ 4,000 57⅞ 6,000 60.

John raised the phone. "Tony! What's going on? Is that our stock?"

"Yeah, Johnny. The last two trades were yours. You've got a total of twelve thousand six hundred so far, but we've got competition. Some shmuck down on the floor is buying a block for a fund. I'll try to talk to him."

Two more smaller blocks of GM went by on the tape.

"Johnny. That son of a bitch may try to break up the cross. I can't do any more until I talk to him."

"What's going on?" Although he was not totally familiar with New York Stock Exchange trading practices, Bertrand realized that there was a problem.

"There's another buyer in there. Tony's afraid he may try to break up the cross." John explained that since a cross has to be done on the floor, the broker must first openly offer the stock he wants to buy. Then he announces that he is buying it from himself. If another broker has a buy order, he can simply interrupt by shouting, "Take it!" when the verbal offer is made, before the first man can "take" his own offering. "Our man is trying to get to the competing broker and talk sense into him."

"Will they try to make a deal?"

"Nothing that friendly. Tony will probably suggest that the fellow had better get out of the way unless he would like to see *his* crosses broken up for the next few years. It often works. After all, they've got to come back and work with each other every day." Tony came back on the line. John listened, then turned to Bertrand. "They got to him. I didn't ask any questions, but I know he'll leave us alone."

The tape sped along, electronic numbers moving from left to right until they disappeared. Then the transaction they were waiting for appeared. AFI 122½ 2s 123 KLM 43 GM 60¼ 4s 60½ 2,000 61 5s 61¼ 85,000 61½.

"It's done! We did the cross." Bertrand looked to John and extended his hand. Both men laughed and cheered as if their favorite team had scored the winning soccer goal or touchdown. John spoke into the phone for the last time.

"Thanks a lot, Tony. Great job. See you Monday."

John and Julien Bertrand walked out of the trading room. All of the traders were now aware of the GM trade and turned and smiled at them as they walked out.

"John, can you stay for dinner tonight?"

"Thank you, Julien, but I'm expected in Paris. Let's do it another time. In fact, I'd better get moving if I want to catch the six ten flight."

The bank's limousine crossed the bridge by Geneva's renowned water spout and continued on the short trip to Cointrin Airport. In the back seat, John Haddad ignored the scenery; he was engrossed in his own thoughts. First blood had been drawn. With John Haddad's help, the Saudi Arabians had begun to acquire the largest industrial corporation in the world.

Back in Paris, John intended to pay full attention to Charlotte and not make any more side trips or excursions in pursuit of business. They decided to make no plans for a heavy dinner, but rather to walk up the Champs Elysées to Fouquet's, a sidewalk café dignified by one Michelin star, which was open until all hours and where you could get anything from a glass of Perrier mineral water to a ten-course banquet. Although the French had become very modern and fast-moving in the last couple of decades, still the pace in Paris was of a different quality from that in New York. On a spring Friday night in New York, people jammed the highways with their cars, heading for the beaches, mountains, anywhere, just to get away. But in Paris the fine weather brought out the walkers . . . the *flâneurs*. The word is not translatable because its meaning includes the concept of strolling, but it also implies a certain attitude. The attitude is one of basking, of examining everyone and everything that meets the eye, of being in a good mood. The *flâneurs* were out in force on the Champs Elysées, and John and Charlotte joined them, arm in arm, aiming for the brightly lighted Arc de Triomphe shining like a jewel at the far end of the double row of leafy trees along the avenue.

They finally arrived, with all deliberate speed, at the mass of sidewalk tables under Fouquet's red and gold awning. They chose a convenient table from which they could easily see the passersby. Drinks were ordered from the fast-moving waiter, who was back in less than a minute with two Scotches and not quite enough ice. All was as it should be. Peace and anonymity.

Behind them, John heard a loud voice, a nasal Brooklyn accent bellowing at an approaching female companion. He wondered if he recognized the voice or was this just another crude New York tourist out to give Americans a bad name? No, the voice was familiar. John turned around discreetly and recognized a short, fat man with black, curly hair. It was Arnie Alpert, late of Woodside, Queens, and now a hot fund manager who operated out of Amsterdam. John had known Arnie Alpert for years, going back to the days when Arnie was a student at Boston University and worked as a waiter in a popular Cambridge hamburger emporium that John frequented. He was always looking for stock tips, even then, and he suddenly quit his waiter's job after cleaning up on some little electronics company stock he heard about in the restaurant from the son of the company's founder.

John whispered to Charlotte, "Let's go."

She looked puzzled for a moment, then connected John's order to his apparent recognition of the man behind them. John caught her look and added, "I'll tell you later." Without saying a word, Charlotte began to assemble the paraphernalia she had placed on the table and prepared to leave.

Just then a thought crossed John's mind, and he gently touched Charlotte's arm as she was rising. "No, honey, I changed my mind. Let's stay, OK ?"" Charlotte sat down and gave him a quizzical but affectionate look.

John turned around, smiled, and said, "Arnie, what a surprise to see you."

"Johnny baby! Watcha doin' here?" Alpert jumped up and waddled over, bumping two other tables on the way and earning angry glances from their occupants. He pumped John's hand, paying no attention to Charlotte at all.

"Arnie, I'd like you to meet Charlotte Grogan. Charlotte, Arnie Alpert."

"Howja do, honey, why don' you and Johnny join us at our table? You gotta come over and meet my chicks." He grabbed the two Scotches in one hand, the waiter's saucers that were on the table to keep count of the drinks in the other, and led the way back. Soon they were ensconced in a tightly packed crowd, and Arnie introduced them to Rhonda and Susan by their first names. He didn't seem to know the girls' last names. The talk was trivial, but Arnie was the loud, jovial host, refusing to hear of anyone but him paying for anything.

Arnie was delighted to have bumped into John. He knew where John worked, and he had always wanted to do business with Thompson, Caldwell. But Thompson, Caldwell was not exactly enamored of Arnie. He ran a mutual fund whose shares were sold only outside of the United States because he couldn't get SEC approval. He did most of his stock buying in New York, but dealt with less prestigious firms who didn't care where their commissions came from as long as they came often. He was not above some slightly shady shenanigans in the market.

John asked him how his business was doing, and Arnie adroitly avoided an answer. But John had remembered that Arnie's various funds held a large amount of General Motors stock, and this would be another source if he could get him to part with it at a price.

"Arnie, did you see the volume in GM today?"

"Yeah, I was tempted to get in there and unload a little . . . but there was a cross on the floor and I couldn't get in in time. The stock went up three points from yesterday's close."

"If you could unload some stock, what kind of size would you be coming in with?"

"Johnny, I'll level with ya, I'm gettin' the squeeze right now. My redemptions are way higher than sales, two of my best salesmen quit, and I have to raise some fast cash. I can't sell most of the shit I'm holding in this market, so I have to sell some blues. The best blue I have is GM, but I'd have to net about sixty-three on a couple hundred thousand to make it worth the trouble."

"You have two hundred thousand to sell at a limit of, let's say sixty-three and three-quarters, to get you out of trouble?"

"Yeah, right, that's it."

"Suppose I said that I could bid for the whole block . . . would you sell it to me?"

"You bet your ass I would!"

"OK, Arnie, let's find a phone. New York is closed now, but we can cross it on the coast. Just one thing . . . I know you understand, but I'd rather not have the sell side on this one. You call whoever you want in LA and tell them to expect a bid at sixty-three and three-quarters to hit the floor of the Pacific Stock Exchange in about forty-five minutes. I'll call the order in to my Los Angeles office, and our guys will meet on the floor. At least on the coast there's no danger of anyone stepping in between on a cross this size."

"Johnny my man, you are OK. You're pulling my ass out of a bind, and you're ready to move two hundred large, between drinks, from Paris to LA. I gotta admit, that's class!"

They hurried across the street to the TWA offices where there was a row of public telephones, excusing themselves to the women and promising to be back in a few minutes. John placed a collect call to Thompson, Caldwell's Los Angeles office and got the block trader on the line. "Jerry, I have a tricky one for you. I want you to put a bid to buy two hundred thousand GM at sixty-three and three-quarters on the floor of the Pacific. Have your floor man hang in near the post and wait until he sees the guy from . . . hold it a second. Arnie, who's selling for you?"

From the next booth, where he was talking to his broker, Arnie leaned out and said, "Robbins and Liebling—in ten minutes."

John turned back to his phone, "Jerry, it'll be the guy from Robbins and Liebling. He'll come with an offering to hit our bid. And you can clean up whatever is in between and still take the full two hundred, got it?"

"I have it . . . is this the same account I heard about from Tony Cassetti this morning?"

"The very same. Please get the account number from Tony. I don't want to talk names at this end right now, dig?"

"I read you loud and clear. Where do I report the trade?"

"Call the Hotel Meurice in Paris, *M-E-U-R-I-C-E*. I don't know the number. I'm registered there, so just leave a message that says 'two hundred done,' or if you have a problem, just say 'partial' or 'nothing done.' I'll get back to you, and, please, no names in the message!"

"We're rolling on it, John. I'll get off now, and thanks for sharing some of the action with us out here on the coast!"

He hung up just about the same time as Arnie did, and

they walked back across to Fouquet's together. "Johnny, how about a drink? I need one!"

"I'd love to, really, but I'm pretty tired from chasing around the last few days, so you'll have to give me a rain check. Do you plan to be in New York any time soon?"

"Not soon. There are a few people in New York who I'd just as soon stay away from, if you know what I mean. Anyway, I live like a fucking king in Amsterdam! I like it better here on this side."

Charlotte looked grateful at being rescued from the conversation with the two women, and she and John extricated themselves gracefully from Arnie's group and hailed a taxi. When they got back to the hotel, the message was in the box with the key. It said, "Two hundred done."

Chapter 8

"MR. GRAYSON's office," said the woman in a tone that appropriated and amplified the importance of the man she served. "Yes, John. Well, I'll see, but he's very busy. Hold on." She was back on the line in twenty seconds. "He says you can come right up if it's that important."

John and Charlotte had flown to Washington from Paris the previous day, and John connected almost immediately to a flight to New York. He had not slept well; the jet lag would take a few days to wear off. In the meantime, he could not let his temporary discomfort delay the project.

The executive offices were two flights above the Corporate Finance Department, and John went up the firm's internal staircase rather than wait for an elevator. The fifty-fourth floor of the Fidelity Building, where Thompson, Caldwell's senior executives worked had that special quality calculated to impress visitors with the importance of its occupants. The dark carpets seemed an inch thicker than elsewhere, old paintings on the fabric-covered walls were illuminated by individual overhanging lights, and the well-groomed male receptionists spoke in hushed tones into their dark-brown telephone instruments. The reception area was suitably designed and furnished to demonstrate the firm's good taste and financial resources. The wide floor-to-ceiling picture window offered a dizzying and unobstructed view of the city and the contrasting green expanse of country to the north. Two pre-Columbian statues dominated one side of the room and provided balance against the frail, modern Giacometti sculptures facing them from the other side. The furniture was modern and comfortable, but unmistakably lush and expensive.

Elliott Grayson's office was divided into three distinct parts: a working area much like most offices, containing a large mahogany desk and chair; a conference table with eight chairs at the far end of the large room; and, in the middle, a living room arrangement with a sofa, tables and lamps, and two armchairs. Grayson often received visitors in the last and most informal of the settings, but he remained seated behind his desk as John came in. In any other kind of business, it would have been unheard of for a junior officer like John to have access to the chairman of the company at a moment's notice. But in the securities industry, no chief executive would refuse to listen. Any employee could come across valuable information by chance. Frequently, time was a factor, and the meandering of vital facts through the stops on an organization chart could be harmful and costly.

Nevertheless, John Haddad had never before invaded Grayson's sanctuary in this manner, and he found the chairman in an impatient frame of mind. As John approached the desk and sat down in a straight chair facing him, Grayson made sure his tone was brusque.

"Hello, John. What's on your mind?"

Elliott Grayson had become chairman of the board of

Thompson, Caldwell four years earlier following the most bitter boardroom fight in the firm's history. The issue was whether or not the firm should go public by making an offer to sell its own stock on the market. The proponents, led by Grayson, argued that selling stock to the public would make it easier for the firm to raise needed capital. They also pointed out that by allowing Thompson, Caldwell officers to sell some of their own shares, they would be considerably enriching themselves. Others on the board wanted the firm to remain privately held, keeping their affairs away from the glare of outside stockholders and the regulatory agencies. Predictably, greed won out, and Grayson ascended to the chairmanship in the corporate reshuffle that took place just prior to the first public offering of Thompson, Caldwell stock.

There had always been some questions about Grayson's motives in leading the fight for taking the firm public. It was now generally assumed that he did so only as a means to split the board and win the top job. After all, he didn't need the money himself; he was a third-generation investment banker, and his forebears had done well. His grandfather had insured young Elliott's privilege not to work a day in his life, if he so chose, by the establishment of three generous trust funds. The grandson was not, however, disposed to the jet-set life or any of the other activities that his happy circumstances allowed. Grayson was ambitious and competitive. He had a consuming desire to win, and if his determination was seldom questioned, his methods often were. Now, at forty-eight, he had achieved his goal of running one of the leading Wall Street firms, and he was completely dedicated to it.

Most of Grayson's character traits were the very ones that would achieve success in the Wall Street game. But his flaws were dangerous ones. He looked on himself as being the very spirit and guiding force of the firm, in the same sense as De Gaulle had thought of himself as being of France. This made it difficult if not impossible for him to recognize the contributions of others, and he had a tendency to credit the reputation of the firm, *ergo,* himself, for anything that went right and to blame subordinates for anything that went wrong. On the few occasions when he was able to bring himself to grant credit to others, the recipients of his approval were always members of the small ruling clique of socially acceptable executives that Grayson nurtured.

In response to Grayson's question, John Haddad related the events leading to his trip to Beirut, the meeting with Marwan Suwadi, his own selection, the meetings with the Oil Minister, and, of course, the plan. But he shrank from telling Grayson about the half million dollars that the Saudis had offered him. It was a violation of Stock Exchange rules for John to take the money directly from the Saudi Arabians. The proper way was for the Saudis to pay the money as a fee to Thompson, Caldwell. Then the firm could compensate John according to its own policy. But knowing how remote the possibility was of getting a fair share from Grayson and being sure that El-Bahar intended the half million as a personal fee for himself alone, John decided to keep quiet about it. There were Wall Street firms where John would not have hesitated to reveal everything, certain he would be fairly treated, but Thompson, Caldwell was not one of them. The private incentive payment from the Saudis would remain private. When John finished telling him about the plan, Grayson was incredulous.

"This is unreal. Are you sure it was the Oil Minister himself?" Grayson thought it was entirely possible that John had been hoodwinked by some impostor with larcenous intentions. His inability to credit John with bringing in such an impressive deal only reinforced this attitude.

"Of course, I'm sure. I've already bought some stock for them, about three hundred thousand shares. I checked, and the trades have been paid for by Morgan Guaranty, as the Saudis said they would be."

"How long do you think you can get away with accumulating shares in the open market? You'll have to make a tender offer, and damn soon."

"There will be a tender offer, but not right away. I have several other problems to work out before any public announcement—and I have to report to the Oil Minister in a couple of weeks." John was purposely reminding Grayson that there was an authority behind the scenes to be reckoned with.

Reluctantly, Grayson was forced to allow John some leeway. "Well, you'll have to pick your own timing, but I want to be kept informed."

John moved on to what he wanted. "I'll need one or two people to work with me on the deal. Apart from them, I must request that no one else inside or outside the firm be aware of the plan until it is publicly announced."

"There's a board meeting tomorrow. I really should inform the board. Surely you can trust their discretion?"

"I'm afraid I can't. Frankly, I've learned of an awful lot of board decisions through the grapevine, days before you've announced them. We can't afford to have that happen in this case."

"All right. I won't tell them." Grayson's tone of annoyance conveyed his resentment at losing the chance of making this spectacular revelation.

"One other thing, Mr. Grayson." John controlled his voice for what he was about to say. "I know it is customary for any employee who brings in a piece of business to share in the profit the firm makes on it. I've thought about it, and I think it appropriate and justified for me to receive half the fees and commissions the firm makes on this deal, especially the tender offer."

Grayson stiffened as though he had been stabbed. This Haddad was definitely not taking the subservient attitude Grayson expected. He had to be brought down to earth, but without losing the business and without being granted a lion's share of the profits. "Look here, John," Grayson said in a fatherly tone, "I think it's too soon for us to be splitting up the profits. In the first place, the deal hasn't been done yet, and we don't know whether it will be successful. We might wind up with no more than the commissions on a few hundred thousand shares of stock trading. But assuming that all goes well, there are a few other things to consider. Thompson, Caldwell will spend a lot of money on legal expenses, advertising, your special staff, and more. Don't forget the expense side of the ledger! Then, too, you are a salaried officer of the firm, and it is your job to bring in new business. Now what you have told me today proves that you are performing very well, and we'll take that into account at bonus time. After all twelve and a half percent of the fees will go into your department's bonus pool. You'll get your fair share." Grayson felt he had done an admirable job of stating his case.

But John was not at all mollified. "I know all that, Mr. Grayson. But I think this is a hell of a lot different from the usual case. This deal could mean more profits to the firm than we earned in the last ten years, and I brought it in. I think that's worth much more than my usual junior share of the bonus pool."

"All right, John, now you listen to me." There was anger in Grayson's voice and he didn't care if it showed. "Do you honestly think that you got this deal on your own?" Without waiting for a response Grayson went on, telling John that the main reason he was chosen was because he represented Thompson, Caldwell—that the firm's reputation was his stock-in-trade and that he should count himself lucky to be in the firm. The most frustrating aspect of this conversation to John was that he knew Grayson actually believed he was telling the truth. Grayson had simply been unable to accept the possibility that John Haddad's personal qualifications had clinched the Saudis' choice. John saw that there was no chance of convincing Grayson he was wrong. He congratulated himself for not revealing his own private fee and resolved to press his claim again at some future time when he had some advantage to wield that Grayson might respect. In the meantime, he was committed to staying at the firm to complete the project. Deep down he cursed himself for knowing beforehand that this was how Grayson would handle the matter. He might as well get on with the job and let the profits take care of themselves when the time came.

John allowed Grayson to finish his speech, mumbled an assent, and went back to his office. There was no point in brooding about something he couldn't change. John's thoughts swung to the positive side, and he began to think about whom he would choose for his staff.

Chapter 9

SINCE Grayson had agreed to let John pick his aides from the personnel of the Corporate Finance Department, John had one hundred and eighty-two people from whom to choose. The only proviso had been to avoid pulling senior people out of the middle of any crucial projects. Grayson had also authorized any additional office space that might be needed, as well as secretarial help, and the services of whatever other staff members might be required on a priority basis. At least John could be confident that there was not a better talent pool in town for the job he had to do.

John would not, of course, select anyone who was very senior to him. There could be no question as to who was the captain of this team. After thinking about it for the better part of the day, he decided on his two choices.

Leon Curtis was twenty-six years old and had come to Thompson, Caldwell directly after graduation from Harvard Business School. He had been with the firm for nearly three years. The son of a Chicago bus driver, Leon Curtis was one of the very few black professional employees at

Thompson, Caldwell. He was also one of the brightest trainees in the firm and had already distinguished himself on the job for his insight, intelligence, and trustworthiness. In high school and college, Curtis had been a fine basketball player and had received bids to join the pros in the NBA. But he had turned down the fast money and glamor for the chance to go to Harvard, and had never regretted it. He would make a good member of the team.

David T. Hill was the son of a prominent Los Angeles lawyer. A graduate of Princeton and the Stanford Business School, he had been with the firm four years and had worked on several tender offers. Dave Hill was twenty-eight. John knew them both well, and although their backgrounds could not be more different, there was a special chemistry between them, a quality that would be necessary to make a team effort work.

After politely notifying Lee Curtis' and Dave Hill's superiors that they were being drafted out from under them for a special project under the aegis of the chairman, John called each one of the two men and invited them to lunch, smiling to himself at his choice of the lunching place. Since it was still nice weather, without the stifling humidity of the summer, John was taking them out to Central Park for a hot dog lunch. He didn't want any interruptions for this first meeting with his new aides. In the office there was no escape from the numerous phone calls and from the friendly intrusion of his many colleagues who would stop by for a chat on their way past his door. On most occasions, John welcomed the diversion and seldom grumbled at being temporarily distracted. Today was different, and it didn't hurt that the weather was ideal, sunny with a balmy temperature in the mid-seventies.

Lee Curtis and Dave Hill arrived at John's office promptly at noon, whereupon John reached for his jacket and led them out.

"How about that nice little Italian restaurant on the corner?" Lee Curtis suggested.

"No . . . " John replied, shaking his head.

"You're right, John," Dave Hill chimed in, "an occasion like this calls for something fitting, especially since you're buying! La Caravelle, maybe?"

John grinned at Dave's reference to one of New York's best and most expensive restaurants. "Not this time, fellas. We're going to get a little exercise and a lot of privacy. I'm taking you for a hot dog lunch in Central Park."

John was greeted by a duet of falsetto groans, as the elevator arrived at the ground floor and they stepped out. They were soon headed uptown on Sixth Avenue toward the park.

Armed with two hot dogs each, they found a quiet, shady spot of grass free of any souvenirs of New York's hefty canine population. The familiar skyline of the tall buildings surrounding the park protruded from beyond the green foliage all around them. Jackets off, ties loosened, sleeves rolled up, they sat down Indian-style facing each other. John talked as the other men munched their hot dogs, wiping mustard off their faces with the flimsy paper napkins supplied by the vendor. There were strollers nearby, but not within hearing distance, and scattered groups of blue-jean-clad frisbee players sent their plastic projectiles spiraling through the air.

Curtis and Hill were in a good mood, and not at all prepared for what was coming. They had speculated together on what they were being reassigned for, and had come to the conclusion that it was probably some minor project that required extra bodies. Because of John's lack of seniority, they couldn't possibly have guessed at the importance and size of the deal. As John got deeper into the story of what he was about to do, their attention became riveted. He had not yet mentioned that General Motors was the company to be taken over. Lee finally asked.

"What company are we going to acquire, John?"

John took a bit of his hot dog, cold by now, and then extended his arm fully to his right and slightly behind him.

He was pointing at the soaring white tower of the General Motors building on Fifth Avenue. The two other men followed his arm with their eyes and gaped.

"You can't be serious." Dave wondered if his friend had not been joking. Or perhaps he had misunderstood the meaning of John's motion.

"I'm dead serious. We're going to handle the takeover of General Motors."

"Holy shit!" Lee put his hot dog down on the grass and stood up.

"Before we go any further, let me tell you guys that I had full discretion in picking anybody I wanted. This is going to take an enormous amount of work and time. You both will have to be available just about twenty-four hours a day, and you can forget about any private social life for a while. But since you're both bachelors, I figured you won't mind the hours and that you'd like to be in on this caper. If either of you wants out, you're free to say so right now."

Dave Hill was shaking his head slowly. "Are you kidding? This will be the hottest thing in the business, not to mention the most fun."

Lee Curtis nodded, emphatically agreeing. "Man, I'm in. I wouldn't miss it for anything!"

John let out a sigh, happy to see they were with him. "OK. Now I picked you both because I knew I could trust you to help me get the job done and keep quiet in the meantime. Not one word to anybody leaks out until we're ready, got it?"

They both nodded, waiting for him to go on.

"Look, I've got to meet with El-Bahar on May 9 in London, and I want to give him some kind of plan. I've already bought some stock, but only a little. We'll have to go for a tender offer at some point, probably very soon."

"No question about it." Dave Hill sat back on the grass, seeking a comfortable position. "Let's see, there are about two hundred eighty million shares of GM outstanding, right? We'll have to tender for at least half that . . . Wow!"

He had just mentally calculated the value of the stock, as John had done in Beirut.

"You know, I was just doing some work with the Vickers Favorite Fifty." Lee Curtis was referring to the list of fifty stocks most widely held by financial institutions. "I remember that institutions hold only about eight million shares of GM, which is not a hell of a lot. Even if you got most of the institutions in the country to sell you their stock, you'd still have only maybe three percent of the company."

"Right, Lee. But I want to get as much stock as I can before we have to spring the tender offer. I'll buy the stocks from institutions or in the open market, as long as I don't draw attention to what we're doing."

Dave's face was grimly serious. "Don't worry, we'll be very careful and very quiet. All we have to do is let one word slip, and those bastards in Institutional Sales will be whispering in the ears of their favorite buddies at the banks, looking to make Brownie points."

"I don't expect any instant ideas or plans," John continued, "but I'd like you to divide up the work for the time being. Lee, I want you to work on acquiring the existing blocks and other purchases on the floor of the New York and the other exchanges. I'm giving you full authority to buy as much stock as you can find, provided you can buy it discreetly. Get an idea of the daily volume of trading, and don't be the biggest order on the specialist's book all the time. Use our facilities on the other exchanges—those guys are half asleep most of the time. Dave, I'd like you to start working on the tender. Talk to our lawyers and get back to me on any unusual legal problems."

"Should we start work on the tender document itself?"

"Yes. But, for God's sake, be sure not everyone in the whole law firm knows about it. In fact, I'll talk to the senior partner myself to impress on him the need for secrecy."

"Even normal tender offers are complicated," Dave said, thinking out loud, "this one will be unbelievable!"

"Your main concern," John said, pointing his finger at Dave, "is that I can't afford any bad surprises. You've got to anticipate every legal maneuver GM might come up with to fight us off. Our procedures and documents have got to be so legally pure that the SEC will stand up and salute when they see them."

"OK, John," Dave replied, "I got the message." He looked at John with new eyes, and a respect even greater than he had felt for him before. Dave had always admired John's quick mind and his skills as an investment banker. But most of all, he respected John Haddad for shying away from interoffice politics with apparent distaste for those of his contemporaries who practiced it. Here was a man who expected to succeed on his abilities or not at all. Now Dave wondered what it would be like to have John as a boss. Can you suddenly start working for a man who has been a friend? No problem, he thought. Besides, Haddad was giving him the chance to work on the biggest financial deal ever—a takeover that would be talked about for generations. No problem at all.

"When we get back," John said, "I'd like you guys to move into the office next to mine. We'll tell everybody around the firm that we're working on a merger for one of our clients and that we can't reveal the names. That's enough to keep the curious off our back. OK. Let's go to work."

John got up and brushed the grass from his trousers. The others did the same. They picked up their jackets and began the walk back to the office.

While Dave and John made small talk, Lee Curtis was engrossed in his own thoughts. He had been selected to work on the single-most-important financial coup in history. If he did his job right, his future would be solid and insured. There would be no end to the demands for his services. After all, he would be one of the men who had taken over General Motors, and his price would be high.

There was something about John Haddad, Lee thought.

He was more than a regular guy. Many of Lee's co-workers had been conspicuously friendly to him since he had joined Thompson, Caldwell, but Lee recognized most of their gestures as patronizing displays of pseudoliberal acceptance. Lee was still the house black, and he knew it.

It wasn't that way with Haddad. His friendship was genuine and sincere. Lee couldn't explain why. He just felt it. To his already warm feelings for John, Lee would add gratitude for having been selected to join the takeover team. He resolved that he would not let John down.

As they reached the edge of the park, Dave and John noticed that Lee had been silent, gazing all the while at the towering, white General Motors building.

"What are you looking at?" Dave asked.

Lee kept staring at the guilding. "Man, I just wondered what a minaret would look like on top of there."

Chapter 10

CLARIDGE's in London was probably the finest hotel in the world, not so much because of the quality and size of the rooms, which were exquisite, but because of the discipline, training, and courtesy of its staff. True, most visiting heads of state and other dignitaries stayed there, but the hotel staff's greatest accomplishment was the ability to treat all guests with the same deference and attention that other hotels usually reserved for monarchs.

John Haddad had not been a guest at Claridge's for four years. The last occasion was during the floating of a Eurodollar deal for a large American company, whose president had insisted that the entire group be housed together in his favorite hotel. John had been to London several times since then, but even his reasonably generous expense account would not have been sufficient to allow him to indulge in a stay at Claridge's.

John approached the reception desk observing that nothing had changed since his last visit. The furnishings were not elegant; they looked like the standard comfortable furniture on an old luxury steamship, perhaps the *Queen Mary* in her heyday. The desk clerk, resplendent in his morning coat, offered his help.

"I just arrived from New York. I believe you're holding a reservation for me."

"Yes, indeed we are, Mr. Haddad." The young man glanced down at a few cards and picked one up. "Do you still reside at East Sixty-seventh Street, sir?"

"Yes, I do." Every guest who had ever stayed at Claridge's has a file, and each file is checked against incoming reservations to insure that special requests and desires will be satisfied without the guest's needing to ask again.

"Fine, Mr. Haddad. It will not be necessary to fill in the registration form. May I ask only that you sign here. We will see to it that the London *Times* is delivered to your door in the morning, and we will send up the New York *Times* and the *Wall Street Journal* as soon as they arrive in the evening, as you requested the last time. Do have a pleasant stay, sir."

The room was large and tastefully furnished. The only concession the hotel made to modern standards was the color television set, discreetly sequestered in a cabinet behind closed doors.

John found a sealed envelope with his name on it on the antique desk. He knew it would be from El-Bahar. As he reached to open the envelope, he hoped that it would not be an invitation for this evening. He had taken the day flight to London, and it was now close to midnight. Although by his own watch it was only seven p.m. New York time, he was anxious to get to sleep and be alert for the next day's meetings. He unfolded the note:

MR. HADDAD,
We hope you had a pleasant flight.
We will look forward to seeing you
tomorrow morning at 9:30. Our party has taken the fourth floor. Please
meet us in Room 404. Regards,
BADER MAHMOUN

The following morning, John knocked on the door of
Room 404 and was admitted by a smiling Mahmoun. The
Oil Minister and Mustafa Attifi, both impeccable in British
worsteds, rose to greet him.

"I'm glad to see you, Your Excellency." John was smiling. "I see from the London *Times* that you are in town to
discuss Britain's balance of payments problems."

"Yes, what a problem! At present oil prices, England
pays us over eight billion dollars a year, and now they want
some of it back. But what can I do? They have very few
products of interest to us. I cannot very well buy eight billion dollars' worth of Wedgwood china! But that is of no
consequence to you. Let's sit down and hear what you have
to tell us."

They settled around the imposing fireplace in comfortable chairs, and Attifi opened the conversation. "John, I see
you've been buying some stock. I trust the settlements have
been made on time?"

"No problem at all, Mustafa. I wish all our clients were
so prompt and efficient."

An Arab servant brought the coffee while John unzipped
his leather case and withdrew his typed papers.

"Did you prepare a written report for us?" The Oil Minister seemed a bit surprised.

"No, these are my notes. I can give you a written report if
you like."

"Don't bother. I hate reports. I'd much rather discuss
business problems verbally."

107

"Well, gentlemen, since we last met in Beirut, I have started to carry out the plan, but we have a long way to go. Through private purchases of blocks, and some in the open market, I have now accumulated a total of one million two hundred thousand GM shares. I know that sounds like a lot, but it is less than half of one percent of the company's stock."

The men sat back and listened. John talked, explaining the problems they might encounter and possible ways around them. He stressed that buying up the stock as he had been doing up to now was a slow process. Each major purchase increased the chances that someone could find out that GM was being accumulated in unusually large quantities. Moreover, once they had acquired five percent of the stock, by whatever means, they would have to register the fact with the Securities and Exchange Commission. A holder of five percent or more of a publicly traded company's stock was considered an "insider" by the SEC.

"So, at some point soon, we will have to make a tender offer."

"John, what if we made the tender offer through a Swiss bank or some holding company? Then no one would have to know the identity of the buyers until we chose to reveal it." The Oil Minister fidgeted with his coffee cup as he spoke.

"We really can't do that, Your Excellency. U.S. law requires that the party making a tender offer be fully identified. We shouldn't take any chance of violating the securities laws. You know there is likely to be a lot of opposition to this. If we slip up on a technical violation, they'll use it to stop us or at least to delay us substantially."

"What kind of opposition do you expect?"

"I expect the typical, uninformed, visceral public opposition that comes from people who read headlines and don't think, encouraged by reporters who know little of finance. This kind of opposition translates itself into the reactions of congressmen, whose only true concern is their own reelection."

"But if we offer to buy stock in the company, and at a much higher price than a stockholder could normally expect to receive, do you think he will refuse our money because we are foreigners? With due respect to your countrymen, John, my experience tells me that windfall profits are always welcome."

"Oh, I have no doubt you're right about that. I didn't mean that stockholders wouldn't tender. What I anticipate is a strong reaction on the part of Congress to legislate against a foreign takeover of General Motors."

Shiekh El-Bahar's brow was furrowed. "Obviously, if the United States government passes a law that says we cannot acquire General Motors, I don't see how we can get around it."

"Well, now you know what's been my principal concern since we started. Frankly, I've thought about this constantly to find an acceptable solution. At one point, I thought I had the answer. What if Saudi Arabia retaliated against the United States by reimposing an oil embargo if the U.S. Congress forbade Saudi Arabia from taking over GM? It sounded good for a while, but I didn't have to be an experienced diplomat to see that it wouldn't work. If Saudi Arabia did that, she would appear to be a spoiled rich kid who couldn't get his toy. World opinion would be against her, and the United States is still a dangerous enemy to have, especially when the rest of the world sides with her."

"You are quite right, John. We would not even consider such a step under these circumstances. If you are really sure that your country would legislate against our buying GM, then we may have to abandon the whole idea."

"No, you don't. I thought of another solution. I'm very confident this one will work."

John went on to outline his proposal in detail to the Oil Minister, choosing his words carefully because the plan required specific action by El-Bahar himself. In a few minutes, he completed the explanation and waited for the response.

As the conference was going forward in El-Bahar's suite, Hans Sloman entered the lobby of the hotel and went up to the desk. The clerk raised an eyebrow at his request for a room next door to John Haddad's. But a five-pound note and a mumbled explanation implying a confidential transaction by the Swiss banker served to calm his fears. After all, Sloman was well known at Claridge's. Once installed in his room, Sloman listened carefully at the wall. Not a sound in Haddad's room. Sloman picked up the telephone and gave the number of the room next door. He held the receiver through several rings until the operator came back on the line and assured him that Mr. Haddad was not answering. Satisfied that John was not in his room asleep, Sloman armed himself with cigarettes, matches, and his Barclay's credit card. He stepped into the hallway, looking up and down to make sure he was unobserved, then quickly went to John's door. Slipping the plastic card against the latch, he quietly let himself into the room. Sloman settled into the armchair, pulled an ashtray to a convenient place at his elbow, and sat back to wait.

After pondering John's idea, El-Bahar replied, "John, this idea is very bold. I wonder if you realize how dangerous it might be. We would be risking a wave of rumors all over Europe—perhaps even an accurate guess or two. I would have to handle it all myself, at the highest levels. Also, I cannot go around brandishing our 'oil weapon' too obviously. The king himself has forbidden it." As he was expressing his doubts, El-Bahar was also thinking to himself that he would enjoy the challenge. He loved to engage in the subtleties of delicate diplomacy, especially when he knew he would hold most of the bargaining chips at the beginning of the game. What John was asking was quite logical—indeed the only way to prevent the U.S. government from stopping the takeover at the outset. The Oil Minister let John stew a minute more before agreeing. "But I think I can manage it pretty well. I'm willing to try and see how it goes."

John was greatly relieved. This had been the biggest hurdle he had anticipated, and now he had cleared it. He was confident El-Bahar would succeed in spite of the minister's modest disclaimer. "Thank you. I hoped you would, Sheikh El-Bahar. I really do think it will work and it will not put your country in any compromising position."

"All right, John, where do we go from here?"

"As I said earlier, we're going to have to make a tender offer at some point, probably soon. I would like to have discretion as to when. Also, I think we should tender for no more than fifty-one percent of the company. That means about one hundred forty million shares. It's not likely that we could buy all of the stock, and it would probably be politically unwise anyway. This way you would control the company but still leave almost half the stock in the hands of the American public."

"As far as I'm concerned, you have full discretion. Just be sure to advise me in advance of the tender offer so that I may inform my government. Most of our cabinet members do not know of the plan. I think I mentioned that to you in Beirut."

"Yes, you did. I'll give you as much notice as I can, but I hope you understand that it might be as little as forty-eight hours. Once the decision is made, we'll have to move very fast."

"That will be fine, John. Do you expect any problems besides the political one we discussed before?"

"Not really, but that doesn't mean there won't be any. I've tried to anticipate all the contingencies, but you never know. Tender offers are tricky and complicated. This one, of course, will have such impact that it will set precedents."

"What sort of steps are required for a tender offer?" Attifi

111

had spoken, and now the attention of the other men shifted to where he was seated. "I mean, it seems to me that all you have to do is put an ad in the paper and offer to buy the stock."

"Far from it, Mustafa." John would set him straight in a hurry. "If it were that simple, an advertising agency could do it for us just by booking the space. A tender offer is one of the more complicated financial undertakings. It requires the best lawyers, accountants, bankers, and investment bankers, and they all must keep silent throughout the preparation. Most tenders are made at prices well above the current market. If there is a single leak before the offer is announced, the stock price will start to rise abnormally as the 'insiders' buy stock in anticipation of the higher tender offer price. Once that happens, you have the SEC breathing heavily down your neck."

"It would appear, then, that the tender offer will require a good deal of advance preparation. Won't that take a long time?" Attifi had asked a very good question.

"That's precisely the point. I have already arranged for all the advance work to be done. We will be fully prepared in another few days. Then, when the right time comes, I can just push a button and the offer becomes effective within twenty-four hours. Incidentally, the legal bill alone will run into the millions. I used to think that investment bankers were the highest-paid talent on Wall Street. They're not—the lawyers are."

"All right, John." El-Bahar had been listening quietly to the exchange between John and Mustafa Attifi. "I'm satisfied that you are doing your best, and I remain confident of your success. Proceed with the plans for the tender offer as you have outlined them. Consult with Attifi on all matters involving payments for services of lawyers and accountants as well as for the stock itself. For my part, I will begin to work on your project to keep the United States Congress from blocking the takeover. It will require my staying in Europe a little longer, but I will rather enjoy it."

112

"Thank you, Your Excellency. I'll return to New York as soon as I can and get to work. When will I see you again?"

"I have some speaking engagements in the States in a few weeks—when are they, Mahmoun?—yes. Actually it's about a month from now. So I will see you then unless something urgent comes up beforehand. You know how to reach me."

John sensed that the meeting was over and rose to leave. "Incidentally, Your Excellency," John said as he and the Oil Minister walked to the door of the suite, "we have established a holding company through which to purchase the stock and make payments. I've called it Islam Investors Limited."

"That's a nice touch, John."

El-Bahar was pleased with John Haddad, more so than he had indicated in words. Now he showed it as he put his arm around John's shoulder and walked him down the corridor to the elevator.

John turned the key and opened the door to his room. The curtains had been drawn and it was quite dark inside. Obviously, the chambermaid had been by. As he took another step inside, he noticed through the darkness a faint puff of smoke reflected in the dim light of the corridor fixture. It might have been a leftover butt, forgotten by the maid, but that was unthinkable at Claridge's. The only other possibility was that someone was in the room who didn't belong there. With that chilling realization taking hold, John quickly turned around to walk out the door. Before he could get out, his wrist was grabbed.

"Please don't go, Mr. Haddad. I have been waiting for you." The voice was deliberate, trembled a little, and had a trace of German accent.

John jerked his wrist loose and swung wildly in the direction of the voice. As the man moved forward to block the blow, the light from the corridor revealed him to be stout and middle-aged with a round face and balding head. He wore wire-rimmed glasses. The sight of him reassured John that he was not in danger of being overpowered easily, and there was no weapon in sight.

"I don't know who you are, but you'd better get the hell out of here fast."

"I must talk to you, Mr. Haddad. Please be patient."

John turned the light on and saw the man more clearly. He looked vaguely familiar, but John couldn't identify him. He faced the man in the doorway with clenched fists, deliberating on the next course of action. The idea of bodily throwing the man out was gaining.

"Mr. Haddad, please. I'm not a criminal, I'm a banker. I know why you are here. Listen to me." The man was pleading.

"All right. Say what you have to say and get out." John had the presence of mind to realize he'd better discover how much the man knew.

"Shall we sit down first? I'm afraid we are making somewhat of a spectacle here in the doorway." Without waiting for a reply, the man returned to his armchair at the far end of the room. John followed him at a cautious distance, then sat at the foot of the bed facing him.

"My name is Hans Sloman. I apologize for the rather dramatic meeting, but I cannot afford too many niceties at this point, and waiting in the lobby for you to come by would have been—shall we say—inconvenient. Fortunately, I am known here at Claridge's, and a plausible explanation allowed me the convenience of occupying the adjoining room."

"I'd appreciate your coming to the point."

"Fine, fine." Sloman was nervous and sweated profusely. He removed his glasses and wiped his brow with a clean white handkerchief. He was wearing a rumpled dark suit, several seasons out of style, with a white shirt and dotted tie. "The point, yes, the point. Mr. Haddad, I know that you are here to see Sheikh El-Bahar and I know what your business is with him."

114

"If you're looking for a handout, you came to the wrong place. Besides, I think you're bluffing." El-Bahar's presence in London was well known.

"Have you bought any shares of General Motors yet, sir?"

"I don't know what you're talking about." The man obviously knew a great deal. John's hopes of quickly disposing of the intruder began to wither, but he knew it would be important to keep his composure. Play the game, see the hand.

"I think we've fenced enough. You know perfectly well what I mean. You have been hired by the Saudi Arabians to buy control of General Motors for them. If you persist in denying it, you will just be wasting our time."

"I'm not admitting anything, Sloman. I don't know who you are or what you want, and I have a plane to New York to catch in a couple of hours."

"I mentioned to you that I am a banker. You may be surprised to know that I manage a small private bank in Zurich. We have many clients in the Middle East, and like human beings everywhere, they talk. Swiss bankers are like parish priests. Because of bank secrecy, clients assume they can tell us absolutely everything in confidence." Sloman relaxed and lit a cigarette. "You see, Mr. Haddad, there are many professional people at the Saudi Ministry of Oil, and they are well informed enough and rich enough to have Swiss bank accounts. I think you understand what I'm saying."

"Yes, I understand quite well that you have talked to someone at the Saudi Ministry of Oil. And I understand that you are trying to use some information to extort something from me. I am quite surprised that you dare do such a thing when you know that with one phone call to the Swiss Banking Commission I can have you practically drummed out of your own banking community for this! Why don't you say what you want from me?" There was no use denying it anymore. Sloman was clearly very well informed.

"Due to some unfortunate circumstances, I find myself in

great need of money. I would like to make a business deal with you. Do you understand?"

"Sure, the business deal is called blackmail. So why do you need me? You know damn well that if you go out and buy some GM stock, you stand to make a sure profit."

"Ah, my dear sir. It is all too true when they say that to make money, you must have money already. That is, alas, not my case at present. I need a very large amount. Twenty million dollars, to be exact."

"What? You came to me to try and extort twenty million dollars! You must be out of your mind. I can't produce that kind of money. I'm dealing for a client, not for myself."

"I could, of course, wreck your takeover scheme. But that's not quite all I could do. You see, I know a good deal about you, John Haddad. You are a very bright young man. You are also a very devoted son. Who else but a devoted son would take a grave risk so that his father would have a chance to make a little money on a stock deal he was masterminding? You do remember the PAPCO-Siesta Inns merger, don't you?" Sloman's client, Ahmed Sharif, had been very thorough in his research.

The disclosure he had just heard confirmed that Sloman's connections in the Saudi Arabian Ministry of Oil were good and far-reaching. So he knew about the Siesta Inns purchase of stock by John's father. That unfortunate bit of information, which had remained a secret for so many years, was getting around much too much for John's taste. More important, it spelled real danger. Sloman would have to be taken seriously, not only for the sake of the takeover but for John's own skin.

"Look, Sloman, I'll level with you. I'd like to trust you not to reveal the things you've mentioned here. But I can't raise twenty million dollars for you. What do you want me to do?"

"I know you don't have the money. But there will be far greater sums changing hands in connection with your scheme—billions! I don't know exactly how you can provide my twenty million either. But I think you're smart enough to find a way, and I know you have plenty of incentive to succeed. I can allow you approximately six weeks."

"Wait a minute. I don't see how I can do it now or even in six weeks. Why do you need so much money? Can't we settle on a more realistic amount?" John was hoping he could draw down some of his special fee and pay the Swiss off with it.

"I'm afraid not, Mr. Haddad. You see, my bank has become involved in some unfortunate losses in the currency futures market. We have lost nineteen million dollars. If the extent of the loss were known, it would mean the end of our bank. On a more personal level, it would probably be the end of me and of the son of my best friend, whom I have vowed to protect. I have a little more than six weeks before our financial statements are due to be prepared and audited. I must raise the money before then."

"I guess we are going to have to trust each other then. I will trust you to be quiet, and you will have to give me some time to see if I can help you with your problems. I can't do any more than that right now."

Sloman nodded. "Frankly, I did not expect you to have an instant solution. I will trust you to find one. Remember, however, that I must have the money in six weeks. I am desperate, Mr. Haddad, so I urge you to take me very seriously."

"Oh, I do, Sloman, I do. I'll be in touch with you in three weeks—four at the most—with some sort of proposal." John knew he had no choice.

"Then here is my card. It has both my home and office numbers, although you have a better chance of finding me at home these days. I will look forward to hearing from you."

Sloman rose and instinctively used both hands to brush the cigarette ashes from his lap. The remains of his most recent cigarette dangled from his lips. He put it out and walked slowly to the door. He slouched pathetically as he went out of the room, giving the appearance of a man whose demeanor had not always been like this, but whose recent unfortunate circumstances had imposed it on him.

John hurriedly packed. It was nearly noon and his return flight left in two hours. Strangely, he found himself with more sympathy for than anger against Sloman. The man was indeed pathetic. John had never heard of the Surit Bank in Zurich, which was the name on Hans Sloman's card. Losses in currency speculation, however, were not confined to small banks. There had been a rash of bank failures in past years, including some large ones like the Herstatt in Germany and the Franklin in New York, all directly attributable to excessive currency speculation. Years earlier, when currency exchange rates had been relatively fixed, the potential losses in buying and selling foreign currencies on margin had been minimal. But since exchange rates began to float freely, there was no limit to these losses.

Sloman was probably a conservative banker who had failed to supervise an overly ambitious trader. John doubted that Sloman himself would have gambled recklessly. He was not the type, but he clearly felt responsible for the losses, no matter who had been to blame. It was doubtful that John could raise anything near the twenty million dollars Sloman needed. His strategy would be to stall Sloman as long as possible, perhaps even remit small amounts of money to keep him satisfied until his information on the GM acquisition became worthless. John was sure that Sloman couldn't know how quickly the tender announcement was approaching. On the day of the announcement, Sloman's information would no longer have a value. Sloman would still be able to ruin John with what he knew about his father's purchase of Siesta Inns, but John didn't believe the man would do it. In the meantime, the threat to the takeover was bad enough. Hans Sloman had to be regarded very seriously.

John felt that he couldn't bring himself to tell the Saudis about this threat and that it would be best to try to handle it himself, mainly because he thought that his own ability would seem diminished in the eyes of El-Bahar if he came running with this sort of problem at the outset. There was plenty of time to turn to the Saudis for help if all else failed. He hoped that he could somehow find a legal way of letting Sloman make something out of the deal without hurting anyone. After all, denouncing John to the authorities would only be an act of spite by Sloman. He couldn't hope to get any money out of such a revelation, and he didn't seem a spiteful man.

Chapter 11

THE French Ministry of Finance was located on the Rue de Rivoli side of the Louvre. The setting was dramatically elegant for a Finance Ministry, and the present minister, Comte Christian de Chaloncy, had a bearing that suggested he was born in the palace, not appointed to it.

The view from the minister's office was of the sort you dreamed of in Paris, overlooking as it did the courtyard of the Louvre and offering a splendid view of the Tuileries Gardens whose trees were in bloom on this sunny spring day.

De Chaloncy had no time for the view. He was busily preparing for a luncheon meeting called by the President of the Republic at which the Minister of Finance was to out-line a new program to combat inflation. There had been a few wildcat strikes in the automobile industry and at the RATP, the Parisian subway and bus authority. Ever since May, 1968, when the workers led the country into a near revolution, French government officials took strikes, even small ones, seriously.

De Chaloncy might well have had time to prepare for his

meeting with the President, but now he was to be interrupted again, this time by the Minister of Oil of Saudi Arabia.

Who but one of those Arab sheikhs would have the gall to request an appointment on one day's notice? De Chaloncy thought to himself. He raised his shoulders in the classic French gesture of despair, as he contemplated the scattered papers and notes on his Louis Seize desk. One could not say no to those people. It was too dangerous to risk provoking them and have them cut off the oil flow. They are so unpredictable.

Every time he thought about the Middle East, De Chaloncy was reminded that the high cost of France's oil imports had caused serious problems in the French economy. Inflation was rampant, workers were restless, and the balance of payments was in deficit, all because of those arrogant Arabs. De Chaloncy could scarcely conceal his dismay that France, a nation whose culture and artistic achievements had inspired the world, was forced to humble herself before the desert tribes that sat on the earth's largest oil reserves.

A *huissier* entered and announced, *"Son Excellence, le Ministre du Pétrole de l'Arabie Séoudite!"*

Anwar El-Bahar walked in, dressed conservatively in one of his British tailored suits.

"Sheikh El-Bahar, how good to see you again." De Chaloncy spoke in English, the only language that he and El-Bahar had in common. His accent and tone of voice imparted the sense of superiority that comes so easily to members of the French nobility.

"I'm glad to see you too, Monsieur le Ministre," El-Bahar addressed the French minister in a cool, businesslike manner. It may be an ingrained characteristic of certain Frenchmen to consider that they are more intellectually and culturally endowed than others, but El-Bahar felt that they should not flaunt it.

"I only wish," De Chaloncy continued, "that I had had a bit more notice of your visit so that we might have planned to spend some more time together."

El-Bahar had expected some rebuff for the short notice on the appointment, but De Chaloncy had not even been subtle.

"Yes, well, unfortunately, the present circumstances did not allow it. I know you are busy, so I will get right to the purpose of our meeting."

As he sat on the antique chair, El-Bahar, feeling quite in command of the situation, explained to the French minister exactly what he wanted him to do. When El-Bahar stopped talking, De Chaloncy was shocked at his request, since an icy confrontation with the United States would be sure to follow. Obviously, these Arabs were preparing some kind of financial coup, but the Oil Minister had not revealed any details.

"You realize, of course, Sheikh El-Bahar, that you are asking us to assume an unfriendly diplomatic posture toward our ally, the United States."

"It occurs to me, Your Excellency, that it will not be the first time that France has done so."

"Well, of course, we've had our differences," De Chaloncy snapped. "But I do not think you appreciate, my dear Sheikh El-Bahar, that although I sympathize with your point of view, it is not in France's best interests to provoke a financial war with the United States."

"There will be no financial war!" El-Bahar looked into the minister's eyes as he spoke, explaining both the righteousness of his views and the reasons that the United States would not, and could not, challenge the position El-Bahar wanted France to take.

"You know, Monsieur le Ministre," El-Bahar concluded, "we Arabs never ask a favor unless we are prepared to give one in return."

"Oh?" This time De Chaloncy's interest was real.

"We are aware of France's current problems of inflation and balance of payments deficit," El-Bahar continued, "and we are sensitive to the fact that the high price of oil is a contributing element. So if you will agree, Monsieur le Ministre, to what I have asked of you, my country will grant

121

France a twenty percent discount on your normal oil purchases for one year."

De Chaloncy's face registered no emotion. He did not speak. The offer was astounding. It amounted to a "gift" of nearly one billion dollars. Moreover, the lower oil price would reduce France's balance of payments deficit, since France would have to pay out one billion dollars less for oil than last year. Indeed, a tempting offer.

On the other hand, De Chaloncy considered the possible repercussions. There was no doubt that the position they wanted France to assume was fair, few would deny that. It was unfriendly, that's all. Would there be any lasting strains with the United States as a result? Probably not, the minister thought. Then a question occurred to him.

"Sheikh El-Bahar, if it is not indiscreet to ask, may I know if you plan to make the same request of other European countries as you have made here?"

"I plan to ask all of them to do the same," El-Bahar said.

That made it a lot easier. It was one thing for France to face up to the United States alone, and quite another if she were part of a group of European nations, all holding the same view. De Chaloncy steepled his hand in a prayerful mode and looked up.

"I will speak with the President later today. My recommendation will be to accept your proposal, on condition that at least three other European governments also agree. I will recommend acceptance based on your oil price offer as well as in the interests of the continually improving relationship between our two countries."

"Fine, Monsieur le Ministre. I can assure you already that you will be joined by more than three other countries. France will not be alone." El-Bahar rose. "I will be in touch with you when the time comes to fulfill your part of the arrangement. Of course, the oil price concessions must remain a secret."

"Agreed."

The meeting ended with a cordial handshake, and El-Bahar was ushered to his waiting limousine below.

Throughout the week, sporadic press items reported that the Minister of Oil of Saudi Arabia had been observed going in or out of the Finance ministries in Rome, Bonn, Brussels, and Amsterdam. Indeed he had, and he had also visited several other countries where his presence had not been noted. The Dutch had been the most difficult. Since they were partial beneficiaries of the North Sea oil finds, the incentive of the lower oil price had not been as powerful. But in the end, Holland went along. The oil price discount meant a savings of three hundred million dollars to the Dutch. That was hard to turn down.

Italy had been the easiest. El-Bahar had been received as if he were a chief of state, rather than the Oil Minister, and Italy's beleaguered Finance Minister was so desperate that El-Bahar thought he might also have agreed to an invasion of the United States to gain the oil price concessions.

Satisfied with his efforts, El-Bahar sat in his favorite chair aboard his green and white 707 as they prepared for the flight back to Riyadh. Mahmoun handed him a Scotch and water, the last one he would enjoy for a while. He did not drink in Saudi Arabia.

"Mahmoun!" El-Bahar beckoned. "Send a telex to John Haddad in New York. Tell him I have been to most of the European capitals, and I am confident that the Europeans will cooperate."

Chapter 12

JAMES LARKIN rose from his desk and stretched. The claustrophobic atmosphere of his cubicle was annoying him. His desk was covered with papers, and there were stacks of documents on the floor. He gazed out through the windowed partition surrounding his work area, beyond the endless row of neatly aligned desks. At the end of the wide room he could see outside. Another gray day in Detroit. A low, heavy cloud cover had kept the sky dark, making the city seem even more colorless than usual.

Larkin sat down. He could not afford to waste any more time, even though he had worked straight through his lunch hour. The General Motors annual stockholders' meeting was less than two weeks away, and since he was chief proxy clerk, this was his busiest time of year. A handful of stockholders would attend the meeting in person, but most of GM's one million four hundred thousand owners would either ignore their annual right to vote for directors of the company or send in their proxies authorizing management to vote for them. A tiny minority even sent in proxies voting against management proposals, usually in years when the stock price had not gone up.

At fifty-eight James Larkin had unique knowledge of the ownership of General Motors. He not only knew which institutions in the United States and abroad held his company's stock, he also remembered how long most of them had owned it. When occasionally an insurance company or bank trust department sold its holdings, Larkin was saddened and felt almost betrayed. He did not feel that way every time someone sold GM stock; there were too many shareholders for that sort of emotion. But when he knew that the seller had held General Motors for a long time, it did hurt a bit. He took his job very seriously.

Having been with the company for more than thirty-four years, all of them in the corporate secretary's office, Larkin understood the importance of his job to the management of the company. This was not a delusion of false importance. James Larkin could pick up the phone and talk to any senior executive of the company. After all, he was the man who knew who owned the company's stock, and to any company, that information was vital.

According to a traditional American corporate practice, the company's management chooses the members of the board of directors. In theory, the stockholders elect direc-

124

tors, but by skillful solicitation of proxies from the share-holders, the management can usually be assured of the nec-essary votes at the meeting to elect whomever they please.

One of Larkin's most important responsibilities was to solicit as many of the proxies as he could for GM's manage-ment. For this, he did not waste time on holders of only a hundred or even a thousand shares. Instead, he methodical-ly phoned most of the insurance companies, pension funds, and major banks that were GM's largest shareholders.

In the past a company official could simply have looked at his register of shareholders to see who owned the compa-ny's stock. For years, however, owners of stock had been avoiding the cumbersome procedure of having certificates registered in the owner's name. Most stockholders were content to let the securities stay in "Street" name, that is, in the name of a brokerage firm, and retain the broker's month-ly statement as evidence of ownership. This procedure worked out quite well and avoided the inefficient paper-work and antiquated securities transfer procedures that a change in the name on the certificate required. One result of this shortcut bookkeeping was that a company like General Motors might show on its corporate books that a brokerage firm was the owner of several hundred thousand shares of GM stock. The real owners, of course, were that brokerage firm's clients, who were merely leaving the stock registered in the broker's name as a matter of convenience.

Major institutional holders of stock had yet a more efficient means of circumventing the awkward transfer procedures. The Depository Trust Company in New York held securities for the large stockholders, and registered all of the stock in a common name: "Cede." Then, when an in-stitution bought or sold stock from another, the exchange was recorded on the books of the Depository Trust Compa-ny, but the certificates stayed registered in the name of Cede. Thus, if a client of one brokerage firm sold ten thou-sand shares of General Motors to a client of another broker-age firm, the change was made by simply subtracting the ten thousand shares from the total held by the selling broker at the Depository Trust Company, and adding that same amount to the total shares held by the buying broker. A simple bookkeeping entry, and no one bothered to change the names on the actual stock certificates.

But since the certificates were registered in a common name, Cede, a company like General Motors would not know which institutions owned what shares until the Depository Trust Company told them. So it came as a surprise to Larkin when, during a conversation with an official at Depository Trust, he learned that Morgan Guaranty Trust Company's ownership of General Motors' stock had risen from one million two hundred thousand shares to nearly twice that amount. Even for Morgan, that was a hefty increase in ownership. Moreover, Larkin was missing proxies for over a million of the bank's shares.

He dialed the area code and number for Morgan Guaranty's New York offices and asked for Sandy Nelson.

"Hi, Sandy. Jim Larkin. I hear you guys got wise and added a lot of GM stock."

"Yeah. I saw that too." Nelson was a contemporary of Larkin's and had put in about as much time at Morgan as Larkin had at GM. They had known each other for thirty years.

"I'm missing proxies on over a million of your shares, Sandy. Can you help me out? The annual meeting's coming up very soon and . . . "

"I know, Jim." Nelson interrupted. "I didn't forget. The missing stock belongs to a single client, and we're trying to get hold of him to see what he wants done with his proxies."

"A single client!" Larkin did not remember any instance in the past when a single new shareholder had acquired anywhere near as much GM stock.

"Yeah, I know. I was surprised too. Anyway, we've been calling Thompson, Caldwell about it. All the stock came in from them."

Larkin hung up, deep in thought over the information he

had learned. A fresh stack of papers was brought to his desk, but he paid no attention to it. He knew that the acquisition of over one million shares of GM was highly unusual; it was his job to know that. But he was not paid to speculate about who was buying the stock or why they were buying it. Worries of that kind were the province of senior management. Larkin reeled the names and functions of the top GM executives through his head, like a microfilm being projected on an illuminated screen. A name came to mind. He picked up the company phone directory and looked up the number of Frank M. Johnson, executive vice-president. He had no problem with Johnson's secretary and was connected almost immediately. Although he had spoken to Johnson a number of times over the years, Larkin carefully identified himself on the phone to the senior executive.

"Sure, I remember you, Jim. What's the problem?"

"Well, no problem really. It's just that I found out today, while I was soliciting proxies, that we have a new holder of over a million shares since last year. I thought I should tell you that."

"A million shares? Are you sure, Jim?"

"Yes, sir. Morgan Guaranty is holding them. They didn't buy them for one of their own funds, though. The stock was all bought through Thompson, Caldwell and Company in New York for an outside client."

Johnson hesitated a minute, then assumed the fatherly voice he had perfected while raising his four children.

"Well, Jim, I'm glad you told me about it. Nothing to be concerned about, of course. Probably a big mutual fund just realized what a great company we are."

Johnson was still chuckling as the conversation ended, but his facial expression stiffened when he put the phone down. No one had ever bought a million shares of General Motors in such a short period of time. The mutual fund theory was so much baloney; Johnson had said that for Larkin's benefit, not wanting to reveal his concern and provoke a rash of rumors. Johnson knew damn well that the purchase of all that stock meant possible trouble. Maybe another company was trying to get a small foothold into General Motors. Maybe someone was going to buy a few million shares, then start a proxy fight. Maybe a lot of other things. They all sounded bad or threatening. Johnson pressed his intercom button:

"Millie, look up the name of the chairman of Thompson, Caldwell and Company in New York and put in a call to him, please."

Elliott Grayson was on the line in minutes. Johnson identified himself, explained why he was calling, and asked Grayson if he knew who was buying the General Motors stock. Grayson lied effortlessly, feigning ignorance of the large purchases but promising to look into the matter and get back to Johnson as soon as he could.

For the second time in less than thirty minutes, Johnson had a sinking feeling as he set the phone back on its cradle. The chairman of any goddamn brokerage firm would know about a million share purchase by a client. That son of a bitch Grayson had lied. Johnson thought about alerting GM's president but decided such a move would be premature. He did not want to acquire a reputation as an alarmist. He would give Grayson three days to call back and see what he had to say.

After the call from Frank Johnson, Elliott Grayson summoned John Haddad and informed him of the conversation. He told John that he had stalled, not admitting anything. He had bought a little time.

Back in his office, John mulled over the recent developments. It had to happen sooner or later. He congratulated himself for having done most of the advance work ahead of time. Now, if he was compelled to do so, he could activate the tender offer in a few days, a procedure that normally takes weeks and even months. So what was the situation? Grayson could not ignore the call from an executive vice-president of General Motors. He might stall for a few days, but no more. Any longer and the suspicions of the GM executives would be aroused and the questions would keep coming. It was Monday and John estimated that he had until the end of the week to make the tender offer. After a few minutes, he decided that the tender offer for control of General Motors would be announced the following Thursday.

The phone rang, his direct outside private line. It was Charlotte.

"Hi, doll. I hope I'm not interrupting anything. I was hoping you could come down next weekend. The Stevens are having a party and . . . "

"I can't, honey."

"Oh? Why?"

"Guess."

There was silence on the Washington end of the line. Then Charlotte came back on. "God! Do you mean that—" As usual Charlotte's quick mind grasped John's meaning.

"Shh. Don't say any more on the phone," John interrupted. "But what you're thinking is right." He knew she had understood. Another quality he loved in her.

"OK. Look, darling, if there's anything I can do . . . "

"Just be patient, and I'll see you as soon as I can."

When the call was over, John walked into the adjoining office of Dave Hill and Leon Curtis. He stood in the doorway, and the two men looked up at him from behind their side-by-side desks. John did not speak; there were other people around. Instead, he smiled and raised his right hand, fist closed and thumb extended, in the classic "thumbs up" position.

They caught on at once. Dave asked simply: "When?"

"On Thursday," John replied.

Chapter 13

JOHN paced his office while his secretary, Sue Anderson, followed in his wake furiously jotting notes as he spoke, ticking off what he wanted done to set up the kickoff meeting for the tender offer.

"We'll need Bert Simmons from sales and Ted Ball from advertising. Just tell them to cancel any conflicting appointments. Use Mr. Grayson's name if they give you any trouble. Oh, yes, don't forget to notify Mr. Grayson's secretary about this meeting he's calling! Make sure there are plenty of pads for the scribblers . . ."

Sue interrupted. "Now are you going to tell me about where to put the ashtrays and chairs?"

John laughed. "You're right. I'm getting too excited—get Dave and Lee into the conference room right away."

When everyone had arrived in the small conference room and the door had been closed, John opened the meeting by explaining some of the background of the takeover attempt for the benefit of Ball and Simmons. They were dumbfounded, listening raptly to the plan that John was outlining in his precise, logical manner. He did not intend to sound mechanical, but having given every facet of the exercise so much thought, there was no way for him to inject freshness into it. John's talk concluded with a warning to the two men that they must maintain the strictest secrecy, albeit but for a few days.

Having traced the development of the project to the present, John asked Dave Hill how long they could delay informing the Securities and Exchange Commission of the tender offer. He was concerned about possible leaks.

"I don't think we'll have a problem there," Hill said. "We can drop the documents off at the SEC in Washington Wednesday afternoon and tender on Thursday."

"Don't they have to approve it or something?" Bert Simmons, the sales manager, asked. He had to make sure his salesmen did not violate any laws.

"No, Bert," Hill replied, "this isn't like a registered stock offering where the SEC has to sanction the offering. All we have to do is file Schedule Thirteen D with the tender offer documents and a copy of the ads and that's it."

"What if there's something wrong with them?"

"Then we get in trouble with the SEC, and General Motors will take us to court to invalidate the tender offer. That's happened before in other tender offers, so I can assure you, we've been goddamn careful."

"All right, Dave," John said, resuming control of the meeting, "then you'll see that the SEC gets the documents on Wednesday afternoon." John looked down at a piece of paper on which he had handwritten the points he wanted to cover. He looked up at Ted Ball, the advertising manager.

"Ted, I'll need a full-page ad in the New York *Times* and in all editions of the *Wall Street Journal* on Thursday. You better throw in the Detroit *Free Press*, too. Oh, can we avoid editorials about the tender on the first day? I want to delay that as much as possible."

"Sure, John," Ball answered confidently, "I'll just block the space now, and I won't tell them what it's for. For an extra fee we can delay transmittal of the copy until late Wednesday afternoon. We'll just miss the early editions."

"OK. That should do it."

The door to the conference room opened, and Elliott Grayson walked in. He went directly to a chair at the round table and sat down. John went on with the meeting as if there had been no interruption.

"The next item on the agenda," John continued, "is the tender price." He looked over to Lee Curtis. "What's the last sale on GM, Lee?"

"Sixty-one and a half. I checked it just before coming in."

"OK. Fine. Then I think we stick to our original thinking on the tender price: ninety dollars a share. That all right with you, Bert?" The question was almost rhetorical.

The sales manager looked up and rolled his eyes. "Jesus, with a premium like that, we should get a hell of a lot of stock. I think it's fine."

"Well, if for some reason we don't, I have discretion to tender at even higher prices. We'll start at ninety dollars, though."

John ticked off the item on his checklist. Curtis and Hill scribbled notes. Grayson sat expressionless, sitting back, arms folded.

John went on. "We will tender for fifty-one percent of the stock outstanding. There are two hundred eighty-seven million six hundred seventeen thousand shares of GM, so we'll tender for one hundred forty-seven million shares, which is a rounded-off figure." There was no comment from anyone around the table.

"We have to fix a solicitation fee. I'd like to make it fifty cents a share." John looked around the table for a reaction. Grayson spoke almost immediately.

"I think that's too low. On a tender at ninety dollars, the fee is always higher."

The solicitation fee is the fee paid to brokers and dealers for tendering shares to the dealer-manager, which Thompson, Caldwell was in this case. The fee was designed to encourage other stockbrokerage firms to get their customers to tender the shares they held. The fee earned by the brokerage firms was then usually split with that firms' salesmen, whose clients had been induced to sell their shares.

"I know that, Mr. Grayson," John replied, "but a normal tender doesn't usually involve one hundred forty-seven million shares."

"There's a potential problem if the fee's too low, John." Bert Simmons spoke, and the others looked over to him. "Your see, when the offer is announced, they'll suspend trading in GM stock for a while, then it will open up again, probably somewhere in the eighty to eighty-five dollar per share range. If the solicitation fee is too low, a lot of salesmen will suggest that their clients sell the stock on the Exchange. The salesmen will earn a higher commission that way."

"Yeah," Dave Hill said, "but why would a client sell his stock on the Exchange at eighty or eighty-five if he can get ninety by tendering it to us?"

132

"Good question, Dave," Simmons said, not really thinking that it was. *These corporate finance guys know so little about sales practices, it's scary,* he thought. "You see, in every tender offer, the price of the stock on the Exchange hardly ever goes up to the tender offer price because there's always the chance that something could go wrong."

Simmons went on to explain that if a client tendered his stock and a court found something wrong with the tender offer, the whole operation would be off, and the stock would go right back to the price it was at originally. Or, if too many shares were tendered, there was a risk that not all of a client's stock would be purchased by the tenderer. So, a client had to weigh the advantage of selling his stock immediately at a price less than the tender offer price, against tendering his stock in the expectation that the tender offer would succeed. As the stockholder thought it through, the salesman's judgment would weigh heavily in his client's ultimate decision. In an imperfect world, the salesman's advice might well be influenced by the alternative that provided the greater commission to him.

"I see your point, Bert," John said. "I guess we'd better raise the solicitation fee to seventy-five cents. Will that do it?"

Bert Simmons made a mental calculation for a moment, then nodded affirmatively.

"All right," John continued, "but I still want to keep the fees reasonable, so I'd like to set a dealer-manager fee of ten cents a share."

The dealer-manager fee would be paid only to the dealer-manager, Thompson, Caldwell, by the tenderer, the Saudi Arabian government, for each share tendered, regardless of origin. The solicitation fee of seventy-five cents per share would go to any brokerage firm that tendered shares on behalf of its clients. Thompson, Caldwell would earn far more money on the dealer-manager fee, since it got all of that.

133

Elliott Grayson was incensed at John's suggestion.

"I don't go along with the ten-cent fee," Grayson said authoritatively, "it's much too low."

No one at the table dared comment; this was John Haddad's party.

"May I again say," John said, "that this isn't a normal deal. Even at ten cents we make over fourteen million dollars. I believe that's more than the firm has made in any single year."

"That's beside the point," Grayson snapped. "That fee is unnecessarily low. The Saudis can well afford a higher price."

"It's that kind of reasoning that makes them suspicious of Americans," John said with a trace of anger. "Sure I want the firm to make money out of this. But I also want to be fair. We'll hurt ourselves in the long run if we try to squeeze the last dollar out of them. I know how they think."

Grayson shook his head in disgust. Here was an opportunity for the firm to earn an extraordinary amount of money, and one young junior officer was about to blow it. Did Haddad not understand that Thompson, Caldwell had nothing to lose by charging a high dealer-manager fee? The fee was not contingent on whether the Saudis were actually successful in taking over General Motors. The fee would be due and payable on each and every share that was tendered to the Saudis, regardless of whether *they* got enough stock to control the company. Grayson saw this as a chance to milk the Arabs. He thought of them as aliens and therefore ripe for plucking, something he would never try when dealing with domestic companies whose executives were often his cronies. He had, before the meeting, privately decided that the fee should be twenty-five cents a share, and he was angry that John was letting the Saudis off so easily.

The other men at the table looked down at their notes and papers, not wanting any part of the conflict. Grayson finally decided he would gain nothing by engaging in an argument with an employee in front of an audience of other executives. He simply said, "I have to go upstairs," and rose to leave. The last person he looked at before walking out of the room was John Haddad. The look lasted only a fraction of a second, but it was intense enough to send a shiver down John's back.

Bert Simmons and Dave Hill exhaled a long sigh, glad it was over. Hill then said, "You know, it's customary to advise the management of a target company in a takeover attempt shortly before it's made."

"I know, Dave," John said, "but I'd hardly expect the GM people to stand up and cheer at the news. They'd probably just throw us out, and they would have bought a little time to prepare their defense. No, I'm afraid this tender offer is going to be 'unfriendly' all the way. Just one big surprise."

"Oh, Jesus!" Lee Curtis had been leafing through the latest General Motors annual report. "Do you guys know what Thursday is? It's General Motors' annual stockholders' meeting."

"Well, that'll give them something interesting to talk about at the meeting," John said sardonically. "I guess we've covered everything. I've got to call El-Bahar in Saudi Arabia and let him know. Dave, can I see your proposed copy for the ad?"

Dave Hill took a large piece of paper out of a folder and slid it across the table. It read:

NOTICE OF OFFER TO PURCHASE
147 Million Shares of Common Stock
OF

GENERAL MOTORS CORPORATION
For Cash At
$90 Net Per Share
BY

ISLAM INVESTORS LIMITED
(A wholly owned holding company of
the Kingdom of Saudi Arabia)

Chapter 14

TIMOTHY F. HURLEY had not found it easy to become the most famous Irish-American businessman since Joe Kennedy, but he had tried, and through determination, guts, and an old-fashioned hard-nosed business sense, he had succeeded. He had become chairman of the board of General Motors Corporation.

In the process, Hurley had had to survive not only the brutal competition for the most important job in American business, but also some serious handicaps of his own. He had a quick temper and a foul mouth, which were not untypical characteristics of his Irish background, and throughout his career, whatever Tim Hurley could not get his subordinates to do through persuasion and charm, he got them to do through intimidation.

Hurley had come up in the automotive side of the business and scored his greatest achievement when he turned around the faltering Oldsmobile division within three years after becoming its general manager. Before his tenure, the division had fallen on hard times when the adept managements of the Pontiac and Buick divisions added new lines of sporty luxury cars. Oldsmobile had not spotted the change in consumer taste soon enough and had continued to produce stodgy, gas-saving models. Under the decentralized management philosophy of GM, the Oldsmobile general manager was allowed to make the decision, but he was also held accountable for the results. When it became apparent that Oldsmobile had guessed wrong, the general manager was replaced by Tim Hurley.

His performance at Oldsmobile had soon made Hurley a leading candidate for the presidency of General Motors. When the job became vacant, he won it, but there had been a fight. Fortunately for Hurley, he had learned early in life how to handle fights, corporate or otherwise, and he skillfully rounded up the support of the key directors that finally clinched the job for him. A few years later when the chairman of the board retired, Hurley automatically vacated the presidency and at the age of fifty-six moved up to the chairman's post.

Hurley had enjoyed his tenure as president of General Motors enormously. He was especially gratified at the comparisons to Joe Kennedy, and he kept a scrapbook of press clippings devoted exclusively to those stories where the flattering comparisons were made. The pride of Irish-America, he was frequently called upon to speak at Irish-American functions.

By contrast, his wife, Mildred, was reserved and calm, and had none of the outgoing enthusiasm that her husband possessed in such abundant quantities. Mildred Hurley was portly and plain, and totally devoted to her bombastic husband and their three sons, two of whom were in college and one who was in medical school. She was also a light sleeper, which is why she was the first person in the rambling Tudor house to hear the doorbell ring at two thirty A.M. on Thursday, June 13.

She switched on the lamp and then reached over to the other side of the king-size bed and shook her husband's shoulder.

"Tim, wake up! There's someone at the door."

Hurley rolled over and moaned. Then he slowly sat up, his eyes half closed and his abundant gray hair sprouting in all directions.

"Huh? What time is it?"

He reached for his watch on the bedside table. "For Chrissake, it's two thirty in the morning! Where's Marie? Why doesn't she get it?"

"I don't think she can hear it, Tim. I've found her asleep in front of the loudest TV programs!"

"All right, goddamn it, I'll get up." Hurley flung the covers aside in a violent motion, then rose to his full five-foot-ten-inch height. His pajamas were Mildred's favorite, light blue silk with dark blue piping. He wore them only to please her and to justify what she thought of as an extravagant gift from A. Sulka in New York.

He walked to the door of the bedroom and pressed one of the buttons on the intercom.

"Who is it?" His voice, gruff and unfriendly, reflected his displeasure at being awakened in the middle of the night.

"Tim, it's Mike Zonick. I've got to talk to you."

"All right. I'll be right down."

As he descended the marble staircase, Hurley wondered what could possibly prompt his close personal friend, a senior vice-president of the company, to come by in the middle of the night. Hurley was sure it must be a personal problem or—God forbid—an accident in Mike's family.

Hurley unlocked two bolts on the massive front door and opened it. Mike Zonick stood before him in a wrinkled suit, white shirt, but no tie. He looked glum, defeated. He held a newspaper in one hand.

"Tim, I had to come over."

"What is it, Mike? C'mon in." Hurley fumbled in the dark for light switches, then finally found the panel and furiously switched them all on, illuminating the entrance foyer, the large living room, the small living room, and the library. "Let's go in the library."

The library was one of the smallest rooms in the house, although it was larger than most living rooms. There were dark fruitwood bookcases mounted on all four walls filled with beautifully bound books, mostly classics, of which Hurley had had time to read only a very few. They remained standing as Zonick spoke:

"Tim, it's about the company, I guess you haven't heard."

"Jesus, Mike, I thought something had happened to you or your family. What's so goddamned important about the company that couldn't wait till morning?"

"Somebody's trying to take it over." Zonick's voice was

138

emotionless, that of a man who had already endured the initial shock of bad news.

"Are you out of your mind? Take over General Motors?" Hurley was annoyed and worked at controlling his volatile temper.

"I got a call from New York an hour ago. One of our men there was tipped off that a tender offer was being made for GM and it would hit the papers this morning. I didn't want to bother you until I could check it out. Our man said it didn't appear in the early editions but would be in the late city one. So I went to the newspaper distribution depot and just came back with this."

Zonick unfolded the copy of the *Wall Street Journal* he was carrying, still smelling of partly dried printer's ink. Hurley moved around alongside Zonick and watched him open to page six. There they were confronted by the full-page advertisement announcing that Islam Investors Limited was tendering for one hundred forty-seven million shares of General Motors Corporation common stock at 90.

"Jesus Christ!" Hurley bellowed. "What the hell is this?"

"It's the Saudi Arabian government, Tim, that's who. They want to take over General Motors."

"I'm looking at it, but I can't believe it! Of all the goddamn nerve. They won't get away with this." Hurley had taken the newspaper from Zonick and was pacing the library floor, staring at the ad.

"What are we going to do, Tim? I mean, they sure have enough money to do it."

"I know, Mike, but that doesn't give them the right . . . anyway, don't worry, I'm not going to let anyone take over this company, especially Saudi Arabia."

Hurley stopped pacing and sat down in the small sofa near the fireplace. He took a cigar from the humidor on the low table and lit it. Zonick sat in an armchair. They looked at each other for a moment, then turned away. Hurley's blood pressure was rising and it was time to cool off. He

139

knew he would have to regain his composure in order to deal with the threat at hand. He thought in silence for a minute or so, taking occasional slow, deliberate puffs from his cigar. Then he sat up.

"Mike, I'd like you to call Sid Luddington at home. Tell him to have his entire legal department in the office as soon as possible. Get them all out of bed. Christ, we've got the annual meeting today. I wonder if those bastards planned it that way."

"Do you want to postpone the annual meeting?"

"No, I can't do that. But I expect that there's going to be a lot more interest in it than usual this year. The meeting is at three. Be sure to tell the press that I'll have no comment on this before then. Also, make damn sure nobody else at the company makes any statements."

"OK, Tim. Maybe you'd better get some sleep. You're going to need all the strength you can muster." Zonick's tone was sympathetic and solicitous. He was glad he did not have Hurley's responsibilities today.

"I can't go back to sleep," Hurley said, rising to his feet. "I've got a lot of thinking to do. We've got to develop a strategy—a plan. We're going to lick this, Mike."

"I know we will, Tim," Zonick said, rising from his chair. He started to walk toward the door. "I'll tell Sid what's going on and relay your instructions. I'm sure they'll think of something. I'll get hold of the other key people, too. See you later, Tim."

"Yeah, Mike. And thanks for giving me a few extra hours to deal with this."

Timothy Hurley arrived at his office at six A.M. He drove himself to work in his Oldsmobile sports coupé. He would not need his limousine today. It was still dark and Hurley switched on the lights in his office. Then he summoned Sid Luddington, general counsel to the corporation.

Luddington was a tall man with a thin, wiry frame. He

had spent nearly twenty years at General Motors, and had worked nowhere else since his graduation with honors from the University of Michigan Law School. His meek manner camouflaged an exceptionally fine legal mind that, combined with his skills as a diplomat, had earned him the highest legal job at General Motors. In his capacity as general counsel, Luddington was responsible for all of the company's legal problems, and he had a staff of nearly fifty lawyers to help him.

Luddington walked into the office of the chairman of the board and timidly looked around, waiting to be told where to sit.

"Come on in, Sid." Hurley beckoned from behind his oversized desk in the center of the large office. "Have a seat over on the couch."

Hurley rose to join him, picking up a sheaf of papers on his desk. His jacket was off, tie loosened, and sleeves rolled up. He sat facing Luddington on a twin sofa.

"I hope you have some good news for me, Sid," Hurley said.

"Well, there aren't any miracles yet." Luddington unzipped his leather folder. "I went over the tender offer ad in the paper, and there isn't anything glaringly wrong with it. We're still looking at it, though."

"Sid, can they really do this?"

"I'm not sure yet. There isn't much precedent. Sure, some foreign companies have tendered for American companies before, but this is a foreign government trying to buy General Motors."

Hurley did not want to waste time hearing about the finer legal points. He wanted the facts as bare and fast as he could get them.

"I do not want this company taken over by a foreign government, or by anybody, for that matter. Just tell me, what are the legal grounds we can use to stop them?" Hurley's tone displayed his impatience and his lack of sleep.

"There are several ways we can go on this. First, if there is anything wrong with the tender documents, we can stop them cold."

"Is there?"

"Unfortunately, we can't count on that. They had one of the top law firms working with them. It's not likely they slipped up." Luddington removed his wire-rimmed glasses and wiped them nervously.

"We can also exhort stockholders not to tender, but since the Saudis are offering ninety dollars a share, we can't realistically expect too many of them to follow our advice."

"How about national security? We make tanks and other military equipment," Hurley said.

"I looked into that, too. Problem is that our defense business is really a tiny part of our overall revenues. The worst thing that could happen is that the company would lose its 'Facility Security Clearance' from the Defense Department. I daresay the Saudis may not really care if that happens. No, I don't think we have a case there."

"Say, what if we bought a radio or TV station? Foreigners can't own them, so they couldn't buy us out."

"We even considered that, but it's not likely to work. If we bought a radio station now, it would be obvious that the only reason we did it was to block the takeover. And, anyway, the Saudis could simply promise to sell the radio station once they got control of GM."

"Jesus, Sid, you're not very encouraging."

"There are a couple of things we can do, and they might work."

"Let's hear it," Hurley said impatiently.

"First, the Saudis, and whoever they have working for them, probably didn't consider what the workers' reactions to this would be. We've got a lot of Archie Bunker, flag-waving hardhats in this company. Four hundred and forty thousand, to be exact. You might talk to Louis Spinner, the head of the United Auto Workers Union, and suggest that this takeover attempt is un-American. I don't think he'll want his boys working for foreigners." Luddington removed his glasses again, this time to rub his eyes. He was aware of his own fatigue, having been up since four.

"That's not a bad idea. I'll call Spinner this morning. He should be able to put some pressure on his congressman, Jennings." Hurley's voice showed the first trace of enthusiasm of the day.

"That's not all, Tim. I think we can get the government to help us. With all the wealth those Arab countries are accumulating, they could buy GM and a lot of other companies too. Maybe you should talk to the president. You could ask for some emergency legislation to limit foreign ownership of large American companies. Congress can set a limit of something like ten percent. Those Arabs aren't going to have too many people in America on their side on this."

"I had already thought of that, Sid. I'm glad you think it'll work. It damn well ought to. The government can't just let this go by. They'll have to do something." Hurley got up and walked back to his desk.

"I'd better be going," Luddington said, rising from the sofa. "I hope you'll let me see any statement you intend to make. I really should check it over."

"OK, Sid, OK."

Luddington departed quietly.

Hurley placed a yellow legal pad on the desk in front of him and began to work on his statement about the tender offer. He asked his secretary to get Louis Spinner on the telephone. As he was writing on the pad, the buzzer sounded.

"Mr. Hurley, I have Mr. Spinner. I reached him in Miami Beach. We've been deluged with calls from the press, and the TV people are all outside."

"No statements for the press until the meeting, Nancy. I'll talk to Spinner."

After the perfunctory greetings, Hurley said: "Lou, I guess you know why I'm calling."

"Well, Mr. Hurley"—it annoyed Hurley that the head of

143

the UAW would not call him by his first name—"I suppose it has to do with those Arabs buying out your company."

"Right. We're dead set against it, and I think you should be too. Jesus, Lou, you don't want your people working for Arabs, do you?"

"I don't know, Mr. Hurley. What difference does it make as long as they pay the wages on time?"

The son of a bitch, Hurley thought. *The man is like a cash register—just like in the contract negotiations. Nothing means a damn to him except money for his men.*

"Look, Lou. We haven't always got along, but we should see eye to eye on this. I know your boys are patriotic Americans. I know they won't go for this foreign attempt to seize General Motors. Now you have some influence with Congress you could use." Hurley was beginning to sound as if he were making a speech. He stopped talking, not wanting to annoy Spinner by preaching to him.

"Mr. Hurley, I'm as concerned as you are. I just don't know what we're going to do yet. I'll talk to some of the members today, though and call you back this afternoon."

"OK, Lou. Please make it before two thirty. I've got the annual meeting at three."

They rang off. Hurley worked on his statement to the press for about an hour. When he had finished it, he asked his secretary to type it and send it over to Sid Luddington for his comments. He then ordered lunch in his office and ate a sirloin steak with some vegetables. Several of the other senior executives of the company phoned or came by and Hurley spoke with them. Between callers, he phoned each of the twenty-four directors of General Motors. They gave him their support. He continued to ignore calls from the press.

At two ten P.M. his secretary informed him that Louis Spinner was calling from Florida.

"Well, Mr. Hurley, I'm calling you like I promised I would."

"What did you decide?"

144

"I spoke to some of our boys. Then Congressman Jennings called me from Washington. I can't remember the last time I was so popular! Anyway, I told Jennings that our membership would not like to work for those Arabs. You know Jennings is head of the Foreign Affairs Committee, so he might be able to do something. He'll need some support in Washington, though."

"That's fine, Lou. I'm relieved and grateful for your support."

"We're not doing you any favors, Mr. Hurley. That just happens to be the way we feel right now. Our only concern is how those people may affect our members' jobs."

"I understand. Say, I'd like to mention in my statement this afternoon that the UAW opposes the takeover. Is that all right with you?"

"Suit yourself."

Hurley's secretary walked in, a manila folder in hand. It was the company statement on the tender offer, which Sid Luddington had looked over. Luddington insisted on seeing it to be sure it complied with the myriad of securities laws that restricted the actions and words of chief executives of publicly held companies.

Hurley opened the manila folder. In the upper-left-hand corner of the typed statement, Luddington had penciled in "OK," followed by his initials. Hurley looked at his watch: twenty to three. Time to go to the auditorium for the company meeting.

Chapter 15

HURLEY squinted as he gazed beyond the speaker's podium toward the audience he could barely see. The lights of the television camera crews were blinding. His vision soon became accustomed to the glare and he was able to open his eyes.

The auditorium was packed. Row upon row of people stood in the rear, behind the seated stockholders. Hurley estimated that there were at least eight hundred persons in the room. As he prepared to speak, the din of the crowd diminished, and a red light on one of the TV cameras went on.

Hurley began by introducing his board of directors with a short biographical sentence on each member. There was an oil company chairman, a black lady, an insurance company president, and a California banker, among others. Then Hurley delivered his speech, the one he had prepared before the takeover attempt. As he reviewed the company's earnings and achievements over the past year, he sensed the restlessness of the audience; this was not what most of them had come to hear. He spoke for twenty minutes and his prepared speech was over. Then he shuffled through his papers to find the statement on the tender offer.

"As most of you are aware," he began solemnly, "it was announced this morning that the Saudi Arabian government is tendering for majority control of General Motors." The audience stilled and sounds of *shh* were heard. "This brazen attempt to seize control of America's largest corporation was conceived in secrecy. Your management had no knowledge of it until this morning. I have discussed the matter with the board of directors and we have unanimously decided to oppose this tender offer in the most vigorous manner. The tender offer is also opposed by the United Auto Workers Union, which represents over four hundred thousand of our employees. In our opinion, this covert, underhanded attempt to control General Motors is an abuse of economic power on the part of a wealthy Arab state. It underlines the urgent need for greater international controls over the use of oil revenues.

"On behalf of your board of directors, I am today calling upon the President of the United States and the Congress to prepare and support emergency legislation to prevent the takeover of General Motors by the Saudi Arabian government. It is clearly inimical to the national interest for our largest industrial corporation to be acquired by a foreign power. Finally, I urge our shareholders to put aside the financial temptation of the tender offer and be motivated by a higher sense of patriotism and loyalty by refusing to offer their shares to the Saudi Arabian government. Let us unite, and in a spirit of solidarity, let us demonstrate that neither General Motors nor the American character is for sale."

The applause was deafening. Half of the audience was on its feet before Hurley's voice had stopped reverberating through the public address system. An official announced that Mr. Hurley would take questions from the audience. He had to repeat the statement; the applause had drowned him out.

When the noise had calmed to background chatter, a floor official extended the boom microphone to the first questioner, a middle-aged man.

"Mr. Hurley," the man said, "the stock didn't trade at all today on the New York Stock Exchange. What if a stockholder needs money and has to sell his shares? He can't sell if the Exchange won't let it trade."

Hurley turned around and nodded to Wes Fullerton, the company's financial vice-president. Fullerton rose and went to another podium.

"The Stock Exchange suspended trading in General Motors today due to an imbalance of orders. In layman's language, it means there were too many buy orders for the stock and not enough sellers to meet the demand. In such cases the Exchange suspends trading until it can match buy and sell orders at an agreed upon price. I understand the stock will open tomorrow."

Another stockholder rose to speak, and elderly woman Hurley recognized immediately as Wilma Plankett, a professional heckler at stockholders' meetings. There were a half dozen such hecklers in the country. They owned one

147

share each of hundreds of corporations, which gave them the right to attend annual meetings. Although they were nationally known and were sometimes bodily ejected from stockholders' meetings, these hecklers had often studied the company's performance and balance sheet well and possessed a thorough knowledge of the company's affairs.

"Mr. Hurley." Mrs. Plankett's voice was commanding. "Did it not occur to you, sir, that the Saudis may have chosen to buy General Motors because they believe that a more dynamic and aggressive management would help the company?"

Hurley rolled his eyes. This was the third year in a row he had had to stand there and calmly listen while Mrs. Plankett hurled her verbal rotten tomatoes. "I don't agree with you, Mrs. Plankett." He hoped this use of her name might flatter her. "I believe our record this year speaks for itself. I went over it in my earlier remarks."

"Well," Mrs. Plankett said indignantly, "that is nothing more than your opinion. I have some statistics here"—she opened a file and began to read—"for example, the profit margins of the five next largest industrial corporations are all higher than General Motors. Furthermore . . . "

Hurley paid no attention as Mrs. Plankett bellowed on. God, he thought, I don't need this today. He started the stopwatch on the podium. Mrs. Plankett would have two minutes.

When the time was up, Hurley banged the gavel. "Your time is up, Mrs. Plankett. Thank you for your question."

Hurley recognized five more stockholders. All of the questions related to the tender offer. One stockholder simply wanted to tell Mr. Hurley that he would not tender a single one of his fifty-two shares to the Saudi Arabians at any price. Another wanted to know what Hurley would do if Congress did not pass emergency legislation. Hurley did not expect that problem to occur.

When the stockholders meeting had been adjourned, Tim Hurley met with reporters for forty-five minutes. He answered their questions honestly, but sensed that the reporters did not believe he was telling them everything he knew. They never believe that anyway, Hurley thought. No matter; he didn't care. From now on, all of Timothy Hurley's energy would be devoted to preventing what he thought of as his corporation from being taken over by the Saudi Arabian government.

John Haddad finished reading Hurley's speech, which had been reproduced in full on the screen of his monitor, transmitted line by line by the Dow Jones service. *Damn good speech,* he thought as Hurley finished. Dave Hill and Lee Curtis, who were sitting alongside, made mocking clapping noises. They might have been at a Knicks basketball game. Dave looked to John, who remained emotionless.

"Hey, coach, what's the matter? This is a big moment."

"We made a mistake," John said.

"A mistake? Shit, Hurley played right into your hand. You knew damn well he would ask for legislation."

"It's the unions, damn it, the unions. I didn't think of that." John's face was ashen. "Hurley's got the UAW on his side. You can't run a company if the workers won't work!"

In a series of flashes, John recalled his meeting with El-Bahar, his clever plan for dealing with the legislation threat, his adroit handling of the large purchases of GM stock. And now this—with all of his careful planning, John had neglected to consider the reactions of the people at General Motors, the workers who were the lifeblood of any company. As the thought ran through his mind, John could feel the takeover slipping away from his reach like sand rushing through his fingers. Was it too late? He wondered if this blunder had irrevocably cost him the deal.

In his low mood, John called upon his optimistic nature for some counterarguments. Granted, he had not foreseen the labor problems; you can't expect to think of everything. The issue now was what to do about it. Was there a way to swing the unions to his side or, at best, moderate their op-

149

position? John would divert a good part of his efforts to doing just that. He only wished he could be assured of the outcome.

"Well, we've got to do something, and we ought to be thinking about what it's going to be." John smiled as he looked at his telephone. All five buttons were lit. "I hope the girls aren't having too hard a time with the press. Remember, no statements to anyone except for the press release Lee drafted. There's no reason to say any more."

"Yeah, right," Dave Hill said. "I guess we'd better keep a low profile. Feelings can run high on a foreign takeover of GM, expecially after Hurley's speech."

"I should call El-Bahar and fill him in. This reminds me of those 'good news-bad news' jokes. The good news, Your Excellency, is that we're going to buy the company"—John mimicked a phone conversation—"the bad news is that the company will suffer an immediate, massive strike."

"Maybe he'll have some ideas," Lee Curtis said.

"I hope so. Let's get back to work."

The small jet aircraft landed at Washington's National Airport and taxied to a hangar in a remote corner of the field. It was early evening, and Hurley needed a good night's rest before his meeting with the President in the morning. The meeting would not be publicized so the company took the precaution of arranging for its chairman to disembark away from the crowded terminal. As the plane stopped before the hangar, a black Cadillac limousine moved swiftly to meet it.

Chapter 16

THE President decided to see his congressional leaders in the Oval Office. Always play for an advantage, no matter how slight. The ambience of the White House, despite the events of a few years earlier, retained its aura and bestowed upon its occupant implications of power beyond that of other mortals. The trappings, combined with the fact that the President was in his second term and therefore not likely ever again to seek the approval of the electorate, gave him great assurance that his opinion would prevail.

Following his meeting with Hurley two days earlier, the President had been convinced that a takeover of General Motors by the Saudi Arabian government should be opposed politically. Hurley had done a good job of presenting his case, thus reinforcing the President's previous leaning. Now he had summoned the Senate Majority and Minority leaders, the Speaker of the House, the Chairman of the House Ways and Means Committee, and the Chairman of the House Foreign Affairs Committee. The Chairman of the Senate Foreign Relations Committee, who was en route to Japan, had been unable to be present.

When they had arrived, the usher seated the guests around the fireplace. The President sat in his familiar wing chair.

"Thank you for coming, gentlemen." The President smiled graciously. "I met with Tim Hurley a couple of days ago. I share his concern that a foreign takeover of General Motors would not be in the national interest. How do you feel about it?"

"I don't think any of us would disagree with you on that, Mr. President." The Senate Majority Leader was not in the habit of contradicting the President. He owed his leadership position to the President's sponsorship, which had catapulted him over the heads of several other senators senior to him.

"Just one moment, if the senior senator from California would yield?" The voice of the Minority Leader, cold as the winter ice of his native Nebraska, cut in. "I see nothing so sinister about a stock purchase made in a free market by the Saudi Arabians. They're spending the very dollars they have earned by selling us their crude oil. This will put fresh capital in the hands of the American stockholders who sell their stock to the Arabs, which will then be available for investment in other industries. General Motors is not exactly 'portable.' It'll still be there the next morning! Even if the Arabs get control, they'll be subject to the same rules and regulations of running a public company as the present management. Naturally, I understand why Mr. Hurley has already been here urgently trying to seek help in keeping his job, but I don't see anything to cause the Congress to rush into some ill-considered prohibitive legislation."

The Speaker of the House, more sensitive to the niceties of public opinion upon which he depended to return him to his comfortable office every two years, cared less for the advantages of incoming petrodollars. "The American people don't want foreigners coming in here and taking control of our most important companies. The public doesn't understand capital flows and all that economic gibberish. They expect their government to slam the door on these Arabs, and I agree!"

The President turned to Sam Jennings. "And what is the opinion of the Chairman of the House Foreign Affairs Committee?"

"I have to go along with the Speaker, Mr. President. I've had a couple of conversations with Lou Spinner, the head of the UAW. Many of his members are my constituents. They don't like this any more than we do. My staff has already started work on legislation to stop the takeover."

The President continued the discussion, eliciting all the leaders' opinions, conducting the meeting as though it were a genuine consideration of alternatives. But privately he had decided long before to seek legislation barring the Saudi project and was only going through the motions. When he saw that the different points of view had been expressed and that now they were being repeated without anything new being offered, he brought the discussion to a close.

"Fine," he said, "then the consensus is in favor of a bill stopping the takeover. There's been a lot of clamor for a statement from the White House, but I wanted to talk to you fellows before I put one out. This will make it easier and your support will be welcome." He avoided the eyes of the dissident Minority Leader.

"Do you intend to make a televised announcement?" The House Ways and Means Chairman asked the question.

"No, I don't think so. I don't want to overdramatize this thing. I'll have my Press Secretary release something on it tomorrow. You gentlemen can start on the legislation, and maybe we can end this whole matter without undue fuss. The main thing is to write a bill that applies to a company the size of General Motors, but does not prohibit foreign investment in smaller companies. Also, I hope you can avoid allowing any unrelated amendments being tacked on. I'll have the Secretary of State talk to the Saudi Arabian ambassador and explain our position as diplomatically as possible."

"Well, that seems to cover it," the Majority Leader said, moving forward in his chair, awaiting the signal to rise.

"Thank you again for coming," the President said.

The noise in the newsroom seemed to get louder as the deadline for the six o'clock news approached. The news tickers sounded as if they were clacking faster and the tempo of the news personnel quickened. Charlotte Grogan was used to the pace, and she did not let the more frantic atmosphere of the late afternoon schedule affect her work habits or her judgment. She had one and a half hours of typed news stories in front of her, and they had to be condensed to forty-two minutes, allowing for commercials, then matched and timed to the film clips. She slashed a major story on the trade agreement with Cuba from five to two minutes, not that it was unimportant, but the ageless Walter Cronkite would be giving it prominent coverage on the national news so that full coverage on the local news segment was unnecessary. A story about a D.C. murder and another about a mugging, she cut altogether. Alas, these events were

153

hardly news anymore. Charlotte then came upon a story that engaged her full attention. One of the station's reporters had learned that the President had met with some congressional leaders that morning and that a Presidential statement on the GM takeover would be forthcoming. It had been reliably reported that the President would strongly oppose the takeover attempt and that emergency legislation to forbid it was already in preparation. Charlotte Grogan picked up the phone and dialed John's number in New York.

"John? This is your lonely and neglected Washington spy. Do you want to hear the hottest and latest White House rumor?"

"I don't know what I'd do without you, Charlotte. What's happening down there?"

Charlotte proceeded to fill him in on the anticipated Presidential blast. John listened carefully, grateful that he had prepared for this development long ago.

"Honey, you've given me some very precious time. Now I can get moving on this right away instead of waiting until tomorrow. Is there any charge?"

"No charge for now, Mr. Haddad, but I'd like to collect some of your valuable time when the Saudis are finished with it." Her words were in a joking vein, but John could tell from her tone that she wasn't too happy about not seeing him as often as before.

"Darling, you're very sweet to call me. I promise I'll make some time for us as soon as I can. Right now I don't have a free second."

When their conversation had ended, John placed a call to Riyadh, Saudi Arabia. He chose the words he would say first with great care. There would be an apology for getting the Oil Minister up in the middle of the night, for Saudi Arabia was seven hours ahead of the time in New York. He would then inform El-Bahar that the time had come to activate the strategy they had agreed upon in London.

* * *

The reception at the Brazilian Embassy Residence was crowded with diplomats, State Department officials, newspapermen, and a few business leaders. It was one of the better dinner parties on the diplomatic circuit that month. For one thing, people were genuinely having fun in the special ambience that only the Brazilians could create. Every one of their parties seemed like carnival in Rio, and invitations to the Brazilian affairs were highly coveted.

Although the party was ostensibly for Brazil's Minister of the Interior, who had been visiting Washington, the featured guest of the evening was the American Secretary of State and his very attractive young wife. Fortunately for the conduct of American foreign affairs, the secretary and his wife actually enjoyed Washington receptions and attended almost all of them. Their sociability enhanced the secretary's relationships with foreign ambassadors and helped him to become one of the best-informed secretaries in American history.

As he walked to the bar for a refill, the secretary thought he heard someone calling his name over the loud, rhythmic sounds of the Brazilian band. He turned and saw Jean de Villars, the French ambassador.

"Hello there, William." Most ambassadors who knew him well called the Secretary of State Bill. This was de Villars' way of being informally formal.

"Hello, Jean. Say, are you coming to see me tomorrow? Our French desk chief told me you wanted to see me urgently."

"That is correct, William. I will be there at ten A.M."

"Fine. Anything serious?"

"Yes, I think so. But I don't want to be gauche and ruin your evening by telling you about it now. Let's enjoy the party!" The French ambassador walked away and was soon engulfed by the crowd. Another group of people who had been hovering around the secretary closed in and began to speak to him. The music played louder, and several guests felt impelled to dance. The secretary gave no further thought to whatever the French ambassador might have to say in the morning.

At ten past eleven in the morning, Ambassador Jean de Villars left the office of William T. Girard, Secretary of State of the United States. Bill Girard sat on the comfortable sofa in his office and spoke into the extension phone nearby. He asked his secretary to try to get the President on the phone, and, according to custom, she buzzed him before the President came on the line so that the President would not be kept waiting.

"Good morning, Mr. President," Girard said, straightening up. "Have you released the statement on the General Motors takeover yet?—No?—Good. That's good. I request that you not release it until we have had a chance to speak.—Yes, sir, it is important.—Fine. I'll be right over."

Girard was struggling with his jacket as he walked out of the office. He told his secretary to alert his chauffeur that he was on his way down.

Girard arrived at the White House in minutes and was ushered right into the Oval Office. The President greeted him and showed him to the area beside the fireplace.

"What's the problem, Bill?" The President asked the question with no trace of concern.

"Jean de Villars, the French ambassador, came into see me this morning," Girard began. "It was about the Saudi takeover of General Motors."

"Why would that be of concern to the French?"

"The French object to our passing legislation barring the acquisition of an American company by foreigners. They contend that it is unreasonable that Americans should be allowed to buy foreign companies, but as soon as a foreigner threatens to buy an American company, we start passing laws against it."

"But this is no foreign company, Bill. This is the Saudi Arabian government."

"I know," Girard continued, "and I told de Villars that.

156

He wasn't moved. He said that some American companies are as powerful as many foreign governments, and, besides, who can know what the internal relationship between a company and its government really is."

The President said nothing for a moment, different thoughts running through his mind. Then he looked up. "Well, what do they want us to do?"

"It's what they *don't* want us to do. They don't want us to bar the acquisition of General Motors by the Saudis."

"I still don't see why it's so goddamn important to the French." The President looked puzzled, then his expression changed. "Wait a minute. Do you think the Saudi Arabians put them up to this?"

"Yes, I do. Saudi Arabia supplies an awful lot of Western Europe's oil needs. That gives them tremendous bargaining power."

"Then maybe we should diplomatically tell the French that we appreciate their views and all that, but we just can't allow General Motors to be taken over. That way the French will score their points with the Saudis for having tried."

"I'm afraid that won't do," Girard said gravely. "De Villars made a veiled threat. If the United States prevents a foreigner from buying an American company, France may reconsider the status of American investments in France."

"He said that?"

"Not in so many words. He was very diplomatic, of course. But the meaning was unmistakable. He had some impressive statistics, too. American companies own fourteen billion dollars' worth of assets in France alone. Total American assets abroad are estimated at almost ten times that much. Incidentally, those figures are from our own Commerce Department."

"I see your point, Bill. Considering the size of our assets abroad, subject to the whims of foreign governments, we obviously have to take that kind of threat seriously. Jesus, I read the other day that the total value of General Motors was seventeen billion. Even that seems like peanuts compared to the total amount of U.S. investments in foreign countries."

"Right. And in many countries the American assets are the most productive ones those countries have. Industries like packaged foods, drugs, chemicals, computers, automobile manufacturing, and farm equipment are often American-dominated. Some foreign governments would love to have an excuse to take them over."

"This is a fine mess," the President said. "I gather you feel that other foreign countries may follow suit and threaten retaliation if we don't let the Saudis get GM?"

"I'm afraid, Mr. President, that it's more than just a feeling." Girard pulled a small piece of paper from his coat pocket. "According to Villars, the countries that have the largest amount of U.S. assets are Great Britain, France, the Netherlands, West Germany, and Belgium." He held up the piece of paper, a note from his secretary. "This morning my office received requests for appointments from the ambassadors of each of those countries."

"So that's it," the President said angrily. "It looks like our loyal European trading partners have gotten together to poke their fingers in our domestic affairs." The President's anger was real. In the years following the Second World War he had been a college student, and he had traveled through Europe in the summer of 1946. He remembered the immediate respect and warm smiles on the faces of the French, the Belgians, whenever they got a glimpse of his green American passport or heard his obviously American high school French. The United States had bailed them out with blood and uncounted dollars over thirty years ago, but the Europeans had the typical debtors' short memory. Now these ambassadors, who were of his own generation and had seen the same things he had, were putting the pressure on his beloved country for the sake of expediency. He shook his head, glad that his second term was coming to an end and that he could step away from the ugliness of politics soon.

"We have to remember," Girard continued, "almost every major American corporation has some assets abroad. If we jeopardize those assets, we are going to create one hell of an opposition movement from the industrialists. General Motors may be the largest, but it is still only one company . . ."

"I know what you mean. This time the Europeans have a club over our heads, and they know there is very little time available for negotiation. Once that tender offer becomes effective and the shares start changing hands, trying to undo it would be a nightmare . . . endless lawsuits . . . all the rest. Do you think we'll have to sacrifice General Motors as the lesser evil?"

"I think it's inevitable," Girard said. "Let them have working control of the company. After all, the physical assets are largely here, and no matter who runs a public company, they are still subject to public scrutiny every quarter. Once the Arabs have paid a high price for the shares, they will be motivated to improve earnings just as much as the present management."

The President smiled. "You're using the same arguments I heard here the other day from the Minority Leader. I hate to give him the satisfaction! But it looks like our hands are pretty well tied. I'm going to have to step aside as far as this acquisition is concerned, but I sure as hell don't want this to be a trend. Now if the Saudis made some deal with the Europeans to get them to threaten us, let's make it damn clear that this is the last time it's going to happen. They can collect from the Saudis on this one, but I want some kind of commitment from those countries that we're not going to have to go through this routine every time. Remind them that we haven't forgotten the screaming from all over Europe the last time Congress proposed the removal of our troops from Germany, and that they still appreciate their 'most favored nation' status with us on trade. Don't give away our foreign assets for nothing."

"I'll try, sir." The secretary was heartened by the President's fighting retreat. It was tactical, but not strategic.

"I guess I'll have to call the congressional leaders and bring them up to date on this," the President said. "They're not going to like it, but unless one of them has a better idea, they'll have to stick to it. Once Congress knows what the stakes are, few members will be in a position to support any legislation against the takeover. Every one of them has constituents who would be severely affected by a massive European retaliation."

"I'm sure they'll go along with you, Mr. President. You know how to put it to them."

Girard left the office, a preoccupied look on his face. No sooner had the door closed behind him than the President's thumb was mashing the button that summoned his secretary. The President rattled off his instructions to her throughout her progress from the door, across the carpet, to the side of his desk.

"First, get me yesterday's congressmen on the phone . . . in order of seniority! Then, tell the press office to announce a press conference for me tomorrow. And make sure they arrange to plant an early question on the General Motors thing. I want to spend a good deal of prime time on it." The President, having made his decision, was in high gear, in full command.

Chapter 17

THE new office tower of the Royal Iranian Oil Company in downtown Teheran was tall enough so that a casual observer would have difficulty counting the floors. Inevitably, dizziness would set in at the repetitive images of the little rows of squares, and the dazzling sun reflecting from the windows would only make the counting harder.

But if he persevered and found that there were thirty-two floors, he still probably would not suspect anything when he went inside and saw that the buttons in the elevators were numbered only from one to thirty. He would assume that the two missing floors were utility areas or served to accommodate the building's massive air-conditioning system. He also probably wouldn't notice the two keyholes in the elevator's panel, at the top above the buttons.

The two keyholes were the means of access to the thirty-first and thirty-second floors, headquarters of the notorious SAVAK, Iran's secret police. Although SAVAK did not have the traditions and longevity of some of its colleagues in other countries, like the KGB or the Deuxième Bureau, still it was rapidly making a reputation. In the late sixties and early seventies SAVAK had grown, under the sponsorship of the shah, into a modern, computerized, efficient, and completely ruthless organization. Its trainees were blooded by being assigned to carry out personally the weekly executions behind the high walls of Teheran's Administrative Detention House, known to the public as The Tomb. From this they graduated to infiltration of institutions in neighboring countries, information retrieval, codes, political assassination and kidnapping, acting as *agents provocateurs* and accomplishing various other missions deemed to be in the interests of the Peacock Throne.

Najib Meshedi stood by the window of his thirty-second-floor office, shielded from the glare by the deeply tinted green of the glass. In the government hierarchy he was known as the Deputy Minister of Finance, a position of very great responsibility, especially since Iran, like the Arab states, had begun to accumulate multibillion-dollar surpluses through the sale of her oil. But Meshedi's real job was known to only a few. The Shah, the Minister of Finance, and the Chief of Staff of the Armed Forces were the only people outside the SAVAK who knew that Meshedi was its director. True, other departments of government dealt with SAVAK daily on hundreds of different projects, but the director was always referred to by his title, never by name. The official office of the Deputy Minister of Finance was a few floors below, in the same building, and Meshedi was able to put in frequent enough appearances there to convince even the most skeptical that he was on the job.

Meshedi's task that morning was a challenge because it combined both his public and his secret functions. He had personally been ordered by the Shah, in the throne room of the Gulistan Palace, to stop the takeover of General Motors by the Saudis. The Shah had not found it necessary to tell him whether to use SAVAK for the undertaking. His only supplementary instructions had been to keep the budget down as low as possible for the operation. The Shah did not want Iran to wind up owning General Motors. His experience with the administration of Krupp in Germany after Iran, building on its original twenty-five percent purchase in 1974, had raised its control to fifty-five percent and inherited all the management problems of the giant steelmaker, did not make him eager to be saddled with another big Western company's problems. The Shah had made it clear to Meshedi that he didn't expect the public or the press to get wind of Iran's involvement in preventing the takeover, and that no reckless gambles on the stock exchanges or excessive risks were to be run.

Meshedi knew that this assignment had to be accomplished by stealth. There was no way that the Iranian treasury could compete with the Saudis buying power in a real slugging match. And, in any case, that had been ruled out by the Shah's reluctance to own too much General Motors stock. But the risk to the Iranian Army's advantage over the Saudis in tanks was too great to allow the takeover to succeed.

Najib Meshedi had reached his position of great power, perhaps even the greatest power in the country after the Shah's, by a policy of enormous caution. He never made a decision in anger and never committed himself to a course of action any earlier than absolutely necessary. He had survived numerous factional political struggles around the throne, particularly when the old Shah had died and the new one had brought in his entourage of sycophants. Most of the old ministerial level had been forced out, but Meshedi had been young enough and smart enough to ingratiate himself quickly with the new order, liberally using the secret SAVAK files to help him fight off any dangerous challenger. Unlike many of his contemporaries in the financial world in the Middle East who had been educated in the United States, Meshedi had attended the Ecole Polytechnique in Paris when his father was the Iranian ambassador to France. The result was a thorough grounding in world affairs, with less stress on competitive capitalism and more on the realities of getting things done. The French had long ago abandoned the high moral tone still heard around the streets of Cambridge, Massachusetts, when they trained their diplomats and businessmen.

The Meshedi family had always belonged to the governmental class in Teheran, and every generation had contributed to the officer corps, the diplomatic circles, and the cabinet. Meshedi had never married, and now, at the age of forty-five, he didn't really expect to. SAVAK took all his energies, and he could not afford the vulnerability of having a wife and family. At the same time, his bachelorhood made him every Teheran hostess' favorite "extra man," and he could often be seen, wearing his resplendent ministerial uniform, tall and distinguished-looking, sunburned, with a strong nose and graying temples, striding into elegant gatherings with his look of habitual assurance.

Meshedi pushed the buzzer to summon his chief assistant and secretary, Mohammed Pak.

Pak hurried into the room. "Yes, Director. You rang for me?"

"Yes. Sit down. Now listen carefully to me and don't interrupt. First, I want a dossier assembled on a certain John Haddad, employed in New York by a Wall Street firm called Thompson, Caldwell and Company. Bring it completely up to date with whatever information you can find. There must be something on him in the Finance Ministry you can start with because his firm has a branch office here in Teheran and all their officers must be registered.

"Next, get me the latest annual and quarterly reports on

General Motors. And have their local man . . . what's his name . . . come and see me as soon as possible. I want to question him on the tank deliveries.

"Next, I want to see the latest reports from all our agents in Saudi Arabia, particularly anything having to do with the Oil Ministry.

"Finally, I want a list of our senior-level operatives with the following qualifications. Fluency in the English language. Suitable cover easily arranged for a trip to the United States in a few days . . . and, of course, availability. And, if possible, I want an agent who knows something about finance or the stock market. Any questions?"

Pak knew better than to ask the purpose of these inquiries. He had read the newspapers too and realized that the GM deal was dangerous to Iran's interests.

"No questions, Director. I will do everything as fast as possible."

After studying the list of agents and their qualifications, which had arrived on his desk in minutes, Meshedi picked up the telephone and dialed a number. The connection was made. Meshedi barked out, "Have agent Tabriz sent to my office immediately!" and dropped the phone.

Then Meshedi summoned Pak again and instructed him to book him and Tabriz to New York on the early morning flight two days hence and to reserve his usual suite at the Carlyle.

Chapter 18

CONGRESSMAN Samuel Jennings received the telephone call from the President just as he was finishing lunch in his office, a sad affair of cottage cheese and canned peaches prescribed by his doctor as an antidote to the rich dinners and many cocktails of the Washington circuit. The President was brief. Unfortunately he would be unable to support legislation to block the GM takeover. Furthemore, if such legislation reached his desk, he would be forced to veto it. The reason? There had been threats of retaliation in kind from the leading industrial nations of Europe. The President was urging congressional leaders not to attempt to put through antiforeign investment legislation for the time being. Perhaps the problem could be worked out diplomatically at a later date, but not now, and not against the General Motors deal.

Jennings had no problem understanding the President's line of reasoning. The arguments were compelling. It was clearly not a good idea to introduce a bill that might trigger a massive retaliatory move against American business interests abroad. He knew that he had to inform Lou Spinner, the UAW chief, of this development, and he was not looking forward to doing it. When Jennings' secretary had located Spinner and had him on the line, the congressman picked up the phone on his desk and spoke softly into it. He explained to Spinner what had happened and, hearing no sounds or comments at the other end, continued to speak until he had no more to say.

"Are you still there, Lou?" Jennings wondered if they might have been cut off earlier in the conversation.

"I'm still here, Congressman. Just thinking, that's all."

"Lou, I am asking you to explain to your membership the how and the why of this situation. I'll be doing the same after the President makes his announcement, and I'd like to have your help with my constituents."

"Listen, Congressman. We don't like the idea of a foreign takeover of GM, and that's that. Now you may have your reason for not wanting to legislate against it, but that's your business. I can't change my position. There are people in my union who feel even more strongly than I do about this . . . they're willing to try to stop it any way they can. I believe it's better for everybody if I stay in office as president of the union and control some of the hotheads down here. And I can't do that without opposing the takeover."

Jennings spent the rest of the afternoon seeing some visiting constituents and posing for pictures with a Michigan Boy Scout Troop. He did not stop thinking about the conversation with Spinner. At face value, Spinner's determination to block the takeover was very real. The implied threat in his remarks about the hotheads in the union could mean a big strike, even violence or sabotage. It was not the kind of problem Jennings wanted to contemplate. He had a responsibility to his constituents, to be sure. Yet as Chairman of the House Foreign Affairs Committee he was expected to act with a perspective and scope far wider than the factional interests of one congressional district in Michigan. In any event, he knew that following his conversation with the President there was no chance for any antitakeover legislation to pass in the near future.

Jennings turned the same facts over and over in his mind until they began to lose their meaning. No new insights presented themselves. Well, he thought, I just hope Skinner's people don't do anything foolish.

That same evening at about seven o'clock, John arrived home looking forward to a peaceful evening away from the phone calls and constant office hubbub surrounding the ongoing tender offer. The administration's failure to attack the Saudi takeover attempt and the absence of any congressional announcements had raised his hopes that a substantial amount of stock would now come in, and that it would not be necessary to raise the price too soon.

As he walked into his living room, he bent to turn on one lamp on a side table, continued into the kitchen to make a drink, and came back and turned on the television set to watch the evening news. He sprawled on the couch, put his feet up on the coffee table, and looked up to see the familiar face of Walter Cronkite coming into focus. In the first minute of the program it was obvious that there would be no story affecting the takeover, and John allowed himself to sink back into the cushions and relax completely.

The television set was on a table to the right of the fireplace, and during the first commercial John looked away from the screen, reached for the ceiling with both hands, and indulged himself in a luxuriant stretch and a massive yawn. As his eyes descended from the ceiling toward the screen again, in the dim light of the single lamp and the glow of the television, he noticed that something looked out of place over the mantel. Idly, he got to his feet and walked around the table to get a better look.

The oil painting of his parents hanging above the fireplace had been slashed in a huge *x* and a triangle of canvas from the bottom quadrant was hanging away from the wall, the point of it swaying slightly like a palm frond. Startled, John ran to the door way and turned on the overhead light to see it more clearly. There was no doubt that this had been done deliberately. John quickly dismissed the thought that his twice-a-week cleaning lady could have gone berserk with a knife in the apartment that afternoon. He reached for the phone to call the police, then reconsidered and dropped the receiver. The first thing to do was check out the apartment to see if anything was missing or if anything else had been damaged. Those were the first questions the police would ask.

He went to the door to check the lock, but there was not a scratch or mark to indicate any tampering. Then he went around looking at all the outside windows of the apartment. There was a smudge of dirt on the sill of the narrow window of the bathroom and some paint chips on the floor. Someone had forced the window open from the outside fire escape, and once past the dried paint he had had no trouble because the window lock was frozen open.

John looked through the closets and drawers in the bedroom, and finding nothing out of place, he examined the living room again. On his desk, which faced into the room in front of the window, he found another sign of his late visitor's presence. There were a group of framed photographs on the desk, one of Charlotte standing on the deck of a yacht on the Potomac, one of his grandfather in his ceremonial village elder's robes, and one each of his mother and father—his mother in her rocking chair at home, and his father standing proudly in front of his newest Haddad Shoe Store on Nostrand Avenue in Brooklyn. The glass had been smashed from the frames of the photos of his parents, and the prints had been slashed with the same blade as the painting, because there were flecks of oil paint clearly visible along the cut edges of the paper. None of the other photographs had been touched.

A pang of fear struck John as he realized the implications of this petty destruction in his apartment. His first impulse was to grab the phone and call his parents, but then he had a second thought. There could be a tap on his phone, for all he knew. He dashed out the front door and down to the corner phone booth. At least from there he wouldn't be overheard. He promised himself to have his phones checked by a professional de-bugger the very next morning, and then checked again every two or three days to make sure. He would bill the firm for this little service in the interests of security.

John dropped in the dime, dialed the number of his parents' apartment, and waited nervously as the phone rang once, twice, and a third time before the connection was made.

"Hello, yes?"

"Mom, are you all right?"

"John! You haven't called for a week. What do you mean, am I all right?"

"Mom, listen to me, is Dad at home?"

"Yes, darling, he's right here beside me. How are you . . . so busy you can't call your old parents once in a while?"

"Mother, please. I have something important to tell you both and I want you to pay attention."

168

"All right, John, we're listening."

John paused to compose his thoughts, then went on. "This is something about business that may involve you. It has to do with the General Motors takeover. I have good reason to believe that some of the people who oppose the Saudis are trying to threaten me by threatening your safety. I want you to take a quick vacation, right now, just to get away for a week or two."

It took John another five minutes on the telephone to convince his parents that he was serious. Then, while they were making reservations on Delta Air Lines to fly to Sarasota that same night, John was busy arranging accommodations for them in a quiet hotel on Longboat Key, a sleepy backwater resort island to the south of Sarasota. By ten o'clock he was able to confirm that their flight had taken off from La Guardia on schedule, and only then did John call the Nineteenth Precinct to report the break-in to the police.

The detectives assigned to come up were prompt, and they dutifully took down the bare facts as John recited them. He told them he had sent his parents out of town to insure their safety. At first, the detectives seemed to be more interested in the insurance valuation of the oil paintings than in the reason for the vandalism. But then John asked them for the name of a reliable private detective who might be available on short notice. They offered to call a recently retired colleague of theirs who was now living in Florida. Within a few minutes it was arranged that the Florida detective would check into the same hotel where John's parents would be staying and keep an eye on them without letting them know he was working for John.

Only after they had left was John able to sit down and try to think through his fears. First, there was nothing he was involved in other than the GM takeover that could possibly have caused this implied threat to his parents. So the question was, what was the source of the threat? Could it be some enemy of El-Bahar's that John had never even suspected? Could it be some desperate scheme of the Swiss banker, Sloman, as a last resort? And who else might be threatened? He considered calling Charlotte to make sure she was safe, but then reconsidered. Since they were not even engaged, it was unlikely that anyone would use her to get at him. John was exhausted, and his mind was too muddled to think any further. He stretched out on the couch in the living room, kicked off his shoes, and allowed himself to doze off, knowing he would be awakened in a few hours by the telephone when his parents called to tell him they had arrived safely at their destination.

Chapter 19

ON Friday, John Haddad, for the second time in his life, faced the prospect of addressing a press conference. Unlike his first one, which was part of the strategy of the Siesta Inns merger, this conference was in response to the demands of the press. Not only the financial papers but the leading newspapers of the United States and all the major financial capitals, plus the wire services, had made such a clamor in the offices of Thompson, Caldwell that finally to still the raging beast of the fourth estate John had agreed to come forward. He had no prepared statement, and agreed only that he would answer questions. It took a conscious effort on John's part to prepare himself for the ordeal because he had been distracted trying to anticipate what the next step would be in the attack on his parents that began with the slashed pictures and could very well end in something worse.

There was no room large enough to hold a press conference of this size in the Thompson, Caldwell offices, so the firm had taken an auditorium in the Park Lane Hotel on Central Park South for the purpose. Anticipating those incoming millions in the form of dealer's fees, Elliott Grayson had authorized the serving of canapes and cocktails, thus insuring at least some initial goodwill on the part of the press.

After Grayson's inconsequential opening remarks, the podium was turned over to John Haddad. John stepped up, leaned down to speak into the microphone, which had been adjusted for Grayson's height, and said, "Gentlemen and ladies of the press, we are here at your request to discuss the tender offer for General Motors stock by our clients, Islam Investors Limited. Please proceed with your questions."

John had almost forgotten to say "ladies" at all, but the last moment he had seen a bright dab of pink in the fourth or fifth row like a flower growing out of a crack in the sidewalk, surrounded by the concrete grayness of the suits of the financial writers.

As he fielded the questions from the *Wall Street Journal,* the London *Times,* Agence France Presse, Reuters, and the others, John watched the pink dab out of the corner of his eye, looking for a question from her side of the room so that he might have an excuse to study her more carefully. The New York *Times,* in the form of a corpulent, balding, cheerful fellow, stood up in front of her and asked his planned question, satisfying John's wish. The questioner was rewarded with a long and complete answer, but the whole time John was looking past him at the stunning girl in pink, making sure she caught his eye.

She had glossy thick straight black hair, parted in the center and falling behind her back in a curtain that reached almost to her waist. He eyes were amber, flecked with gold, and set wide apart above a delicate sloping nose with slightly flared nostrils. Her cheekbones were clearly outlined, and her smooth, tan skin set off her crimson, pouting mouth, which suddenly burst into a dazzling smile as she realized that John had noticed her.

She was wearing a pink silk knit spring dress that clung to her perfectly formed body and made it very obvious that

171

she wore no brassiere. John could see the darker hue of her nipples through her sheer fabric, and suddenly this press conference had new possibilities.

She raised her hand after John had finished answering the *Times* man, and he immediately pointed to her. She said in a rich, husky voice, "I am Lila Rashid of the Middle East News Wire Service. I would like to ask Monsieur Haddad how, considering his youth, he happens to have been chosen by Saudi Arabia for this most responsible task?"

"Miss Rashid, I am afraid that you will have to put that question to your sources in the Middle East. I don't think it would be proper for me to comment on it."

John handled a few more questions, most of which had already been answered or required predictions of the future on his part that he was not prepared to make. He wound down the session by announcing that drinks were being served in an adjoining reception room and that he would be in there to circulate and chat with the distinguished members of the press. There was a rush for the bar.

John strode into the outer lobby to a pay phone and placed a call, giving the operator his credit card number. Soon he was speaking to his father.

"Is everything peaceful down there, Dad? Are you enjoying the beach?"

"Yes, yes, son. It's beautiful weather, everything is fine. I don't know what you are so afraid of, but I'm grateful for the vacation. Don't worry, and go back to your meeting."

"Dad, are sure there's nothing unusual, no strange people around?"

"No, no strangers, no nothing. Just sunshine and your mother. Except for the reason we are here, it's just like a normal vacation."

John made one more call to his detective, to make certain that everything was as it should be. Reassured, he rang off and went back to the press group, feeling relieved and happy that his parents were safe. Whoever had slashed the pictures wasn't bothering his parents in Florida at least. He found Lila Rashid near the bar and, walking up behind her, took her elbow, steered her away from the others, and said, "I'm sorry I was forced to avoid your question. Didn't you know I wouldn't answer that kind of thing? If you're from the Middle East, you must know that the Saudis are very careful and thorough about their investments and who handles them."

"I'm Lila, Mr. Haddad, and I accept your explanation. You know, I really don't care very much about the details of your deal and the technicalities of your stock market. My readers at home wouldn't understand too much of that. I'm more interested in the personality of the American who has the trust of the Saudis to handle their money, especially such large sums of it, so independently. Would you consider giving me a . . . how do you call it . . . an exclusive personal interview for my Middle East subscribers?"

"Please call me John, Lila. I'd be delighted to give you an interview, if you avoid the technical elements. How about having dinner with me? I'll spend another fifteen minutes here walking around a little while you finish your drink, then I'll meet you at the taxi entrance on the Fifty-eighth Street side of the hotel."

"I would love to dine with you. But are you sure you would not prefer entertaining some more important members of the press?"

"Let me be the judge of that," he answered.

As John made the rounds of the hard-drinking press men still clustered around the bar, he was careful to greet each important publication's representative with a word or two of what sounded like "inside" information. Then leaving the further care and feeling of the press to his assistants, he went to meet Lila Rashid.

John chose a quiet French restaurant, Le Perigord, for dinner with Lila. There were two Perigords, one loud and noisy where people jostled each other to see and be seen on Park Avenue, and one quiet and pleasant one on East Fifty-second Street near the East River where the chef was better and the atmosphere relaxed. Since it was rather early, they had no trouble getting a corner round table with a curved banquette.

John felt a little guilty, like a married man unexpectedly finding himself alone with a girl far too attractive for his wife to "understand" about it if she knew. But he quashed the feeling, reminding himself that he was not yet married.

John ordered the *hors d'oeuvres variés,* Dover soles stuffed with purée of mushrooms and bathed in champagne sauce, and an appropriate Pouilly Fumé, 1971. Lila Rashid settled close to him on the banquette, putting her handbag on the other side away from John and allowing her leg to press gently against his. Her scent was strong, musky, and very provocative. John had difficulty concentrating on her fairly innocuous questions and was well aware that she knew exactly what she was doing.

"Don't you take any notes when you interview someone?" he asked her. "How can you remember everything we say?"

Lila grinned and pulled her large handbag onto her lap. She reached and pulled out a tiny tape recorder the size of two packages of cigarettes. "I have it all down right here, John."

"Well, I'm not saying another word until you turn that gadget off." He reached over and pushed the off button, placing the little machine on the table where he could keep an eye on it.

"Then business hours are finished," said Lila, "and we can now be friends." She tucked her arm through the crook of his elbow and put her cheek against his shoulder, reaching for her wineglass with her other hand.

John decided not to resist her gesture. She might take offense if he rudely pushed her away, and it was not unpleasant having her there. Lila kept up a conversation that required little response from John as the dinner was quickly and efficiently served. He was more aware of her physical presence than of what she was saying. This pleasant stranger made no pressing demands on him and seemed interested only in his well-being. Before he knew it, the coffee had arrived and Lila was insisting that he order a good cigar. She dipped the rounded end of the long Uppman briefly in the brandy, produced a gold cigar cutter to neatly make a V-shaped incision, and lighted it for him the correct way, without puffing on the end at all, but merely by holding a match to the tip and turning it slowly in the flame until the whole tip glowed evenly. The cigar was the most satisfying John had ever smoked, and he knew that much of the pleasure came from the manner of presentation.

As they walked out to First Avenue to find a taxi, one glance from Lila confirmed their unspoken agreement. John gave the driver the address of his apartment without even asking her where in New York she was staying. As she preceded him into the apartment, she went right through the bedroom into the bathroom and closed the door behind her. John was left in the living room, staring at the rectangle of lighter-colored plaster over the mantel where the oil painting had hung. He had sent the painting out to be repaired the previous day. The spot was a chilly reminder of his parents' danger.

The sound of the toilet flushing made him look back, just as Lila emerged from the bathroom and walked out to meet him. He was not prepared for the sight of her. She stood in the middle of the room, looking at him with a tentative smile. Her pink dress, stockings, and panties were neatly draped over her left arm. She was wearing only her pink silk pumps.

Lila had an even tan over her whole body, without a trace of any mark where a bathing suit might have cut off the sunlight. Her waist was very narrow, but her hips flared wide, then tapered to her nicely turned calves. Her breasts jutted forward without sagging and her back was straight.

"Where should I put these?" She asked in a little-girl voice of mock innocence.

John walked up to her, took her clothes, and dropped them into a chair. He took her by the hand, led her to the bed, and with one motion, swept away the bedspread and turned down the sheet. Lila slipped under the covers, and he went around to the other side of the bed, hitting the light switch as he went by and plunging the room into darkness. John quickly rid himself of his clothing, kicked off his shoes and stripped off his socks. He was under the covers and reaching for her as she rolled over to meet him. He was aroused and eager, but at the same time amused. She was challenging him to a contest and it happened to be in bed.

In the next few instants John discovered what an amateur tennis player must feel like having accidentally walked onto a court occupied by a Wimbledon champion. The pro has to be in control of the game. Lila was definitely a pro. She was on him without giving him a chance to draw breath. And her instinctive movements were made to insure his comfort while she made all the effort.

Lila would bring him just to the verge of a climax and then ease off, making him wait. Then she would wind him up again, until at last he clutched her around the waist with both hands and forced her down upon him, not letting her escape as he surged up to meet her. Feeling his superior strength, she finally relaxed, letting him have his way. She leaned down over him, matching her thrusts to his, letting her hair fall in a perfumed curtain around his face and bringing her lips close to his.

John was awakened with a start by the loud jangling of the telephone on the table next to the bed. He was forced to reach across Lila's inert form to grasp the receiver and grunt a response into the phone.

"We have a person-to-person call for Mr. John Haddad." The operator's voice had a distinct Midwestern twang.

"This is he." John cleared his voice and blinked his eyes, his brain slowly focusing.

"Go ahead, please, we have your party," singsonged the operator.

A hoarse man's voice came on the line. "Mr. Haddad?"

"Yes, who is this?"

"You don't know me, Mr. Haddad, and my name doesn't matter. I have something to say and I think you'd better listen. It's concerning certain parties who are staying at the Sea Breeze Bungalows. Do you get my meaning?"

John jumped out of bed and stood up, now wide awake. The voice had just named the motel where his parents were staying on Longboat Key.

"OK, I'll listen. Say what you have to say."

"That's fine, Mr. Haddad, I knew you'd understand. I have two associates sitting in a parked car across from bungalow Number 14 at the Sea Breeze. Right now their instructions are to harm no one. The only precaution they have taken is to persuade your retired policeman to go home . . . he's not coming back. Now I would like you to go downstairs to the coffee shop next door to your apartment and talk to another associate of mine. He's waiting to hear from you. His name is Carlo Lanzini, and he has a proposal to make. Do you understand?"

"I think I understand perfectly. For Christ's sake, don't do anything until we talk. I'll go see your man right away!"

"I'm glad to hear you're willing to listen, Mr. Haddad. This is just a business meeting, like any other, right?"

"Right, I'm on my way."

John turned to Lila, who by this time was sitting up and looking at him, trying to understand what was going on, but, of course, not able to from hearing only John's part of the conversation. "Lila, you'll have to get dressed now and go back to your hotel. I'll get you a cab. Something urgent has happened and I'm going to be tied up today."

"What a pity. I thought we could spend a nice peaceful Saturday in bed!" Lila looked up at him with a sultry smile. John leaned down and grabbed her hand, then yanked her out of the bed.

"Oh, no, you don't, young lady," he said, "I'll see you later . . . maybe tonight, if you're free. But right now I have no time."

He gave her a gentle push toward her pile of clothing, then hurried to the bathroom to wash his face and brush his teeth before going downstairs. He pulled on a pair of slacks and a sport shirt, stepped into a pair of loafers, took Lila's arm and strode into the hall. At the street, John whistled down a taxi, put Lila into it, closed the door, then leaned in the open window.

"Wait! Lila, where are you staying?"

"I'm at the Carlyle."

"The Carlyle? They must pay good salaries at your agency!"

"I don't pay for the room. My boss stays at the Carlyle and wants his wage slaves within shouting distance. When will you pick me up?"

"I don't know exactly. I'll call you." The taxi took off, and John turned, his face now set in a grim mask as he pushed open the glass door of the coffee shop.

Chapter 20

THE only person in the coffee shop besides Harry, the counterman, was sitting in one of the booths lining the far wall, with his back to the door. He didn't turn around as John entered, and the only part of him that was visible was the back of his head—covered with short, bristly black hair—and a thick, muscular acne-scarred neck. John walked up to the booth and faced the man. He was about fifty years old, with cruel lines in his pitted face, yellowed teeth, and small eyes. A nose that was too small for the rest of his features seemed pulled back, revealing too much of the inside of his nostrils. He was wearing a shiny, electric-blue suit, with tiny silver threads in it, and an open-necked white figured sport shirt. From his jacket protruded the

178

plastic mouthpiece tips of four cheap cigars. A fifth was lying in the ashtray, sending up a plume of foul-smelling smoke. John's stomach sent the taste of bile to the back of his throat as he inadvertently breathed in some of the smoke.

"Are you Lanzini?"

"Yeah, I'm Lanzini. Siddown, Haddad."

"I want to know what you people are doing and I want to know right now."

"Look, Haddad, I'm just a messenger—I carry the word. You call the shot. I take the word back. So don't give me any indignant shit, and let's talk business."

"All right. I'll listen to what you have to say, but I'll tell you one thing right now. Nobody touches my parents. They're not involved in this situation at all. So lay off them."

Lanzini grimaced painfully. "Lemme tell you what we want, and don't get so hot under the collar. We want you to lay off this General Motors deal. The working stiffs in Detroit don't want no greasy Arabs running the company. They're worried about their benefits and jobs. They're used to dealing with that mick Hurley, and they don' want no changes. You go ahead and buy some stock, run up the price, whatever. But I gotta go back to Detroit with the word that control don't go to no Arabs. Now if you don't go along, then we pass the word to our guys in Florida to get rough. Otherwise they just sit in the limo and watch that bungalow. You got forty-eight hours to decide."

"Lanzini, do you have any idea what you are talking about?" John was afraid of what this man might say or cause in his ignorance.

"Are you stupid or some'tin, Haddad? Do I have to go troo it again?"

"No, no. I know what you said. But don't you understand that forcing me out of this deal won't stop the Arabs at all? I'm just their agent. Eliminate me, and somebody else will turn up to handle it. I'm sure your organization works the same way, doesn't it? What do your people plan to do, declare war on the Arabs? Don't you see you can't stop a foreign government from buying stock in a public corporation by threats against the broker they hire?"

Lanzini was uneasy at John's challenge to his authority. He had delivered many such threats in the past, and the recipient had invariably been convinced to give in or face the painful consequences. But he had never encountered anyone who attacked the strategic value of the threat itself. He was at a loss for words and took refuge in repetition. "My orders are to tell you what Detroit wants. That's it. Don' gimme no arguments!"

"But stopping me personally doesn't stop the takeover. Can't you at least try to explain?"

"I don't make explanations to them. I do what I'm told." Lanzini folded his arms emphatically.

"And what if I notify the police about your threats?" It was the only thing John could think of to say.

"Then we pull out . . . for a week, or a month . . . the cops can't guard you forever."

"How will I get in touch with you after forty-eight hours?"

"We'll call you. We know where to reach you."

"Well, I'll see what I can do. But it won't work." John got up from the table and went out of the coffee shop, back up to his apartment. He picked up the phone and placed a call to Florida. When his father answered, he confirmed the presence of a black limousine with two men in it across from the entrance to the bungalow. John told his father not to worry about it, that they wouldn't bother him.

Next, John placed a call to El-Bahar and, having confidence in the wisdom of the Oil Minister, unburdened himself of the whole story of the slashed pictures, the threat to his parents, and the predicament he found himself in. El-Bahar showed concern for John's parents and asked twice if he was sure they were safe. John could only hope that they were.

"But who would do such a thing?" the Oil Minister asked.

"The man implied it was the unions. But it could be anybody—GM's management, some fanatics, anybody who doesn't want Saudi Arabia to get control of GM. I've got to assume it's the unions, though.

"And you have forty-eight hours?"

"Yes. They must have known that I couldn't call this thing off on my own. I had to reach you and—"

"We will not call the operation off, John." El-Bahar's tone was firm and emotionless.

"Oh, no, I wasn't thinking of that. We do have a problem with the unions, though, and I have an idea of how to handle that, if you'll go along with it." John explained to the Oil Minister what he proposed to do.

After a very brief silence, El-Bahar spoke. "All right, John. I will agree to your proposal. Let me know as soon as possible if it is accepted. Also, John, please understand that I am concerned about your parents and I want them safe. But I am also concerned about getting this takeover done. Be sure to stay in control of the situation. I am counting on you."

Feeling much more confident, John now dialed the long-distance operator and placed a personal call to Congressman Jennings in Washington, hoping that he would catch him at his office on a Saturday and not out on some golf course. His luck still held. Jennings was there. It took only a few moments on the phone to arrange an appointment as soon as John could get on the shuttle to Washington

Less than three hours later John was striding down a wide, echoing hallway in the House Office Building, reading the nameplates on the doors, looking for Jennings' name. As he approached the next paneled door, it opened, and out stepped Harry Grogan, Charlotte's father.

"John! What are you doing here on a beautiful weekend like this? You should be out on the tennis court with Charlotte."

"Well, actually, Mr. Grogan, Charlotte doesn't know I'm here. It's a business thing I have to discuss with Mr. Jennings."

"I see," said Mr. Grogan, "then I won't keep you. Don't be a stranger, John." Grogan walked off down the hall, leaving John regretting that he hadn't made a fuller explanation of his presence in Washington. Obviously Jennings hadn't told Grogan that he was expecting John to come, and John's respect for him went up a notch at this display of social tact.

He went into the office and identified himself to the young receptionist, who immediately ushered him into Jennings' large, sunny office.

"I gave up eighteen holes of golf with Harry Grogan for you, young man," said Jennings with a grin, "so you'll have to make it worth my while."

"I'm very grateful to you for your time, Congressman, and I do believe it is important to both of us." John went on to once again explain his dilemma, the threats against his parents, and the limited time he had left to solve the problem.

"You know, of course," said Jennings, "that I am no longer opposing the Saudi purchase of GM stock. The President has given the leadership of Congress good and sufficient reasons to allow the takeover. It seems the United States has been gently but officially reminded of the principle of reciprocity by our close European friends!"

"Yes, I know a little bit about that side of it. But what about the labor unions in Detroit? Obviously it's someone there who's responsible for the attacks on my family."

"You may be right. But I can't believe Louis Spinner is responsible. Naturally, he was very unhappy when I told him we were dropping our opposition to the Saudis. And even after I explained all the reasons that it would be against the United States' best interests to take this stand, he was unwilling to see it our way. It's very hard to get a union official to understand about protecting other people at the expense of his own constituency. You know, he has to

182

run for office in his union just like I have to run in my district. But it's possible that one of the other union executives, maybe someone who wants to take Spinner's seat, is responsible for bringing these hoods into it."

John believed the congressman and saw that he was sincerely concerned. "Congressman, I think I may have a solution to this problem, and even to the other problem that you were too tactful to mention. Obviously you need the support of the labor unions in your district to get reelected, and as things stand now, they aren't going to have much enthusiasm for helping your campaign. But what if you could make them a very attractive and very specific offer to coat the pill they are being asked to swallow?"

"That depends on what the coating is made of." Jennings smiled. "These boys are getting pretty sophisticated these days, and you can't con them with any double talk."

"No, no! No double talk. I'm talking about a twelve percent across the board wage increase retroactive to the date of the tender offer, over and above any future or past contract commitments.

"I've worked out the economic impact, and the company can afford it. GM's profit margins are so far above Ford's and Chrysler's that the company won't even have to increase the price of the cars to make up for the pay raise. Further, a guarantee of continuity of management and no major displacements of plants or warehouses without consultation with the unions may be offered."

"Now you're talking!" said Jennings enthusiastically. "You could change their attitude from opposition to outright support overnight with an offer like that!" Jennings couldn't imagine Spinner opposing such a generous wage offer. But being more attuned to the thinking processes of labor leaders than John was, he saw even more of a gift for Spinner in the proposal. Once General Motors gave a raise, Spinner would be able to force an equivalent one from Ford and Chrysler, and maybe even American Motors. This was practically a guarantee of reelection for Spinner.

183

"Well, I secured approval for precisely those terms this morning from my principals in Saudi Arabia. And to help your personal cause, they agreed that you can publicly take the credit for doing it. That way, everybody gets something. There's only one condition. Before any announcement is made, Louis Spinner has to find out who sent those hoods after me and my parents and call them off. I'm working under a deadline imposed by them of less than forty-eight hours now, and it won't wait. Tell them this offer expires at nine o'clock Monday morning, and let's see what happens."

John then availed himself of Jennings' telephone to call his parents again in Florida and was happy to learn that all was well, although the long black car was still parked outside the bungalow. He told them that steps were being taken to dispose of the threat, and promised to tell them the details when it was all over. He took his leave of Jennings, who promised to get to work immediately on finding Spinner and passing him the word. John felt the heavy weight of danger ease a little, now that he had taken some concrete action to fight back.

While Thompson, Caldwell's offices were usually closed on Saturdays, John knew that back in New York his staff was hard at work, tallying up their inventory of how much stock had been tendered and at what rate it was coming in. Soon, some hard decisions had to be made about a possible price increase to attract additional shares. If the price were raised, it would annoy and infuriate some of the shareholders who had sold at ninety dollars. Having tendered their stock at that price, they were entitled to no more. Only the holdouts would benefit, and it was precisely to attract them that the price might be raised. Convinced that he had done all he could in Washington and that Jennings would carry on at full speed, John decided to hurry back to New York and catch up with the progress of the takeover.

John felt guilty coming into and out of Washington without calling and seeing Charlotte. Such a thing hadn't happened in more than three years. But he told himself that he would be able to explain it all to her later, and that she would be sure to understand and sympathize when she knew the reasons for his visit. There was little chance that Harry Grogan would forget seeing him in the hallway outside Jennings' office, so an explanation to Charlotte would be in order.

As John hurried through the terminal to catch the early afternoon shuttle back to New York, he stopped at a pay phone, inserted a coin, and rapidly dialed Charlotte's number. There was no answer. Frustrated, he slammed down the receiver and ran for the plane. At least he had tried. No thought of the voluptuous Lila Rashid, who was expecting to hear from him any minute, even crossed his mind.

Chapter 21

AS he walked to work along his customary route Monday morning, John had the feeling that people occasionally recognized him. He attributed this to the photographs carried by most of the newspapers whose reporters had covered the press conference the previous Friday. No doubt about it, John Haddad was becoming somewhat of a public figure. He had avoided interviews and television talk shows and declined a personal invitation from Barbara Walters to appear on the *Today Show,* as well as other invitations to be a guest on *Meet the Press* and *Face the Nation.* But the General Motors acquisition attempt by Saudi Arabia was a hot news story in an otherwise flaccid summer slowdown. Much as he shunned personal publicity and tried to focus the attention of the public on the desirability of encouraging Arab oil billions to be invested in the capital-starved American economy, the press was fascinated by the personality of the American singled out by the Arabs for such a spectacular operation.

John's avoidance of publicity for himself was not the result of any modesty. Self-promotion simply had no place in carrying out the wishes of Sheikh El-Bahar. In fact, the cause might even be damaged, if not by the jealousy of Grayson, then by the possibility of violating some of the very rigid strictures of the Securities and Exchange Commission controlling the form and content of advertising and public statements by the principals when a tender offer was in progress. So far, John had won some battles in the campaign. No legislation would be introduced opposing the acquisition. He hoped the unions would relent, satisfied with the offer of increased wages and the possible guarantee of continuity of operations. But the General Motors management itself continued to fight the takeover through constant appeals to its shareholders. The company's most recent ploy had been to raise the quarterly dividend by twenty-five cents a share, a measure designed to stimulate the loyalty of long-term stockholders who owned the stock primarily as a source of regular income. It would add one dollar a year per share to the dividend and, ironically, was worth over ten million dollars every quarter to the Saudis just on the basis of the stock they had already acquired.

As John neared his office building, the heat had become oppressive. Beads of sweat formed on his forehead, and he felt his shirt become damp and clinging under his suit jacket. He ignored the discomfort and kept his attention focused on the strategy of the takeover. Following the announcement of the increased dividend, the number of shares tendered each day had declined. The first item on today's agenda would be an analysis of the rate at which tenders of stock were coming in.

Since the beginning of the tender offer, John had made a practice of having a regular telephone briefing with Attifi at the Saudi Arabian Monetary Agency. Sometimes the conversation went on for an hour, while Attifi was plugged into a meeting between John and his aides, the proceedings being broadcast through a speakerphone in John's office. Today, they were joined by the two lawyers assigned to work on the tender offer. When everyone was seated, John asked Sue Anderson to place the call to Saudi Arabia. There was no delay; she could dial through directly, a convenience dating back to the launching of a separate communications satellite for the Saudis by NASA, paid for by the Saudi Arabian government.

Within a minute, Attifi was on the line, and John switched on the speakerphone enabling Attifi to hear and be heard by everyone in the room. Sue discreetly closed the door on her way out as John began the conversation by telling Attifi who was in the room this morning.

"The main point we want to cover today, Mustafa, is General Motors' apparently successful attempt at discouraging some shareholders from tendering." John spoke loudly and leaned toward the small microphone in the telephone unit. "As you know, they have raised the dividend, and our incoming stock has dropped off sharply ever since." John motioned to Lee Curtis, who rose and came alongside John's desk. "I'm going to ask Lee to give us a rundown."

Curtis leaned on the desk and read from his notes. "As of the close last night, we had acquired a total of forty-six million six hundred and twenty thousand shares, which is sixteen percent of the company. This is considerably less than we had hoped to have at this stage of the operation. Moreover, the shares are now coming in at a rate of less than twenty thousand a day."

"Is the decline in tenders linked to the increased dividend?" Attifi asked.

"Definitely," John replied, "and GM has really gone wild on publicity. They're trying to make tendering stock to us equivalent to trampling on the American flag."

"How about public opinion?" asked the voice from Saudi Arabia.

"The newspapers are generally against the takeover, although many of them recognize that it's only fair to allow foreigners to buy American companies. But remember that we've made a good offer to the unions, so no one is marching in the streets against us yet."

"What do you suggest, John?"

"We've talked it over on this end, Mustafa, and we're afraid the flow of stock is just about to peter out. If the rate doesn't pick up, I think your only hope will be to raise the tender price substantially." John saw that everyone in the room was nodding in agreement.

"That is acceptable to us," said Attifi. "You are in charge of those decisions. What will be the new tender price?"

"Well, the stock is selling at eight-five on the exchange, thanks to our offer of ninety. I think we should raise it to one-twenty. The market price will also go up, but not until we raise the tender price."

Attifi agreed and wished them luck before the conversation ended, promising to keep Sheikh El-Bahar posted on the progress. But his voice unmistakably conveyed that he did not want to have any bad news to pass along. Everyone remained in the office as objections and details were worked out. Each idea was cleared with the two lawyers before it became part of the ongoing plan. They had agreed that they would wait until Friday, as long as the market price remained below the tender price. If the amount of stock tendered at ninety increased substantially, however, it might not prove necessary to raise the price at all. Meanwhile, the amendment to the tender offer raising the price to one hundred and twenty dollars a share would be drawn up and kept ready for immediate delivery to the SEC on a moment's notice. This way they would be able to respond very promptly to whatever happened in the market. John asked Dave Hill to prepare a confidential memorandum on the decision that they had just taken. The precaution of drawing up an *aide-mémoire* was standard procedure. There were to be three numbered copies only. Copy number one was for John, number two to be shared by Hill and Curtis, and number three was for the lawyers. Grayson would be notified of the new price by telephone.

The rest of John's business day was occupied with various other matters related to the tender. There was a brief conversation with a Morgan Guaranty bank official on payments for the incoming shares. The man had an idea to expedite the deliveries of stock, which John liked and accepted. A file from the clipping service was brought in. It contined several hundred news stories and editorials about the takeover from newspapers all over the United States. Most opinions were against the takeover of General Motors. John glanced through them, paying special attention to those with a red check mark that Dave Hill had placed on the items he thought warranted it. As a sensitive person, John was an able judge of how far public opinion could be allowed to go against them before the operation might be jeopardized. He felt the mood of the key articles and editorials, the letters to the editor, the prominence given to the story. He concluded that current public opinion, although not on his side, was not yet a dangerous threat.

At five thirty Dave Hill handed John a manila folder containing a three-page confidential memorandum outlining the plan to raise the tender offer price to one hundred and twenty dollars by the end of the week, or sooner. John's copy was marked "1" on the upper left-hand corner. He glanced at it, then tucked it into his briefcase.

Feeling confident that the new plans would work out well, John left the building, collapsed into a taxi, and gratefully went home to his apartment, a peaceful refuge from a hectic day. Automatically going through his evening ritual, he had just settled himself in front of the television to watch the news when the telephone rang. He pulled the phone over on his lap and lifted the receiver on the second ring.

"Hello."

"John? John Haddad?"

"Yes, who's calling?"

"This is Lila Rashid. Have you forgotten me so soon?"

"How could I forget you, Lila?" John heaved a sigh, facing up to the fact that he had promised to call her last Saturday. "Lila, I just got home five minutes ago and I've been on the run all day. I'd love to see you, but I'm too exhausted to go out. I couldn't face getting dressed and doing the whole restaurant bit." He hoped she would acquiesce and let him off the hook.

"Do not worry . . . remember that where I come from, the women are trained to take good care of their men. I will come to you in an hour, and I will bring dinner with me. Have a drink and don't move."

John's stomach reminded him that, apart from a soggy little sandwich for lunch, he had had nothing to eat all day. Lila's proposition sounded perfect, especially the part about not moving.

"You sold me, Lila. I won't move a muscle until you knock on the door. And I'll leave it to you to decide what to bring. But don't count on much of anything to be found in my kitchen . . . I don't stock any perishable food."

"That doesn't matter. I will bring everything. Including me, if you want that, too."

John guessed that Lila must have been complimented by her editors on the interview she had written and that they had told her to stay on the story.

He had no sooner hung up the phone when it rang again. Thinking it was Lila calling back for some forgotten question, he said, "What did you forget?"

"This is Charlotte, John. Who did you think was calling?"

"Oh . . . hi, darling . . . I thought it was Lee Curtis from the office," he lied. There was a silence at the other end, then Charlotte's voice, with a note of hurt coming through clearly.

"John, would you *please* tell me what's going on? I know you're under pressure from the takeover, but I have a feeling there's something more."

"No, Charlotte. Really. I haven't had a spare minute."

"You came to Washington Saturday and didn't even call me." Charlotte's voice betrayed her bruised feelings.

"Darling, I did try to call you, but there was no answer. And I tried again when I got home. It was a last-minute trip to see Jennings on business."

"That's too bad. You must have tried at some very odd hours on Sunday. I was home most of the day." Charlotte made no effort to conceal her sarcasm.

"Come off it, Charlotte. Christ, the last thing I need is a fight with you now."

"All right. I might as well tell you. Suzy Chapman called me to tell me about seeing you at Le Perigord the other night. She said you were practically glued to some brunette with no brassiere."

"That was a reporter for a Middle East news syndicate who was at my press conference . . . she's doing a story. Nice friend of yours, that Suzy Chapman." John could see that the conversation was going nowhere. He was beginning to regret the involvement with Lila, who was nothing more than a diversion, a release for his tension. But the diversion was now threatening his relationship with Charlotte.

"John, maybe I'm being too sensitive. But you have to admit that from where I sit, your behavior has been strange. You come to Washington without calling me, but go to see someone I introduced you to who's a friend of my family. You haven't been down here to spend a weekend with me since Paris. Then I get a call about you being seen around town with some sexy girl. What do you expect me to think?"

"Darling, believe me, nothing's wrong. Just give me a chance to finish this project and we'll have all the time in the world to spend together."

"OK, honey," she said, and John could sense the smile returning to her face. "I've got an idea! How about my taking the next air shuttle to New York. We can have a late dinner together."

He saw the ax fall. He had to calm Charlotte down without letting her come up tonight. It was too late to call Lila back and cancel, she would already be on her way. He took the plunge. "Honey, I can't tonight. We're having another meeting later, with Dave and Lee, and it won't wait."

"I see," Charlotte snapped angrily. "Well, you just let me know when you have time to grant me an audience. In the meantime I won't be waiting around for you to call." She hung up abruptly.

John's anger quickly boiled up. He had done everything he could to calm Charlotte down and reassure her, and she had hung up on him. He slammed down his own phone, heedless of the fact that the gesture would not reach the other end of the line. Charlotte had never hung up on him before. If she wanted to indulge in petty tantrums he would let her cool off for a while.

There was a soft knock on the door, and as he walked toward it he heard Lila's voice out in the hall. "Hurry up! Or I'll drop all of this food."

He ran the last two steps, flung open the door, and caught a heavy bag just as it was sliding from her grasp. She stumbled into the room, laughing. Lila was wearing a light beige linen pants suit, a heavy gold link necklace, and the same bag as before, looking bigger and more stuffed than ever.

"What have you got in there?" John asked. "It looks like you're going on a trip."

"Not a trip, just a few necessaries for an overnight stay." She grinned mischievously. "Now you go relax and let me into the kitchen with my dinner. I'll call you when it's ready."

John went back to the armchair, sat down, and sipped his drink, hearing faint sounds of china and glassware clinking in the kitchen. It was too late to change anything that was happening tonight. He dozed off without another thought, comfortable in the domestic illusion that he was home from work and dinner was under way. He only wished that it were a reconciled Charlotte instead of this exotic stranger who had somehow insinuated herself into his life.

Lila gently shook him awake and John blinked, taking a moment to realize where he was and who she was. She

192

smiled and pointed proudly to the coffee table. She had pulled out a big old round brass tray he had wedged in the back of the closet. It sat, covered with a white cloth, on which a neat bed of crushed ice had been laid. In the middle of the ice was one-kilo can of fresh, practically unsalted, pale gray Iranian beluga caviar, the top removed. Two consommé spoons protruded from the center of the caviar. Around the can, Lila had arranged wedges of fresh lemon, a cup of very finely minced onions, and a cup of sieved, hard-cooked egg. On another dish, covered with a napkin, there was freshly buttered toasted rye bread, cut into little triangles. From the kitchen, John's senses were assailed by the perfume of a rich meat dish with a trace of wine.

Wide awake now, he said, "Lila, this is magnificent. I'll have to throw away my Scotch and have vodka with caviar like this. Where did you get it?"

"Oh . . . I have my ways to find things," she said, "and I only like caviar when there's plenty of it. There's nothing worse than those little tiny half-ounce jars people serve. You feel guilty if you take any at all!"

"God, this stuff must have cost a fortune."

"Nothing for you to worry about. We have an ample allowance to pay our news sources."

"What other surprises do you have in there?" he asked, indicating the kitchen with his glass.

"Be patient . . . all in good time."

Together they demolished almost half the caviar, and finally John called a halt, fearing he would be unable to do justice to whatever followed. Lila cleared away the dishes, then returned from the kitchen with a casserole containing a steaming beef ragout cooked in red wine, with sliced mushrooms and tiny pearl onions swimming in the rich, reddish-brown broth. She produced a dusty bottle of vintage Burgundy and a dish of white, fluffy rice. John vigorously polished off his share, and a second helping. Lila poured the wine for him, encouraging him to drink and eat his fill.

After dinner, try as he might, John couldn't keep his eyes open. Lila helped him undress and tucked him into bed. Then, humming a little tune, she went back to the kitchen to clean up the debris.

The sheets were crisp, the bed felt more comfortable than usual, and John relaxed in a peaceful, semiconscious state prior to sleep. He had enjoyed the evening, but a single vision had stayed with him all night. The last thing he thought about before going to sleep was Charlotte Grogan.

When Lila joined John in bed, she tried several ways to arouse him, but gave up when she saw that the sleep he was enjoying was impenetrable. She slipped back out of the bed, took up her handbag, and walked soundlessly on bare feet into the living room. She rummaged in her bag, coming up with a tiny Minox camera no bigger than a cigarette lighter. She went to the desk and opened John's briefcase, which was lying on top of the desk. Going back to make sure the door from the bedroom was tightly closed, she pulled out the papers detailing the plans for raising the tender offer price. Turning on the desk lamp and pushing its goose neck down to shine directly on the surface of the desk, she quickly focused the little camera and photographed each page twice, just to be sure. Then she rapidly put everything back as it was, tucked away the camera after removing the little roll of film that went into an empty lipstick tube in a side pocket, and stole quietly into the bedroom and to bed.

Chapter 22

JOHN woke up the next morning and looked at his bedside clock. Eight A.M., Lila was gone and he had a splitting headache from drinking most of the bottle of Burgundy the night before. He groggily made his way into the kitchen and was pleasantly surprised to find a fresh, hot pot of coffee already brewed in his electric coffee maker, and a note from Lila. The note said, "Call me when you're free." It was signed "L." and was written on a Carlyle Hotel memo pad. He put it down, sat at the kitchen counter, and poured himself a cup of black coffee. He went back to the bathroom and got out two aspirins. After having downed half a cup of coffee and the pills and beginning to feel partially restored to humanity, John went out in the hall to get his newspapers. As he leaned down to pick them up, he noticed a small white envelope lying on top of the *Times.*

Back in the kitchen he slit open the envelope. A cablegram from Hans Sloman. "Situation growing desperate. Ten (10) days left before large deposit required. Urgent you reply soonest. Sloman." The message was an ugly reminder that he still had more problems to solve. He knew that he would have to face up to Sloman, but every time he thought about Sloman's extravagant demands, the solution seemed increasingly remote. Now time was running out and Sloman was demanding money with the threat of possibly revealing John's past indiscretion. John bitterly regretted his own stupidity in bending the rules to help his father. If he had known the cost would be so far-reaching, he was sure he would not have done it.

Now a decision had to be made. Offering Sloman a portion of the half-million-dollar fee he was to be paid by El-Bahar would do no good. That was only a small fraction of what Sloman was insisting on. John had to form some sort of plan to make a substantial profit without in any way damaging the success of the takeover. He still needed some time. He went to the telephone and dictated a reply to the RCA overseas cable operator, asking Sloman for a few more days and promising to be in touch in the middle of the coming week.

Having finished with the cable, John placed a call to his parents' bungalow in Florida. The connection was made, and soon his father's voice came on the line.

"Is that you, John?"

"Yes, Dad, I'm calling to check again to make sure you're both well."

"Your mother and I are fine. But we're eager to return home, son, so we've booked a flight back this afternoon."

"I'd rather you waited until I'm positive you're safe."

"If you're referring to the car outside the bungalow, son, it left over an hour ago. Funny thing. The men even waved at us as they drove away."

John was flooded with relief. The only logical explanation for the thugs' departure was that the threat had been called off. Jennings must have talked to the Detroit union leaders about the promise to increase wages, provided that they did not oppose the takeover. As John had hoped, the union leaders apparently could not resist a settlement that promised more wages to the workers. In fact, it might have been politically disastrous for the union heads to turn it down. Workers always wanted more wages.

"That's great!" John exuded. "I wish you had told me about the car earlier."

"But we tried to . . . but your telephone was busy. So we decided to pack and try again before leaving the hotel."

"Anyway, I'm happy you're coming home. Why don't I meet you at the airport and drive you home? Then we can all have dinner together tonight."

"Good. That's what we'll do. We're on Delta Flight 402 and we are due at La Guardia at four fifteen this afternoon."

John called the office to alert his staff that he would be working at home today and filled the rest of the early afternoon with calls to Jennings in Washington to confirm the settlement and to El-Bahar in Saudi Arabia to relay the news. Feeling much cheered by the recent turn of events, he shaved, showered, and got dressed. Then he called the

East Sixty-fourth Street Hertz office to rent a car for his trip
to the airport to meet his parents.

Chapter 23

WHEN Lila Rashid, as she was known to John Haddad, arrived at the Carlyle that same morning she was confident
that she had done her job well. There was no reason to believe that Haddad thought of her in any way but as a casual,
accidental affair with no hope of a future. Also, she was
quite sure that he couldn't possibly suspect that his documents had been read and photographed during the night.

Lila considered reporting her success immediately, but
knowing her superior's penchant for sleeping late in the
morning and his impatience with incomplete information,
she decided to develop the film and transcribe the contents
first. In her room, she laid out the materials on the desk.
First, a heavy black flannel bag, zippered on one side, with
two elastic-bordered arm holes on the other. Then a bottle
of developer, one of fixative, and a bottle of wash solution.
She placed her bedside clock, equipped with a sweep second hand on the desk in plain view.

With practiced fingers she unzipped the bag, placed the
developer and fixative inside, followed by the tiny roll of
Minox film. The she zipped the bag closed, and slipped her
hands through the two holes into the bag, making sure that
the elastic borders fit snugly and did not allow any light to
leak into the working area. Working blindly by touch alone,
she unwound the film from its protective covering, un-
capped the developer, and dropped the film into the bottle,
capping it again. She waited the prescribed time, then un-
capped the bottle and transferred the developed film into

the fixative solution. Again she waited, concentrating on the passage of minutes and seconds on the clock.

Freeing herself from the restraint of the black bag, with the film now safe from light damage, she made the final transfer into the wash solution and shook the bottle repeatedly. Removing the finished film from the solution, holding it by one end, she waved it in the air until it was dry. She held the film up to the light and could see that the photography had succeeded. The pages of the report appeared as bright white squares, and the typescript as microscopic black lines, too tiny to read with the naked eye.

Lila cleared away the developing equipment and pulled out her flat Hermes typewriter, opening the case and inserting a fresh piece of paper. Then she got out a plastic viewer with two cushioned eyepieces, its own tiny light source powered by a flashlight battery, and mounted with a thick elastic band. She threaded the film into the viewer, adjusted the viewer to her eyes, then slipped the elastic band around behind her head so that the viewer stayed in place.

Without hesitation, the staccato tapping of the little typewriter's keys began, as Lila transcribed the private planning session from the Thompson, Caldwell meeting word for word. Having finished, she put away all the equipment, returned the little roll of developed film to the empty lipstick tube in her bag, folded the typed paper and slipped it into an envelope. Now she was ready to report.

Lila Tabriz, for that was her true name, had distinguished herself at every level in her climb to her present post as one of the three top international agents of SAVAK. She was now thirty years old, and in her eighteenth year of service to her country's intelligence and secret police service. It had all begun when she was twelve. Lila had been sitting down to the noon meal with her parents and her younger brother in their two-room mud-walled house near the small village of Anarak in central Iran. The house was on the side of a hill down the slope from where the Iran Highway Authority was building a new road. Lila's mother had forgotten to buy milk in the marketplace that morning, so she sent Lila running to the village, which was only about three hundred yards away, to get some.

She had already reached the milk seller's stall when she heard the explosion and saw the immense cloud of yellow dust rise from the direction of her family's home. Lila ran back, followed by a handful of villagers, but in spite of their frantic digging they were unable to dislodge the earth that had buried the little house in time to save the occupants. The family was found sitting around the table, frozen in place by the tons of earth and sand that had descended upon them so unexpectedly.

Lila was sent to the state orphanage on the outskirts of Teheran, and it was there that her rare beauty and quick intelligence caught the attention of a SAVAK recruiter. She found herself getting extra attention and slightly better food than the other girls, and being singled out for more advanced education until her seventeenth year. Then she met Najib Meshedi, the unquestioned ruler of SAVAK. Having entered his suite of rooms a virgin on a Monday afternoon, she emerged on Tuesday evening with a much better understanding of what was to be expected of her in the service of the state. At this point she could have allowed herself to merge with the dozens of others recruited for the same purpose, ending up discarded and used up after a brief career.

But Lila had determination and learned very quickly to set herself apart. She volunteered for the most difficult assignments, and then demanded the training that would be required to do them well. By the time she was twenty-two, helped by the fact that her beauty had ripened as quickly as her facile mind, she was high on the list of first-rate agents trusted with the most sensitive assignments. Among her exploits were the discovery of an opium-smuggling ring bringing the shipments on muleback from neighboring Afghanistan; the betrayal of an Iranian petroleum official who manipulated crude oil prices in return for massive bribes; the infiltration of the Saudi Arabian defense establishment and procurement of their plans for naval base construction; and many more. She was fluent in Arabic, Hebrew, French, English, Greek, Turkish, German, and Russian, and was busily engaged, when time permitted, in studying Italian and Spanish. She was an expert photographer under the most adverse conditions, and her mastery of electronic bugging devices was second to none in SAVAK. Lila knew the importance of her present assignment and relished the thought of defeating John Haddad's plans on behalf of the Saudis.

She telephoned Meshedi's suite in the hotel and was quickly admitted to his living room. Najib Meshedi studied the text of the planned amendment to the tender offer and rejoiced.

"At last," he said, "we have an opening to prevent their progress!"

"Is this as helpful as you expected?" asked Lila. "If they are willing to pay one hundred and twenty dollars a share for General Motors, won't that have the effect of attracting much more stock? Enough for the Saudis to get control?"

"Only if no one steps in between. But since now we are apprised of their instructions, we can interfere with no risk at all. My instructions are to avoid big losses in this operation, and I was quite concerned about how to do it. But this gives us the way. Since Haddad will wait another week or so before raising the price, and the current tender offer is ninety dollars, we will buy, starting tomorrow morning, all the stock we can get at ninety-five, slightly above the tender. When we raise the market price to ninety-five, no one will tender to Haddad at ninety, and he will have to go to a hundred and twenty, perhaps sooner than he wants to. So, in effect, he will be paying double what the price was when this takeover attempt began. This could discourage the Saudis enough to make them abandon the scheme.

"Lila, you have done an excellent job, but it is far from finished. I want you to stay on the good side of this Haddad, and do everything you can to keep informed of his plans. Is there a reason you can find for spending more time with him? I mean other than your specialized bedroom talents?"

Lila laughed. "Why would I need any other talents? Haddad is under great pressure, and I am uncomplicated relief for him. But I plan to write up a draft of our 'interview' and ask him to review it before it is published. That should be a sufficient excuse."

"Very well," said Meshedi, "go ahead. And be sure to keep me informed at all times."

He sent Lila on her way and sat down to plan his strategy for entering into the purchase of General Motors stock the next day. He had to pick several stockbrokers, so that there would be no indication that another large buyer was single-handedly trying to obstruct the tender offer. He would begin with Merrill Lynch, the largest brokerage firm in America and the world. Some years before, Merrill Lynch had opened a branch in Teheran when the Iranian oil billions had become an irresistible magnet for investment bankers everywhere. SAVAK maintained several dummy accounts at Merrill Lynch, and the first of the orders would be placed through these. The source of the buying would seem to be several of the Iranian private banks, corporations, and private individuals. There would be no visible connection to any government agency. SAVAK's funds were not subject to scrutiny by Iran's nominal parliament, or even by the Finance Minister.

Then Meshedi would activate agents in several European financial centers and in the United States to proceed with the buying. He was willing to run the risk of having competing orders for the stock hit the floors of some of the exchanges, all coming from him, just to preserve the appearance that they were not connected. It might cost him a point or two more to buy, but the concealment was worth it.

He sat at his desk and drafted a thick pile of cables, carefully worded in code to resemble innocuous business instructions, went down to the elegant lobby of the hotel and submitted them at the desk. Content with a job well done, Najib Meshedi retired to his suite and ordered a sumptuous dinner to be brought up for himself and Lila. Calling her in her room, he summoned her to come for dinner and whatever pleasures he might desire afterward.

The next day, John Haddad, Lee Curtis, and Dave Hill left the office together and went to a little restaurant around the corner for lunch. So far that morning, the volume of GM stock coming in to Thompson, Caldwell under the ninety-dollar tender offer had dwindled to a trickle. When they had left, the market price was edging up to 89¼, dangerously close to crossing the line. Evidently they would have to make the price amendment sooner than they had planned. John would have much preferred to be able to make the new price announcement after the close of business on a Friday, allowing a whole weekend for the news to reach the millions of GM stockholders who were not able to follow the news minute to minute as did the people in the financial community. Now they would have to rely on the stockbrokers—who would see the announcement on their Dow Jones news tickers—to relay the word promptly to their clients who held the stock.

They had been in the restaurant hardly fifteen minutes when the captain bustled up to their table carrying a telephone. He plugged it into an outlet near the baseboard and placed it at John's elbow. "There is a telephone call for Monsieur 'Adad," he announced in his thick French accent.

John raised the telephone to his ear. "Yes?" He listened a moment, said, "Thanks," and replaced the receiver.

John stood up and said, "Let's skip dessert."

Curtis and Hill rose almost immediately, trying to read John's face for a clue. "What's up?" asked Dave.

"GM just traded above ninety on the New York."

"Oh, Christ!" was the last thing Hill said as they walked out of the restaurant. John paused for only a few seconds to sign the bill and followed them out into the bright sunlight of the street.

John and his aides well knew that as long as the tender offer was was in effect at 90, the stock would trade in the high 80's on the open market. The reason was that some owners would be willing to sell a fraction below the tender price for an immediate profit, not subject to cancellation. This way they avoided the risk, however small, that the tender offer might not be purchased.

But when the market price of the stock rose *above* the tender offer price, it was a clear signal. Someone now thought that the tender offer would be raised, either by the original tenderer or perhaps by another party who wanted to compete for the same stock. But John knew that there could be no other buyer big enough to plan a competing tender, particularly so late in the game. There was only one answer. There had been a leak of the plan to raise the price, and someone was trying to make a quick killing, planning to pick up as much stock as possible between 90 and 119, then tender it at 120 when the announcement he had learned of surreptitiously was made.

When they had assembled in his office, John called the trading department and asked to be connected to his firm's booth on the floor of the New York Stock Exchange. He spoke to Stuart Thurmond, Thompson, Caldwell's chief floor broker. If anyone could quickly assess the situation for him, it would be Thurmond, who had fifteen years' experience on the floor, handling every kind of transaction.

John asked Thurmond to call him back from one of the pay phones made available for members' personal calls at the edge of the exchange floor. He explained that he didn't want to discuss his question on the office line running through the switchboard where anyone could punch a lighted button and listen in. John's private line rang two minutes later, and he started throwing questions at Thurmond thick and fast.

"What time did the buying start? What brokerage firms

were representing the buyers? How was the volume of trading in GM? Were there any clues to the identity of the buyer?"

Thurmond answered the questions with his customary professional aplomb. There were three firms buying, all large major wire houses with offices throughout the United States and abroad. There was no way of telling who the clients were, but there was a rumor around that the buying was based abroad. The volume was very heavy.

John put down his pencil after scribbling notes and said, "Tell me what you make of this, Stu. How does it feel to you?"

"Well, all three firms started buying at the same time, even bidding against each other a couple of times. But it didn't feel right . . . like it was planned to look kosher. I think it's just one big buyer trying to cover his tracks."

"Why use three brokers?" Lee Curtis asked, speaking into the extension.

"There isn't any reason, really. One broker could have done the job more efficiently. I guess the buyer thought if he used three brokers, he would look like several buyers on the floor. But he doesn't fool me, because the orders are coming in, one-eighth of a point apart, five thousand shares at a clip. There are no one or two hundred share orders, and no other brokers are buying."

"Stu, is there any reason you can think of why someone would buy GM stock above our tender offer price?" John's question was important—Stu Thurmond did not know that the tender offer price was about to be raised.

"As far as I'm concerned," Thurmond replied, "whoever is buying the stock above ninety must expect it's going higher. There must be some inside information around."

John thanked Thurmond for his help and rang off. Then he looked at Curtis and Hill. "Either of you have any doubts there's been a leak?"

Lee Curtis shook his head slowly, wearing a wry expression. Dave Hill whispered, "No doubt."

"OK then, let's retrace our steps." John sighed. "There were three copies of the memo on raising the price to one hundred and twenty. Dave, you and Lee had one copy. Can you account for it?"

"No problem," Hill replied, "I locked it my desk drawer as soon as it was typed and it was still there an hour ago. I'll be right back." He went across to his office and was back in a moment. "Here they are, both copies, ours and one for the lawyers, which they never picked up from me. The lock on my desk hadn't been tampered with, and the papers were in the same position I left them."

Lee Curtis looked up. "The only other copy is yours, John."

"And my copy has been in my briefcase ever since Dave gave it to me." John swiveled around in his chair and opened his black leather briefcase, lying on the side table behind his desk, first turning the numbers of the combination lock to the correct sequence. The folder containing the confidential memorandum was on top of the stack of other documents and papers. He opened the folder and looked inside. All three pages were there, exactly as he had left them.

The possibilities ran through his mind. He had to dismiss any suspicion of Dave and Lee, first because he believed they were trustworthy, but also because he didn't believe they could have had the time or the connections to mount this kind of massive buying program through third parties. Mustafa Attifi was a possibility; he had had the time and the opportunity. But Attifi had nothing to gain by revealing the new price to anyone. There was a chance that someone had bugged the office, but John couldn't start tearing apart walls to look for listening devices now.

He realized that he had merely been postponing facing up to the truth. Only his own copy of the memo had left the building. The only time the briefcase containing it had been out of his sight was last night in his apartment. And the only person who could have seen the document there was Lila Rashid.

John finally looked up at Dave and Lee, whose pained faces showed they understood and wouldn't say another word to embarrass him. "You guys get on your horses, and down to the SEC with the price amendment right now. I want it in the afternoon papers and on the Dow news ticker within an hour!"

Chapter 24

PRIORITIES have a way of changing fast in the business world, and John was suddenly faced with rearranging his. Something had to be done immediately to verify Lila Rashid's credentials. There was no time to lose. She was the only person who could possibly have gotten a look at his papers. How stupid he had been to believe that a reporter for some obscure news syndicate could spend three hundred dollars on a tin of caviar. *We have an ample allowance to pay our news sources.* Sure. And he remembered how she had kept refilling his glass with the heavy Burgundy wine, after he had had two Scotches and a generous half-tumbler of vodka before the meal.

Being taken for a ride is not the best thing for your ego. But the pain increases when you've been taken by a girl you thought you had charmed and seduced. John cursed. If he was right about Lila, he had behaved like a fool. Not only had he risked his relationship with Charlotte, but he may well have compromised the takeover.

He placed a call to the Saudi Arabian Consulate and asked to speak to Marwan Suwadi. Shortly, Suwadi came on the line.

"John! What a pleasure to hear from you after all this time. How are you?"

"I'm fine, Marwan, and I need some help from you. I suppose you know about my trip to Beirut that you helped to arrange."

"I know that we have instructions here to cooperate with any request you might make for assistance."

"Good. What I need from you is very confidential. We'll have to meet as soon as possible to discuss it face to face. Could you come over to my office now?"

"I'll be right over. John, you're not asking me a favor . . . right now a request from you has all the import of a direct command from Riyadh."

"Great. See you in twenty minutes or so."

John gave Sue Anderson instructions to hold all calls and closed the door to his office after Marwan. They settled down to talk, John behind his desk and Marwan in the side chair.

"What can I do to help you, John? When I told the consul I was coming to see you, he literally chased me out the door to be sure I didn't keep you waiting."

"First of all, this is highly confidential. You can't talk to anyone at the consulate about it. If they ask you, just refer them to Sheikh El-Bahar. I don't think you'll have any trouble."

"I think that's a good enough reference for me!"

John's face was serious and his brow wrinkled. "Now here's what I want done. There is a reporter from the Middle East News Syndicate named Lila Rashid. She is staying at the Carlyle, and I met her at my press conference last week. I want her credentials checked thoroughly." He went on to outline the plan he had in mind, and Marwan nodded in agreement, relishing the chance to get out of the consulate and into some excitement. John finished with a warning. "Marwan, this is not a game. It's serious business. Don't approach it like a Harvard prank, OK?"

"Don't worry, I'll be very careful. You know, I got some experience in investigation when we were screening people for the job you were picked for. I have a good idea of how to go about it."

Marwan had no intention of treating this job lightly. He had always respected John and had looked to him for advice and guidance while they were in college. John had willingly helped Marwan through those awkward first months on campus, and Marwan had been grateful for the opportunity to repay him when John needed the twenty-thousand-dollar loan. John wasn't even aware of the esteem Marwan held for him. No matter. This was a job that Marwan intended to do expertly, not only for John's sake but to prove something to himself.

They shook hands at the door to the office, and Marwan left, promising to report as soon as he had anything to tell.

Marwan hurried back to the consulate and started drafting cables to various people and agencies in the Middle East, which would take some time to send and even longer before he could expect any replies. When the cables were on their way, he went to his phone and started checking Lila's credentials locally. But SAVAK had done a good job of providing her with cover. Lila Rashid was listed as a member in good standing of the United Nations Press Association. She was even a member of the sacrosanct Press Club, which only recently had opened its doors to a very few women members. Naturally, the Middle East News Syndicate's New York offices acknowledged her identity and offered to arrange an appointment for Mr. Suwadi if he had something newsworthy to announce. Marwan declined with thanks and pursued his inquiries. A call to the State Department in Washington confirmed that Miss Rashid was admitted to the United States on a temporary press visa that had thirty days to run and was easily renewable.

Having exhausted his list of American souces for a possible conflicting background on Lila Rashid, Marwan went on to the next phase. For a positive identification he required a good photograph of Lila, which could then be sent by teleprinter to Riyadh and matched against the Saudis' voluminous files on foreign agents of every description. Marwan ordered a consulate car and driver to meet him at the entrance and went downstairs. First he was driven home to his apartment, from whence he emerged in minutes armed with a Nikon 35-millimeter single-lens reflex camera and a long, 300-millimeter telescopic lens. He told the consulate chauffeur to drive up Madison Avenue and park directly across the street from the entrance to the Carlyle Hotel between Seventy-seventh and Seventy-eighth Streets. There was no reason to believe that Lila would be using the side entrance, and if she came out of the bar entrance, it was right next to the main one and he could watch them both at once.

Sitting in the back seat of the car, Marwan removed the standard lens from the camera and installed the telescopic one. He loaded the camera with a fresh roll of 36 exposure film, and laid out another roll beside him, ready for quick reloading. Very few women would match the careful description John had given, and Marwan was prepared to photograph any who were even close. Since John had agreed to make a date with Lila for cocktails at about six, and it was now five fifteen, Marwan was sure he wouldn't have long to wait.

The late afternoon sun slanting in from the west provided perfect light, bathing the sidewalk in front of the hotel with brilliance. Careful not to waste his film and be caught changing rolls just at the wrong moment, Marwan concentrated on every woman coming out of the hotel. Most were much older than Lila: some were young enough, but blond or too tall or, in some cases, too ugly. Marwan had only taken seven pictures, all of well-dressed, attractive brunettes, when Lila came to the door. Directly behind her a man who was a full head taller than she, with dark hair and slightly graying temples, spoke to her, obviously saying good-bye. Marwan snapped a perfect close-up of her face, then, working the lever of the camera, had time for another one of her profile as she turned to speak to the man. The second shot provided a full-face view of the man as well as her profile. Then she was in a taxi and gone, and the man walked north on Madison.

Marwan told the chauffeur to drive him back to the consulate. Once there, he walked quickly to the press department where the darkroom technician was waiting for him.

An hour later, Marwan was back in the consulate car, inching down Fifth Avenue, nervously looking at his watch. The hands pointed to eight o'clock, and John had promised he would be at the Sherry-Netherlands bar until eight fifteen, after which he and Lila would be going on to dinner.

Folding the brown envelope of photographs inside a copy of the New York *Times*, which he had taken from the office for that purpose, Marwan went through the revolving door of the Sherry-Netherlands and turned immediately to the right, opening the door to the bar. It was an L-shaped room, with the long leg of the L running parallel to Fifth Avenue. The banquettes and narrow, crowded black formica tables were along the outside wall, which was pierced by two or three small windows. The bar ran along the inside wall, ending at the corner of the L, where the short leg was considerably wider. At this corner was the piano, now being massaged languorously by a white-haired pianist who had been a fixture there for twenty years.

Marwan edged through the narrow aisle between the tables and the bar, stopping once and leaning out of the way to avoid being hit in the teeth by an onrushing waiter bearing a tray of drinks held just at mouth level. Unable to find an empty stool, he edged a shoulder in between two people turned in opposite directions, and signaled for the bartender. After ordering a drink, he turned his back on the bar and faced into the room, his eyes swiftly scanning the faces of the people lined up along the banquettes on the wall. He spotted John off to the left, at a table in the far corner. John was talking animatedly to a long-haired brunette, and Marwan suddenly felt a thrill of pleasure. Holding his newspaper close to his jacket, he slipped out the sheaf of photographs, looking up from each one and comparing it with Lila in the flesh. There it was! She was the girl who had turned to say something to the tall man behind her. He had two shots of her, one full face and one profile . . . almost like a set of police identification pictures. John looked up and caught Marwan's eye. Marwan nodded once, turned to the bar, laid down a five-dollar bill next to his practically untouched drink, and hurried out.

Minutes later the two photographs were on the electronic teleprinter, being reproduced line for line on a screen in the Saudi Arabian Foreign Ministry's intelligence department. Marwan waited in his office, ordering up a sandwich and some coffee for his supper. He knew it would take the Saudis' computers about an hour to scan all the photos in the memory bank electronically to see if there was one that matched.

Marwan had just managed to finish his sandwich and the last sip of coffee when his telephone shrilled. He grabbed the receiver, cutting off the first ring.

"Yes, this is Suwadi."

"This is Communications, Mr. Suwadi. We have an urgent cable for you from the ministry."

"I'll be right down."

He hung up and walked down the stairs to the communications center, which was manned twenty-four hours a day by relays of technicians. As he approached, the clerk was tearing a message out of the teletype machine. He handed it to Marwan. The cable read: FEMALE SUBJECT NAME: LILA TABRIZ POSITIVE ID. AGENT OF SAVAK, RANK JUST BELOW DEPUTY DIRECTOR, HIGHLY SKILLED AND DANGEROUS. MALE SUBJECT NAME: NAJIB MESHEDI POSITIVE ID. DEPUTY FINANCE MINISTER OF IRAN. SUSPECTED BUT NOT POSITIVELY CONFIRMED TO BE HIGH OFFICIAL OR DIRECTOR OF SAVAK. ADVISE HADDAD PROCEED WITH CAUTION.

211

This was a bonus. The man in the picture, who had been photographed only by accident because he was standing there, was even more important than the girl. Marwan went back to his office and, following John's plan, telephoned the restaurant where he knew John would be dining, asking to have him paged but not to bring a telephone to his table. Soon John's voice came on the line.

"Marwan? Do you know anything yet?"

"Yes. She's an Iranian agent, very top level. Her name is Lila Tabriz. And she was with the Deputy Minister of Finance of Iran, Najib Meshedi, just before she met you this evening. Our people think he may be the director of their intelligence agency."

"Now this is starting to make sense. I think I understand why GM went up five points today."

"Are you satisfied with the report?"

Marwan was fishing for a compliment. He damn well deserved it, John thought. Marwan had performed his assignment as well as any pro could have. Maybe he was more serious than John had suspected.

"You did great, Marwan, thanks a million. I'll write you a letter of commendation when this is all over that will knock your consul's eye out. Gotta get back now . . . good night."

"Good night, John, and don't have too much fun fraternizing with the opposition!" Marwan could hardly contain his pride. Mission accomplished and all that, but much, much more. Marwan felt, for the first time, that he had contributed productively to an important job.

The phone call from Marwan provided John with a perfect excuse. He needed time to think before deciding how to deal with Lila. He went back to the table and told Lila something had come up that required him to make some urgent overseas calls. He called for the check, paid it, told the waiter to serve Miss Rashid some coffee and then put her in a taxi. He apologized profusely to Lila, who said she understood, and he hurried out of the restaurant.

Chapter 25

BACK home, John settled down to plan his next move. He brewed himself a pot of coffee, poured a cup, took it into the living room, and reviewed what he knew about the recent events. Now he understood why the price of GM had gone over 90, and who the big buyer was. It was Iran! Of course! They had all the motives. First, they were having what amounted to a war with Saudi Arabia. Second, they were afraid of interference with their supply of new tanks and other equipment. Then there was the evidence. The Deputy Finance Minister of Iran was here in New York, with *Lila*.

So Lila was an agent. John idly wondered what she would have done if he had ignored her at the press conference . . . she must have had an alternative plan for striking up a friendship with him. Their affair had been meticulously planned by the Iranians. He allowed himself a moment of self-pity for his hurt male pride, then shrugged it off. He didn't really believe that all the contact between them had been purely mechanical on her part. In any case, John felt lucky to have discovered her true role while there was still time to make a countermove. Obviously this Iranian Deputy Finance Minister was so confident that he hadn't even bothered to conceal his identity. He was sitting in New York masterminding the scheme.

The Iranians were attempting to block the takeover by buying GM stock in the open market. Once the market price rose above the tender offer price, no one would tender his shares to the Saudis, since he could do better by selling it to the highest bidder on the exchange, or else hold it, hoping for a further rise.

Now that the tender price had been increased to 120, the market price was moving with it, to around 115. Meanwhile, the Saudis were receiving millions of shares at 120 from the holders who had not been satisfied with the original offering price of 90.

But, John thought, if the Iranians' plan was to break up the tender offer at any cost, they would probably be willing to continue buying, even above 120, or perhaps make a tender offer of their own at, say, 125. They had done neither. The only possible conclusion was that they wanted to break up the Saudi acquisition but not at the risk of being discovered. Neither did the Iranians want to risk an excessive sum of money by continuing to buy the stock above the tender price. They had only done so when, through Lila's stolen information, they had been assured the price would subsequently be raised, and they could not lose. There must be a way to use this reluctance of the Iranians to take a market risk and turn it against them, to his own, and the Saudis' advantage.

As the pieces of the puzzle fell into place, each complementing the other, John's heart gave an extra hard thump. He had found a strategy sure to succeed. Forcing himself immediately into the role of devil's advocate, he cross-examined himself. Would it solve Sloman's problems and thereby the risk of any unpleasantness from him? Yes. Would it trap Lila and her master and neutralize their effort? A resounding yes. Would El-Bahar object in any way to his method? Not likely, since it did not interfere with John's recently revised strategy for the takeover. Was it illegal? Only in the sense that it violated some of the trading rules. Then would he be found out? The only people who would know were not likely to betray him . . . Sloman and El-Bahar. There was no flaw serious enough to warrant canceling the idea, and the potential rewards were enormous. John let out one triumphant yell, then stopped, embarrassed, hoping the neighbors wouldn't think some violent crime was being committed in the building.

The first step was to contact Hans Sloman and arrange a meeting as soon as possible. The sun had barely risen in Switzerland, but John didn't want to wait. He placed a call and was soon rewarded with a sleepy and disgruntled Sloman answering the line.

"John Haddad here. Mr. Sloman, are you quite awake?"

"Yes, go ahead, Mr. Haddad. I hope you have some good news for me. Time is short."

"I think I have a solution to your problem, but it will require a trip to New York for you . . . as soon as possible. When can you make it?"

"First tell me what you are planning, or at least give me a few hints."

John was reluctant to discuss any details on the phone. There was no way of knowing whether someone was listening at either end, and one eavesdropper could ruin his whole scheme. He responded by telling Sloman that he would be able to clear at least the twenty million he needed and perhaps even more, entirely within the bounds of Swiss law. Sloman finally agreed to catch a Swissair flight that would reach New York at about ten in the morning, the day after tomorrow. But Sloman was not too sleepy to be aware of risk. He promised John that in the event of any accident to himself, a written account of all pertinent matters would be found with his personal papers with instructions for mailing to the Securities and Exchange Commission.

The next step was to get hold of Lila. John called her at the Carlyle and, telling her he had disposed of his business calls, begged her to come back to the apartment to spend the night. Knowing she would be required by the nature of her job to agree, John didn't trouble to be too solicitous. After some half-hearted protests she agreed to take a cab and come over.

When Lila arrived at the apartment, John had to make a conscious effort to conceal his anger at her and keep her believing that all was as before. If Lila had known him better, she would have noticed the coldness in his eyes even as he smiled and welcomed her warmly with a kiss. But her curiosity and hope for another chance at picking up some inside information made her less observant than she might

215

have been in other circumstances. Soon after getting settled, Lila started to become inquisitive.

"How is your fabulous takeover coming along? Did you have some bad news?" Lila asked.

"Not so well. We don't seem to be getting as much stock as we should be."

"Well, what will you do?" Lila sensed she might get some fresh information to use.

John laughed. "You don't think I would spill my plans to the press in advance, do you?"

"Oh, John, I'm not 'the press,' I'm your friend. And anyway, I don't really understand these market technicalities. I told you that before."

John changed the subject and avoided talk of the takeover for the rest of the evening, just to pique her curiosity. Later, before they went to bed, being careful that Lila noticed what he was doing, he sat down at the desk and drafted what appeared to be a memo to his staff. He left the memo in his briefcase, checked to make sure it was not locked, and joined her in bed.

Much later, feigning sleep, John felt her side of the bed lighten as Lila slipped out noiselessly. He saw her reach into her bag, then pad softly into the living room. When she had closed the door, he waited until he saw a crack of light appear beneath it. Edging the door open in time to see Lila bent over his desk, the memo illuminated by the desk lamp, he heard the faint click of her camera in the stillness of the night. As she quickly put everything back the way it was, he returned to bed, closing his eyes and breathing deeply and steadily. Her next report to her boss would contain the information that Thompson, Caldwell was planning to raise the tender offer price for General Motors from one hundred twenty to one hundred and fifty dollars a share!

The next morning, at precisely ten A.M., John switched on his electronic quote machine and tapped the letters G-M on the keyboard. At 10:02 GM traded for the first time at 116,

216

up one half dollar from the previous day's close. Soon the stock was trading at successively higher prices, on rising volume, 117, 117¾, 118⅛, 119. At 11:04 A.M. the stock traded above 120, and then quickly reached 123.

Dave Hill burst into John's office. He was shouting, "Did you see the stock? Somebody's doing it to us again!"

"Don't worry, Dave. This time I know what it's about and we can control it. Please don't ask me for any details yet, OK?"

"No sweat, John." Dave went back to his own office, a little disappointed that his hot news had elicited such a cool reaction from John.

John turned his attention back to the screen. GM was still trading at 123. Good old Lila. *I don't really understand these market technicalities.* Bitch. At least the Iranians were now doing exactly what John wanted them to do. Control of the situation had changed hands, but the Iranians didn't know it.

Hans Sloman neatly took his clothes from the suitcase and placed them in the drawers of the bureau. He had been given a room overlooking Central Park, one of the better rooms the St. Moritz had to offer. He was fast approaching the deadline for replacing the squandered capital at his bank, and although he had provided himself with some protection against double dealing by Haddad, he was still very apprehensive. What miracle could this young man produce to save him?

The telephone shrilled, and Sloman flinched at the unexpectedly loud ring. He picked up the receiver and heard John Haddad's voice saying good morning to him. He quickly agreed to order breakfast for the two of them in the room and John said he would be there by ten thirty. Then Sloman found the room service menu and studied it, wondering what to order. In Switzerland it was so simple. You just told the hotel that you wanted coffee or tea, or perhaps hot chocolate, and they brought you a complete breakfast with croissants, rolls, jam, butter, and cheese. But here, you had to choose from a menu that offered such bewildering things for breakfast as home-fried potatoes! Waffles! Steak and eggs! Finally he settled for coffee and sweet rolls for two and put down the phone, glad to be rid of the chore.

John and Sloman sat at a table by the window overlooking the green expanse of Central Park. As Sloman listened intently, John outlined the plan he had developed, step by step.

At first Sloman's face was calm. Then he began to nod affirmatively, and the ghost of a smile tickled the corners of his mouth. He congratulated himself on having taken the chance that Haddad could help him. The boy was brilliant! He had put together a strategy bordering on genius, with practically no risk. There was even an aura of biblical justice about it.

Finally, as John wound up his narrative, Sloman could stand it no longer. Wreathed in smiles, he stood up and clapped his hands. "Bravo, bravo, John! It is extraordinary. A masterful plan!"

John smiled. "I thought you would appreciate the finer points. Does that mean you agree?"

"Of course, of course," Sloman repeated excitedly, "but when do we start?"

"As soon as you can get back to Switzerland and set it up. And don't forget, use several banks to implement the plan, and not your own."

"That will not be a problem. I still have many friends in the banking community in Zurich who will be glad to participate." Sloman looked out the window at the park, then turned back to John and spoke in a low, solicitous tone. "There's something I want to ask you that's puzzling me."

"Go ahead." John sipped his coffee, wondering what was coming next.

"We first met under extraordinary conditions, John. I attempted to blackmail you and I am not proud of it. Now that the tender offer is on, the only information I have

218

against you is your indiscretion about the PAPCO merger." Sloman took a deep breath and went on. "You have revealed a plan that will make me a fortune and recoup all my losses at the bank. Why?"

Before he answered, John took a long look at Sloman. He felt warmth for the man and sympathy for the predicament that had led him to try blackmail, which he was sure was contrary to Sloman's character. "When you threatened to expose the tender offer, I was frankly worried. And don't kid yourself—I would not like the incident involving my father and the PAPCO-Siesta merger exposed. But, Hans, I did that because my father needed the money badly. I didn't have any money to give him, but I did have information. At the time I put my loyalty to him above the SEC rules."

Sloman shrugged his shoulders and spoke to John with affection. "I know that. You know I probably shouldn't tell you this, but I would not have revealed what I knew about you in any case. I would have gained nothing by hurting you."

John smiled faintly and nodded his head. "I never thought you would, but I couldn't risk it."

"Then why did you call me at all?"

"I needed your help—as much as you needed mine. I have no time to set up a new relationship with someone who can handle this for me properly. I need someone in Switzerland with your kind of connections who is as interested as I am in seeing the plan succeed. The whole thing must be done anonymously through a numbered account without so much as a hint of who's behind it. You may retain twenty five percent of the profits. Is that acceptable?"

Now Sloman smiled, his face lighting up. "Entirely satisfactory, in view of the sums involved. I'm happy to work with you, and you can count on my absolute discretion." John knew he could trust Sloman now. He had just showed the man the way to his salvation, and there was not time left for Sloman to try anything else.

When John left the hotel, Sloman booked himself a return on the Swissair night flight to Zurich. The trip to New York had been short, but most rewarding.

Chapter 26

AT last John had a moment to breathe, bolstered by the knowledge that all the threads in the web radiating out from the General Motors takeover were in his hands. He was now able to turn to the problem none of the competitors in the financial contest cared for one whit. The problem's name was Charlotte Grogan.

To begin with, he couldn't blame Charlotte for her angry explosion and hanging up the telephone the night he was expecting Lila. He had tried to suppress the guilt he felt every time he had been with Lila. Rationalizing had not helped much. True, he was not married or even engaged to Charlotte, but there are commitments that go further and deeper than the ones that are signed and sworn to. Their own relationship was like that, and he had broken faith with her. Would he have forgiven her for a similar breach of trust? He wondered.

He thought about telling Charlotte everything that had happened, unburdening his guilty conscience. But he decided that it would serve no useful purpose. Charlotte had guessed that there was someone else; there was no need to hurt her more with the details. If any good had come from this, John thought it was that he now loved and respected Charlotte more than he ever had, and he didn't want to lose her. He had strung Charlotte along for years, monopolizing her time without facing up to the responsibilities of marriage. She had been patient and loving, and although she brought up the subject of marriage now and again, Charlotte never pressed it. Now the time had come for John to make his relationship with her whole, if she would have him.

Once having made the decision, he felt lighthearted and buoyant, in the mood to do something extravagant. Since he had not yet drawn down one penny of the half-million-dollar payment the Oil Minister had promised him as a fee for handling the takeover, John wasn't worried about the risk of depleting his savings account. He left the office and walked quickly to the bank, which was on the ground floor of the same building as Thompson, Caldwell's office. Going to the savings teller's window, he pulled out his bankbook and saw that he had a balance of nine thousand four hundred dollars in his account. He scribbled a withdrawal slip for nine thousand, signed it, and handed it to the teller with his bankbook. She looked up at him and and smiled. "Are you going on a trip, Mr. Haddad?"

"No, this is for something much more important."

"How would you like this paid? It would be an awful lot of cash to carry around."

"Please make it a teller's check, payable to me, and have it certified."

Five minutes later, John was striding toward Fifth Avenue, the certified check tucked securely into his wallet. He had gone by the windows of the famous jewelers on Fifth Avenue many times, often stopping to look at their opulent displays, but he had never actually gone in with the intent to buy. This time would be different. He pulled open the heavy glass and wrought-iron door of Buccellati, the Italian jeweler. John had always noticed that Buccellati's designs were different from the others. They did not content themselves with surrounding one or more massive stones with minimal settings. They managed to make even the largest stones seem to look natural in frames of delicate Florentine gold or set in intricate patterns of smaller stones surrounding the central one. He was confident that Charlotte would agree with his taste.

Soon he was seated in a leather chair, across a counter from a distinguished-looking saleslady dressed in severe black, with a jeweled comb anchoring the upswept arrangement of her gray hair. "What may I show you, sir?" she asked.

The atmosphere reminded John of a Swiss bank. Only two other customers were in the room, and each was conversing in hushed tones with a salesperson. Trays of jewels were discreetly brought out for inspection, looked at, then returned to their cushioned slots behind locked cabinet doors. There were no glass-enclosed showcases displaying a variety of pieces. In the walls were three inset little display windows, each showing a small selection of pieces in matching stones, but that was all the open display.

"I'm looking for an engagement ring," John said, "and I don't know too much about jewelry, so you'll have to help me."

The woman smiled. "I understand how you feel. Don't worry, we will find something perfect for you. But I must ask you one thing which is unavoidable before we start. About how much did you plan to spend on the ring?"

John was taken aback by the question. He had expected to be shown a tray of rings of varying size from which he could choose, then ask the price. But then he realized that the saleslady was tactfully trying to spare him the embarrassment of choosing something way beyond his means and he appreciated it. "Well, I have in mind something that would cost somewhere between seventy-five hundred and ten thousand dollars."

She sat up a little straighter and eyed him with new respect. "Oh, yes, sir, I think we'll do very well indeed for you."

As she was getting up to fetch a tray of rings, John called her back. "Just a minute, I have an idea."

The saleslady returned frowning.

"What do you think of an emerald rather than a diamond? I'd like something a little different from the ordinary."

"Nothing we sell here is ordinary, sir, but your taste is very good. Many of our most distinguished clients have been choosing emeralds lately." She walked toward the cabinets, taking a slightly different direction from the previous one. She was back right away with a tray of glistening green stones, arranged in rows in a beige velvet lining. At first glance they all appeared to be about the same size, but as he looked closer, he saw that the emeralds varied considerably. Some were round, some rectangular, some square, and some oval.

"Are all of these in my price range?" John asked.

"Yes, approximately. Do you see any you like?"

He studied the tray and was struck by one particular ring. It had a round stone, smaller than most of the others. There was a circle of tiny diamonds surrounding the stone, creating a strong contrast in color between the deep green and the sparkling diamond brilliance. "May I?" He looked up at her.

"Yes, please examine it."

John gingerly picked up the ring. It was beautiful, perfect for Charlotte. It was not too big, and Charlotte would not want anything ostentatious. But it was no little chip, either.

"How much is this one?"

"You have chosen very well, sir. Please look at the other stones for a moment. You will see that none of them is completely clear of any flaws, except the one you picked. Although the stone is smaller, it is much better quality."

John was pleased that he had picked a good one. "But you haven't told me the price," he said.

"This ring is ninety-five hundred dollars, plus the tax, of course."

"I'll take it. But what about the size?"

"If it doesn't fit, we can adjust the size in a few hours. You can bring it back any time if necessary."

John pulled out the certified check, endorsed it over to the store, and wrote another check from his checking account to make up the difference. Back in his office, with the little velvet box making a bulge in his jacket pocket, he called Charlotte at the station in Washington.

"John—oh, sure I recognized your voice. I was just surprised to hear from you." Charlotte's tone was cool. It would be a job to appease her.

"Darling, I'm not making excuses, but I've been busy night and day since we talked. I really want to see you."

"When did you have in mind?" Her tone had softened slightly, but she had not yielded.

"How about tonight? I could fly down this afternoon and we could have dinner." He didn't say anything about spending the night, afraid to set her off.

"I can't. Dad's having a few people in for dinner and I promised I'd go."

"Charlotte, I love you. You have to believe me. If you really can't make it tonight for dinner, I'll see you after dinner. And if that's no good, I'll come down in the morning."

"Well, that would be the first time you've been willing to skip work to see me!" In spite of her sarcastic words, John could detect the humor in her voice.

"That's right, lady, you're still number one with me."

"Well, all right, come ahead. Dad will understand. Where shall I meet you?"

"Let's see, it's two thirty now. I'll meet you in front of the television station at five thirty and we'll go on from there."

Grateful that Charlotte had agreed without much resentment, John told Sue Anderson he would be out for the rest of the day, and that he would call in the morning if he was delayed coming in. Sue asked where he could be reached if something came up, but John just smiled and said he couldn't be reached at all.

Three hours later, Charlotte came out through the revolving glass door of the WTOP-TV building on Wisconsin Avenue into the bright sunlight. She blinked in the glare and reached into her bag for her sunglasses just as John opened the door of the taxi he was sitting in and jumped out onto the curb. He walked up to her and put his right arm around her, gently taking the glasses off her face with his left. Heedless of the stares of passersby, he kissed her on the lips, holding her tightly to him. At first she resisted, surprised. But then she gave in and kissed him back, fiercely. Finally, they broke apart.

"I don't ever want to have a fight with you again," she said, tears forming in the corners of her eyes and running down either side of her nose.

"It was my fault," he answered softly. "I got too involved in what I was doing."

"No, no, it was my fault. I shouldn't have gotten mad at you so easily. I should have thought of the pressure you were under. It's just that I felt so left out of everything all of a sudden."

"Come on"—John took her arm—"let's go somewhere nice and dark for a drink and we can talk."

As they walked down the street, Charlotte pulled a small handkerchief out of her bag and smiled. "I have to have something over my eyes to cover the mess I've made of my mascara. Make sure the place we go is dark!"

They walked over to the nearby Presidential Arms and found a quiet table in the cocktail lounge. When their drinks had arrived, Charlotte started asking questions.

"Tell me, how is your deal coming? Is it almost over? I noticed the price of GM has gone way up in the last few days."

"I'll tell you about all that later, if you want to know. But I came here to talk to you about something much more important."

"More important? What other deal are you getting yourself into?"

John laughed. "The other deal I'd like to get myself into is completely different. It's an equal partnership in which I would have half the voting stock and would be co-chairman of the board. A unanimous vote would be needed to make

225

any decisions, and I'd like to plan for some expansion in the near future!"

Charlotte looked at him quizzically. "What kind of kooky company would that be? I don't understand."

"That would be Mr. and Mrs. John Haddad, with some possible little Haddads to come. In case you didn't know it, I just proposed to you." John reached inside his pocket and pulled out the little velvet box.

Charlotte's tears began to spill out again, coursing out from under the glasses she still hadn't removed.

"Honey, don't. . . . Just tell me yes or no." John took her hand.

"Of course I'll marry you, silly," she said through her tears, "it's just that I'm so happy." John reached over and opened the little box, slipped out the ring, and slid it onto her finger, praying that it would fit.

Charlotte extended her arm then arched back her hand, looking down at the ring. "Oh, John, it's beautiful! It must have cost you a fortune! Are you sure we can afford it?"

"Now you're sounding like a future wife. It's too soon for that. And yes, we can afford it. In fact, if all goes well, we'll be able to afford just about anything you can think of."

They sat there for hours, talking incessantly about all the little things neither had wanted to broach before. About houses versus apartments, what color eyes their children would have, and whose parents to call first. John told Charlotte all about the Iranians and about his arrangement with Sloman.

He did not mention Lila, but the guilt was still there when he thought about her and how stupid he had been. He squeezed Charlotte's hand and kissed her cheek, a kiss that asked forgiveness for his unspoken indiscretion. Finally, they noticed that the room had emptied out and that it was almost eleven o'clock. They walked back toward the television station, to the garage where Charlotte had left her car, giving up the idea of going out to dinner. They drove to her apartment and raided the refrigerator instead, happy to be together.

Charlotte called Harry Grogan to break the news, and then let John talk to him. Between them, they had a great deal of trouble dissuading him from rushing right over with a bottle of champagne. Then came the call to John's parents. His mother wept predictably while his father dropped broad hints about having some grandchildren at last. Then Mrs. Haddad took the phone back from him and insisted on giving Charlotte all kinds of advice and promised to teach her how to cook Lebanese food for John. John's own elation was considerably heightened by the anticipation that he would soon be rich and free from the financial worries of a newlywed.

At last, the calls were over, and John and Charlotte went hand in hand into the bedroom, turning out the lights behind them. They made love with tenderness and patience, knowing now that all was well between them and would stay that way.

In the morning John and Charlotte decided not to make any announcements until after the takeover of General Motors had been completed and he could decide on his next step. Charlotte would not yet give notice at the station, and she would come to New York at the end of the week for an evening with John's parents.

As she drove him to the airport, Charlotte asked, "When do you think the takeover will be finished?"

"It's a matter of days, honey. Please be patient."

"Oh, I am. It's just that I need a new car and I figure you'll be able to get me a General Motors one wholesale!"

Chapter 27

THE Special American Airlines DC9 streaked across the morning sky, heading northwest toward Detroit, Michigan. The airplane, one of the few DC9's specially fitted as an executive aircraft with a living room interior, had been chartered by John for the trip. The green and white Boeing 707 of the Royal Saudi Arabian fleet, which had brought Sheikh El-Bahar to the United States, remained parked at Kennedy Airport. Its presence in Detroit would have attracted too much attention. When John had phoned El-Bahar, he asked that the Oil Minister come to the United States as soon as possible to discuss a new tactic concerning the GM takeover. El-Bahar arrived three days later.

Once he was comfortably settled in the Waldorf Towers in New York and had been allowed enough time to recover from the seven-hour time difference, El-Bahar met with John, who outlined his proposal. Attifi was there, and so was Mahmoun, ever faithful to the commands of his master.

John explained that the tender offer had not been going as well as he had hoped. He admitted his own weakness and told El-Bahar about the Iranians and how they had sent a spy to seduce him. More important, he explained, the Iranians had twice interfered with the tender offer by buying GM stock at higher prices. El-Bahar had stiffened at the recounting of John's experience. But when John told him that he had finally outwitted the Iranians, a smile returned to the Oil Minister's face and he nodded approvingly. John purposely did not explain his arrangement with Hans Sloman. That would have to wait until the right moment.

Having presented the facts to El-Bahar, John told him of his new plan to resolve the GM control problem. The Oil Minister hesitated and spoke at some length in Arabic with Attifi. He adjourned the discussion without giving his decision. Later that evening, John met El-Bahar for dinner in the Presidential Suite. The Oil Minister questioned John throughout the meal, raising objections and suggesting modifications to the planned course of action.

El-Bahar was disappointed at first, since the proposal would involve a partial capitulation. But he recognized his disappointment for what it was—a temporary emotional reaction. He told himself that he must concentrate on facts, for El-Bahar had an exceedingly logical mind, and the good sense of what John had told him led the Oil Minister to the same basic conclusion. In the end, John and El-Bahar ironed out their minor differences and found themselves in agreement.

When John had reached Tim Hurley on the telephone, Hurley's tone had been cold, even hostile. Would Mr. Hurley be available to meet with the Minister of Oil of Saudi Arabia and himself as soon as possible? The meeting was to be held in strict secrecy. Hurley grudgingly agreed to a meeting in Detroit the following day.

The big jet made a smooth landing at Detroit Metropolitan Airport and El-Bahar unbuckled his safety belt. His hands were shaking. *How ironic,* he thought. Anwar El-Bahar had met dozens of heads of state, always confident, always in command, always well received. Always well received—that was the difference. Now, for the first time in his professional life, El-Bahar was going to a meeting where he was neither liked nor welcome. No embraces at planeside, no fawning ministers, no pleading for his favor. This time he was the supplicant, not the granter, and he was not sure how he would react in that situation.

A black limousine deposited El-Bahar, Attifi, Mahmoun, and John Haddad at the side entrance of General Motors' mammoth headquarters. A young man, conservatively dressed in a gray suit and blue tie, stood at the door and asked the guests to accompany him to a small conference room. Following a short elevator ride and a walk down a dimly lit, plushly carpeted corridor, the men were shown into a room with a circular table and chairs, wood paneling, a fireplace, and illuminated portraits of past General Motors chief executives.

Tim Hurley entered the room through a side door and was followed by Sid Luddington, general counsel to the corporation. No one said anything for three long seconds.

Finally, John addressed the General Motors chairman and introduced himself and the Saudi Arabians. Hurley introduced Luddington and gestured to the chairs around the table, inviting the men to take seats.

Hurley looked across the table and spoke in a curt tone. "You gentlemen asked for this meeting. We are ready to listen."

El-Bahar recoiled at Hurley's tone. He was not accustomed to being addressed so coldly. He wanted to answer Hurley, give him a verbal tongue lashing, a needed lesson in diplomacy. *But remember,* he thought to himself, *you are here asking for something, not granting favors. Be still.*

El-Bahar turned to John Haddad and nodded, a signal that John was to begin the discussion. Acknowledging the order, he mentally composed himself, but there were butterflies in his stomach and John hoped the nervousness would not show in his voice.

"Mr. Hurley," John began, "we came because we hoped to reach some agreement with you on the Saudi Arabian purchase of your stock. We—"

Hurley interrupted, making an effort to contain his anger: "I hope you know by now that we are opposing this takeover. What possible agreement could there be?"

John was dismayed at Hurley's immediate negative attitude but controlled his reactions. "We did not come to ask you to surrender control. We want to talk to you about a—well, a compromise."

"Go ahead, I'm listening."

"Please let me continue." The nervousness had left and John spoke with confidence. He explained to Hurley that while the Saudis had a perfect right to buy GM stock or even control the company, they were sensitive to the fact that the company's management and public opinion opposed the takeover.

The Saudi Arabians had two problems. They had enormous sums of money to invest and they needed a guaranteed supply of arms, especially the new M-90 tanks.

John opened his attaché case and took from it a single sheet of typewritten paper. "As of yesterday, we owned seventy-four million two hundred thousand GM shares. That's about twenty-six percent of the company."

Hurley and Luddington stared at John in obvious anticipation of what he would say next. John sat back in the chair and continued to speak in a slow businesslike manner. "Now we can go on with the tender offer, or even raise it, until we have complete control of the company. But I have another solution to propose to you, sir."

"Go on," Hurley said.

"We are prepared to cancel the tender offer and freeze our participation in the company at twenty-six percent."

"There must be a catch." Hurley knew there would be a price to pay.

"We want to buy control of your German Opel subsidiary. We'll pay book value."

"What the hell would you want to do that for?"

"We intend to produce M-90 tanks and other equipment in Germany. Sheikh El-Bahar has already discussed this with the German government, and they have agreed to the Saudi Arabian manufacture of arms in the Opel plant facilities, subject to some limitations."

"You know we have an exclusive contract with the Iranians on the M-90 tanks," said an amazed Hurley.

"Of course we do. But once Opel belongs to us, the manufacture of M-90's will no longer be under your exclusive control. It won't be a violation of your contract with Iran. We've checked that very carefully."

Hurley stared at John Haddad for several seconds. Then he sat back in his chair and seemed to relax.

"What about the raise you promised to the workers?" Hurley's voice was still challenging.

El-Bahar motioned that he would answer. "I want that commitment to be kept, if you accept our compromise."

Hurley turned and spoke to Luddington. "Sid, would we get into any trouble accepting this?"

Luddington stared at the ceiling for a moment. "I'll have to look into it, of course, but . . . no, I can't see any problems right off the bat."

Hurley toyed with a pencil, concentrating on the point as he brought it down, making tiny dots on the paper pad. "You must know that our Opel division has been losing money for years, ever since Mercedes came out with a low-priced small car."

"Yes, we know that," John replied, "but we think it can be turned around. Besides, its current profitability is not our major concern."

Hurley went back to his pencil, bringing it up and down until now the dots had formed a shape, a widening circle. He nodded, in apparent response to an unspoken question that he had put to himself. The others sat quietly realizing that the man was deliberating the most important decision of his career.

Hurley looked up. "Your offer appeals to me. I'd sure as hell rather have you fellows own twenty-six percent of the company than all of it. All right. I'll talk to the board about it this afternoon, but as far as I'm concerned, you've got a deal."

John could not hold back a smile, his first since the meeting began. He flashed a congratulatory glance at El-Bahar, who was about to speak to Hurley.

"One last thing, Mr. Hurley," El-Bahar said. "As owners of twenty-six percent of General Motors stock, we would like two seats on the board of directors. One of them will be for me"—El-Bahar looked to his left at John—"and the other will be for John Haddad." At this, Hurley had difficulty concealing his relief. The Saudis could have demanded six or seven seats and gotten them.

There was a mood of celebration in the plane as it flew east to New York. John popped open the third bottle of Dom Pérignon champagne and poured for everyone, including the three stewardesses assigned to the special flight. El-Bahar was visibly pleased and he joined in the buoyant talk and laughter.

At one point, John whispered to El-Bahar that he would like a private word with him. They walked to one side of the aircraft and sat in two facing armchairs.

"Your Excellency, I want to thank you most kindly for giving me the seat on the board. I am very moved and honored beyond words."

"You deserved it, John. Now I am assured of having a friend in the room when I come to the meetings!" He laughed and patted John on the shoulder.

"I've always been candid with you," John said, his voice serious now, "and I will continue to be. I want you to know that I stand to make a considerable amount of money for myself tomorrow when we withdraw the tender offer." John explained his pending project in detail, and how it had come to him after he learned of the Iranian attempt to block the takeover. He told El-Bahar about Sloman and the role Sloman had played. "If for any reason you disapprove, I can probably cancel the operation."

"Far from it, John," El-Bahar said. His eyes looked at John with affection. "It is an extraordinary plan, and after all, since the Iranians will suffer, it is poetic justice, isn't it? But tell me, with the discretionary power I gave you at the outset, couldn't you have done all this without asking my permission?"

John nodded and looked straight at the Oil Minister. "I could have, but I didn't want to."

Chapter 28

"GM OPENING DELAYED . . . NEWS PENDING." The New York Stock Exchange ticker tape carried the cryptic announcement in routine fashion. In brokerage offices all over the world, millions of investors buzzed with speculation on what the news might be.

Minutes later, the Dow Jones news service, which everyone in the securities business referred to as the "broad tape," carried the announcement that a press conference would be held in New York later that morning. Thompson, Caldwell and Company would make an announcement concerning the takeover. Usually reliable sources had indicated that a representative of the Saudi Arabian government would also be present. No further information about the announcement had been made available.

"All right, let him in," Grayson said to his secretary.

"Good morning, sir." John greeted the chairman cheerfully. Indeed it was a good morning for John Haddad, and he hoped that his poor relationship with Elliott Grayson would not be allowed to spoil it. "I have some important—"

"Before you say anything else, would you mind telling me what the hell this press conference is all about? Most people in this firm consult me before calling press conferences." Grayson mixed sarcasm with anger, one of his more typical emotional combinations.

"I came to tell you about it, Mr. Grayson. I'm afraid things moved so fast, we didn't have time to advise you any sooner."

John explained that an agreement had been reached between General Motors and the Saudi Arabians. Mustafa Attifi and John were holding a press conference that morning to announce the terms of the agreement publicly. Grayson listened, expressionless, and did not comment.

For days John wondered how Grayson would react to the final part of the agreement, El-Bahar's ultimate tribute to his young American adviser. Now was the time to find out.

"The Saudis have asked for two seats on the board. El-Bahar will have one of these, and he offered the other one to me."

"He wants *you* to be on General Motors' board?" Gray-

234

son's annoyance seeped through, even on the few occasions when he made efforts to conceal it.

"That's right."

Grayson leaned over his desk and aimed a pencil at John. "Look, you're a bright young man. You must realize that it's hardly appropriate for someone of your age and seniority to sit on the board of General Motors."

John concealed his anger. He slowed the pace of his words, trying to remain calm. "Under the circumstances, sir, I consider it perfectly appropriate. And Sheikh El-Bahar offered the seat to me—I didn't ask for it."

"Your sheikh offered the seat to his investment banker. That's normal. He made the offer to Thompson, Caldwell, not to you personally! Don't you realize that?"

John shook his head, but said nothing. The conversation was going nowhere. How could he convince Grayson that El-Bahar had sincerely and generously granted the GM position to him, John Haddad, not to some impersonal financial institution! No matter what he said, Grayson would simply not believe it.

"There's a great deal of responsibility involved in being a corporate director," Grayson continued, sounding like a preacher giving a sermon. "It requires judgment and experience—a good deal more experience than you have."

Grayson's words hid his true meaning. It was not John's lack of experience that mattered, but rather his lack of status. Investment bankers vied for corporate directorships the way movie actors scrambled for leading roles. If it involved an important and expensive film, the prestige was correspondingly higher. Similarly, the larger the corporation, the more desirable it became to serve it as a director, and, on that score, General Motors was the ultimate achievement.

Grayson would have been flattered to serve as a GM director himself, and why did John Haddad not have the good sense to suggest it to him? Any other subordinate would have recognized this duty instantly. But alas, since

Haddad had not done so, Grayson could hardly volunteer. He would have to appoint someone else, an executive whose background and status were more suited to the job than the qualifications of Mr. John Haddad.

John closed his eyes and a pained expression came over his face. His anger and frustration were reaching unmanageable proportions and he fought hard not to lose control.

Grayson continued to speak, thinking out loud, ignoring John's discomfort. "I think Tom Richardson would make a fine GM director. After all, he's head of the Corporate Finance Department and about the right age. Yes, by God, he's perfect!" Grayson's fist came down on the desk, emphasizing the point. "John, I'd like you to tell your sheikh that we've thought it over, and we think Tom Richardson should sit on the board. I'm sure he'll understand."

John did not look at Grayson. In a controlled low voice, he said, "I don't think I can do that. As I said before, the seat was offered to *me*."

"God damn it, Haddad! They offered it to this firm. There are at least twenty people in the Corporate Finance Department who could have handled that takeover."

"That's not the point."

"I know what the point is. You want the seat for yourself, and you know damn well El-Bahar will give it to anyone we ask him to."

"He will not. And I don't want to talk to him about this kind of petty dispute. He expects more than that from me."

"That just proves what I'm saying—the reason you don't want to mention this is that you know he'll agree to having Richardson on the board. Well, if I have to, I can talk to El-Bahar myself. So make your choice."

"I've got to get down to the press conference. Can I think this over for a few days?"

"Just remember, in this firm, officers may serve as corporate directors only with the prior approval of senior management. I might add that we don't tolerate insubordination."

236

When John left the office to hurry to his press conference, his earlier cheerful mood had vanished. There were several alternatives and he had little time to consider them now. He had tried anyway. Clearly, he had been threatened with dismissal for insubordination. How ironic! Grayson obviously thought he was threatening John's livelihood. John did feel threatened, but for a completely different reason. His coming financial independence through Sloman's handling of the transaction they had arranged together would make his salary at Thompson, Caldwell trivial. But what John did care about was his professional standing in the investment community. He intended to stay in his field and did not want his reputation to be damaged by anyone.

Time was running out and John postponed further thought about his problems until after the press conference.

Meshedi was finishing breakfast in his suite when Lila Tabriz arrived on schedule. He put down his copy of the New York *Times* and rose to greet her.

"You've done a fine job, Lila, and it seems you've even managed to enjoy certain aspects of your assignment." He looked at her lasciviously, his eyes moving slowly from her ankles to her strikingly attractive face.

Lila responded without emotion. "I am happy that you are pleased with my work."

"Yes, yes," Meshedi continued, pacing the living room floor in his silk bathrobe. "Did I tell you that yesterday we bought over two million shares of General Motors at one hundred twenty-five?" Meshedi went on to praise Lila, and how she had cleverly discovered that Haddad would soon raise the tender offer price to 150.

"Did you listen to the radio this morning?"

"No, I hate radio programs in this country. Nothing but loud music. Why?"

"Haddad and the Saudi Arabians are having a press conference at eleven A.M."

Meshedi raised his arms. "Fine. Undoubtedly they will

announce the increase in the tender offer price to one hundred and fifty. Today, I will definitely listen to the radio."

Meshedi strutted into the bedroom. The Shah would be pleased, and His Highness rewarded those who had served him well as intensely as he punished the few who served him badly.

Thompson, Caldwell's conference room was crowded and noisy as reporters and photographers vied for position in front of the empty lectern. Young men and women, casually dressed, carried portable tape recorders slung over their shoulders, microphones in hand. Two television cameras were set up facing the lectern from different angles. Extra lights had been brought in and the heat they threw off overpowered the air-conditioning system. A reporter composed a mock prayer for a short conference, lest the representatives of the press expire from the heat. "Maybe they want to show us what it's like on the burning sands of Saudi Arabia," one wag commented.

John Haddad and Mustafa Attifi walked into the conference room precisely on time. Both men smiled and John nodded to the reporters he knew or thought he recognized. He saw that Lila had not come this time, and so had cheated him of seeing her face when the announcement was made. Taking his place behind the lectern, John spoke into the six microphones facing him. He welcomed the media and press people and introduced Attifi. Then he took a sheet of paper from his suit pocket and put it on the lectern.

"The statement will be very short, ladies and gentlemen, but we will be available for some questions afterward." John looked down at the paper and read. "On behalf of the Saudi Arabian government, we wish to announce that an agreement has been reached between the Saudi Arabian holding company, Islam Investors Limited, and General Motors Corporation, with respect to the former's acquisition of General Motors stock. As a result of this agreement, Islam Investors will not buy any additional shares of General Motors. Consequently, the tender offer is being withdrawn, effective immediately. In consideration of this agreement, General Motors has agreed to sell seventy-five percent of its German Opel division to Saudi Arabia. Islam Investors will continue to own twenty-six percent of General Motors and looks forward to a happy and productive relationship with the company."

As soon as he had finished, reporters crowded around John to ask for more information and probe into the meaning of the agreement. One thing was sure, when General Motors finally traded again on the New York Stock Exchange, it would be at a considerably lower price. Without the support of the tender offer to keep the price up, there was no longer any reason for the stock price to stay at those inflated levels.

The relative calm of his office contrasted markedly with the noise and tempo of the press conference John had just left. He dialed the four-digit internal number that would connect him with Stu Thurmond on the floor of the New York Stock Exchange. When the phone was answered, the first thing John heard was the loud shouting and frenzy that were a traditional part of the floor trading. Then Thurmond came on.

"How does GM look?" John asked.

Thurmond raised his voice to be heard over the background clatter. "It won't open for an hour or so. Indications so far are sixty-five to seventy on the opening."

John thanked Thurmond and hung up. More of a drop than he had expected. GM had closed the day before at 125. It would probably open today at 70, some 55 points lower. In one day, the stock market value of General Motors stock would decline by over fifteen billion dollars. By withdrawing the tender offer, John had precipitated the largest single loss in market value in stock market history. At the same time, he had insured a painful black eye to the Iranians, and although only El-Bahar and Sloman knew about it, he was amassing a fortune for himself in a brilliant financial coup.

John reached for his wallet and removed a paper with Sloman's home phone number in Zurich. Using his private line, which bypassed the switchboard, he dialed the international code and then the number. Sloman answered.

"Good evening, Hans." It was early evening in Zurich. "Have you heard the news?"

"I have indeed, my friend." Hans Sloman was cheerful. "Will the stock open today?"

"In less than an hour. Did you have any trouble, Hans?"

"No trouble. We sold two million shares short at one hundred twenty-five yesterday. Do you know at what price GM will open?"

"The floor tells me sixty-five to seventy."

"God! Do you realize how much we'll make?"

"I certainly do. I want you to start covering your short position as soon as the stock opens."

"I will, I will." Sloman was excited. "I don't expect to get much sleep tonight!"

Lila Tabriz replaced the telephone in its cradle and walked across the living room to where Meshedi was sitting. He did not see her. His hands were covering his eyes, holding his bowed head.

"General Motors just opened at sixty-nine."

Meshedi lifted his head slowly. His face was ashen and he looked several years older. "We will lose over one hundred million dollars." His voice trembled and he cleared his throat to conceal the emotion. The phone rang again and Meshedi answered swiftly. He spoke in Persian. The conversation lasted ten minutes. When it was over, he turned to Lila.

"He told me . . . he said . . ." Meshedi choked, unable to continue.

"What? Tell me, please . . ."

"He said to sell all of the shares at a loss. He wants us to come home. No one should know that we tried to stop the

240

takeover. His Highness does not want to be embarrassed."

"Does he understand what happened?"

"He was not interested in details. He only knows that we failed. Lila, I had to tell him that we would lose over one hundred million dollars!"

Lila bit her lower lip and spoke nervously. "So Haddad knew about me. He set a trap. A one-hundred-million-dollar trap."

Meshedi was not listening. He was on the phone again, shouting orders in Persian. This time the conversation was very short.

"I have given instructions to sell the stock. There are so many shares, it may take weeks."

"I'll fix you a drink." Lila made one for herself as well.

The phone rang, sending shock waves through Meshedi's already deteriorating nerves. After the brief call he took the glass Lila handed to him.

"They were able to sell all of the stock at once. They found a buyer of two million shares at seventy. A small bit of luck."

Lila sat and sipped her drink. She looked at her reflection in the mirror across the room. Although not especially vain, she delighted in having a beautiful, well-proportioned body.

"What will they do to us?" she asked.

Meshedi looked at her hopelessly and shook his head. "I really don't know, Lila. Go pack."

Chapter 29

BILLY MARTIN's Carriage House was filled with happy weekend diners. John and Charlotte sat side by side at the same table they had occupied over three months earlier, be-

241

fore his trip to Beirut. He held her hand as they listened to music and sipped a fine red wine.

She put her head on his shoulder and her hair caressed his cheek. "Glad it's over?"

"Yes, in a way."

"Do you feel like telling me about it? I mean what you mentioned on the phone." Charlotte's voice was soft and docile.

"I'm dying to tell you, darling." And John meant it. He loved her more than ever and wondered how she would react to the incredible news he was about to give her. How would anyone react in that situation? "Do you know what a short sale is?"

Charlotte thought for a moment before answering. "I think so. Isn't that when you sell stock you don't own?"

"Right. Now stay with me for the details." John explained that when a trader thinks a stock's price is going to decline, he can arrange to sell shares he doesn't own. He can borrow stock through his broker to deliver to the buyer. Then, if the stock goes down, the short seller can buy the stock back at the lower price, and use the newly bought stock to replace the stock he borrowed from the broker.

Charlotte's eyes lit up. "I get it! If he sells short at fifty, then buys the stock back at forty to replace the stock he borrowed, he makes ten dollars a share, right?"

"Right!" John raised his glass. Charlotte's glass met his and they clinked a toast to each other.

"So what does all this 'short' business have to do with you?" Charlotte asked.

"Well, just before we reached the agreement on GM, I leaked some false information to the Iranians." John sipped his wine and hoped Charlotte would not ask exactly how he had leaked the information. "I led them to believe that we were going to raise the tender offer price from one hundred and twenty to one hundred and fifty.

Charlotte looked puzzled. "So?"

John continued to talk, savoring every word. "So, they

started to buy more stock in the market at one hundred and twenty-five, thinking it would go up to one hundred and fifty. At the same time, Hans Sloman, the Swiss banker I told you about after my London trip, sold stock to them short. Still with me?"

"Yeah, I think so. Go on."

"Then we withdrew the tender offer and the stock price collapsed."

"Oh, God, now I get it. The stock went down and your friend bought it back cheaper."

John smiled at his fiancée. "That's right, honey. Sloman sold short at one hundred and twenty-five and bought the stock back the next day at seventy. That's a profit of fifty-five dollars a share."

"That's neat. Let's see if I really understand. He sells short at one hundred and twenty-five. So then he gets one hundred and twenty-five dollars for each share, but he has to replace the shares he borrowed. So when the stock price went down, he bought the shares back at seventy and replaced them. But since he sold them for one hundred and twenty-five and bought back for seventy, he kept the difference—fifty-five dollars a share, right?"

"Right again!"

"Great! So how many shares did he sell short?"

John kept smiling and watched for her reaction. "Two million," he said.

Suddenly, she realized. "Two million! That can't be true. That would mean you made a profit of one hundred and ten million dollars!" She stared at him in disbelief.

"You have a way with numbers, you know. A real talent." John laughed.

Charlotte's excitement was mixed with laughter. "You mean it's true, John, really?"

John put his hand on her shoulder, then stroked her cheek. "Yes," he said softly.

Then John explained to Charlotte about his arrangement with Sloman and that the banker would get twenty-five percent of the profits. That left John with over eighty-two million dollars of his own. He had made the money at the Iranians' expense, and considering what they had tried to do to him, he felt no remorse at having profited from their loss.

Charlotte suddenly looked serious. "Honey, is what you did legal?"

"No . . . strictly speaking, it's not. I took advantage of inside information and that's a no-no."

"Could you get in trouble?"

"Yeah, sure. But it's not likely that anyone will find out. The real issue to me is the morality of what I did."

"What do you mean?"

"The rules against using inside information are designed to protect the investors who don't know as much as the insiders. The idea is that everybody should have an equal chance, so that if I sold stock at one hundred and twenty-five to some poor chump who thought it was going up, and then caused the price to go down, that guy had no chance from the start. Now, I agree with that rule and I've defended it publicly. But remember—Sloman sold the stock to the Iranians. I have no sympathy at all for them."

"I guess you shouldn't. They tried to ruin you. But how will you ever explain your tremendous wealth?"

"The Saudi Arabians are notorious for extravagant rewards. That fact alone will do most of the explaining, and I'll pay taxes on it. Why not? I can certainly afford it!"

Charlotte sat silently. She was beginning to understand the enormousness of the coup. Her composure returned slowly, and she grappled with the size of the figure. She might have been able to cope with his earning half a million or maybe even a million. But eighty-two million dollars? What an unfathomable sum! The money would change their lives and their children's lives for generations to come. She thought of how he had done it, admiring his ingenuity and courage. One thing still puzzled her.

"John, how could Sloman borrow two million shares? "It's such a huge amount. . . ."

"Good question, darling. I had Islam Investors lend the

stock to him. He only needed it for twenty-four hours, since he bought it back and replaced it the following day. Sheikh El-Bahar knew what I was doing."

"Oh," she said, still putting the pieces together. Yet they all fitted somehow. There were no loose ends. "What are you going to do with the money?"

John gazed at her with affection. "I'm going to spend a little of it extravagantly—on you, on us, on my parents. I'll also put a lot of money in trust for our kids."

Charlotte looked pleased at the thought of being a mother. "Honey, what about your work? Don't misunderstand me, but I wouldn't want you to retire at the ripe old age of thirty-two."

John put his arm around her and squeezed gently. He told her about his most recent confrontation with Grayson, and Grayson's demand that he give up the seat on General Motors' board. He kissed her on the cheek and added, "But don't worry, darling. I won't retire. In fact, starting next week, I'm going to be working harder than I've ever worked in my life."

Charlotte breathed a sigh of relief. She loved John too much to think of him as an insufferably rich playboy with nothing to do but flit from country to country and vie for mention in the society columns. Thank God he was not that type, and she hoped the money would not change him. "What will you be working at?" she asked.

He grinned and went back to the apple tart in front of him. "That, my darling, will be next week's dinner topic. And brace yourself for another surprise."

Chapter 30

ON most Monday mornings the offices of Thompson, Caldwell came to life shortly after eight, when the ambitious associates trickled in and immediately began to work on the projects they had left late Friday night. Soon thereafter, secretaries arrived and headed straight for the cafeteria for the breakfasts they never found time to make at home.

At least that's the way it went most of the year. In summer, business life was different. The executives, brokers, secretaries, and clerks who had fled the oppressive city heat stretched the weekend to Monday morning, and considered that arrival at their desks by midmorning was a feat deserving of high praise, given the state of public transportation in New York. John Haddad had also been away for the weekend, in Washington with Charlotte, but he had returned to New York Sunday night. When he arrived at the office early the next morning, he found himself alone in his corner of the floor. He looked for Lee Curtis and Dave Hill, but neither of them had yet appeared.

John picked up his copy of the *Wall Street Journal* and scanned the "In Brief" column for the major stories. He found it hard to concentrate on what he was reading. Grayson would arrive in about a half hour, and John planned to phone him as soon as he came in, and ask for a meeting.

Bright sunlight streamed through the window, illuminating the room. John noticed that the arms of the sofa were worn. *I guess that won't be a problem anymore,* he thought. Somebody else may have this office. He turned his thoughts to his upcoming meeting with Grayson. Had he truly anticipated everything? He went over it again. No problem. Could Grayson spring some trick or maneuver that he didn't expect? Not likely. Would Grayson be surprised? Would he ever! John opened his attaché case and checked for the one document he might need that day. It was there.

Lee Curtis poked his head in the door. "Hey, you're in early. Stay in town this weekend?"

"No. Got back last night. Say, Lee . . ."

Dave Hill appeared, briefcase in hand. "Jesus, you guys in already? Got another takeover deal, John?"

"You never know. Listen, I'd like you two to be around

and available this morning. I'm going to talk to Grayson. I'll want to see you right after."

"Sure," Dave said, "but, John, don't blow up at Grayson and get yourself fired. We want this team to stay intact."

"Oh, we'll be together, I promise you that," John said, making it sound like a mock threat, "and there'll be plenty of times when we can run our asses ragged doing deals." John picked up the telephone and dialed Elliott Grayson's number. After John had insisted that it was urgent, Grayson agreed to see him right away. He gave a short wave to Hill and Curtis and went off to the meeting.

Grayson greeted John in his usual curt manner, the kind of greeting designed to put you ill at ease. This was an early warning that you were not particularly welcome and the sooner you left the better. John had never grown accustomed to being insulted by Grayson, as so many other Thompson, Caldwell executives had. Now he didn't care. This would probably be the last time. Grayson never liked John, not only because John wasn't a member of the Establishment but also because Elliott Grayson despised executives who did not keep to their places—and their places called for blind loyalty. If you didn't "belong," then not the slightest variation from dictated rules would be tolerated. John Haddad not only didn't belong, but refused to conform and kowtow to the haughty attitudes and arrogant whims of his superiors.

When John walked into Elliott Grayson's office, he was not offered a chair and he did not take one. Instead, he remained standing in front of the chairman's desk.

"What is it, John?" Grayson said, barely looking up from the newspaper on his desk.

"I've made up my mind about the GM board, Mr. Grayson." There was no emotion in John's voice. His tone was straightforward and businesslike. A normal business discussion.

"Fine." Grayson smiled. His sense told him that he had won. Haddad would capitulate.

247

"I thought about everything you said," John continued, "and I can see how you might feel the way you do."

"I'm not surprised, John. I always knew you were a bright fellow. I mean, that's all we have here, nothing but bright fellows!" Grayson laughed, loud laughter mixed with relief.

John allowed a half smile, which quickly vanished as he continued to speak. "Then I reexamined my own feelings and compared the two. You, Mr.Grayson, want someone else on the GM board because you say I'm too junior." John's tone remained cool and unemotional.

Grayson's joviality disappeared and was quickly replaced by doubts. He started to say something but stopped himself, allowing John to speak.

"Yes, I could understand your concern about my lack of seniority. But had it not been for me, no one in this firm would have that seat."

"We've been through all that."

"Yes, of course. Forgive me. I'll come to the point. Since I feel very strongly that I deserve the GM board seat, and you feel it should go to someone more senior, I want to suggest one way to solve the problem."

"What do you mean?"

"All you have to do, sir, is promote me to a senior enough position in the firm, and let me serve on the GM board. Then the problem of seniority will be resolved."

So that was it, Grayson thought. The impudent little bastard was not giving in. Hardly. He wanted a big promotion! Did he really believe that he could be promoted to a senior executive partner just like that? The board of managing directors of Thompson, Caldwell wouldn't hear of it. At least not from Elliott Grayson.

"That is completely out of the question," Grayson snapped. "You disappoint me, Haddad. For a while, I really thought you had come to your senses. You just let all of this go to your swelled head."

248

John had always been adept at concealing his emotions when he had to, but this time the disappointment showed clearly on his face. Was his proposal really out of line? Was he reaching too far? No, damn it. His demands were reasonable and fair, and if Grayson would not accept them, John would not compromise.

"I've made up my mind, Mr. Grayson. I have nothing further to add."

"You're putting me in a difficult position. I'm sure you realize that."

"It doesn't change anything."

Grayson straightened in his chair and folded his arms. He looked at John with stern, cold eyes. "Since you refuse to cooperate, I can see no alternative but to ask for your resignation."

John turned to walk away, then looked back toward Grayson. "I should have known you wouldn't understand. Well, you'll have to live with your decision."

"Don't you worry about my decisions—and keep in mind that you'll need recommendations to get another job, so I'm warning you to be very careful about what you do and say from now on. *Very careful.*" Grayson picked up a letter on his desk and read it silently. He had nothing further to say to his former employee, John Haddad.

John left the office quietly.

Sue Anderson pressed the flashing button on the call director. "I'm sorry, Mr. Haddad is away from his desk . . . Yes, I'll tell him. Thank you." She filled out another call report, the fifth one this morning. Not that she minded the activity—that's the way it had been since the takeover began. But events had taken an unexpected and awkward turn recently, and Sue Anderson knew that her boss was in trouble. She found it hard to understand. John Haddad had negotiated the largest financial deal on record, and somehow, instead of being promoted, he might be fired. At least that's what the rumor mill was grinding out.

Of course, if he had been a son of a bitch, like some of the others Sue had worked for, she might have understood. But John Haddad wasn't like the others. Not at all, in fact.

"Any news from John?" Dave Hill tapped Sue on the shoulder and she jumped.

"God, you startled me! No . . . he isn't down yet. Lee is waiting in the office."

"OK, I'll join him in there."

When John Haddad finally arrived, he went up to Sue and greeted her cheerfully. "Hi! Any messages?"

"Oh, yes. I'm glad you're back. I mean . . ."

"I was only gone a few minutes, Sue!" John smiled, picked up the messages and went into his office where his two serious-faced colleagues were waiting.

"Jesus, this has been like waiting in the maternity ward." Dave stood up to greet his boss.

"One of you guys having a baby?" John was teasing them, and they knew it.

"Well, I can see from your mood that it went OK upstairs. Whew!" Lee fell back on the chair, exaggerating his sense of relief.

"You mean with Grayson? No, it didn't go too well. He fired me."

"He *what?*"

"The son of a bitch."

John raised an arm. "Hold it, fellas. It's not the end of the world."

"God damn it, John." Dave shouted, and Sue discreetly closed the door to the office, remaining outside. "You can't let him do that. Christ, I feel like going up there and—"

"Hold it. Listen, I appreciate what you both are saying, but I've already thought this through."

Lee Curtis had also thought about this moment, so the words came easily. "If you're going to another firm, John, I'd like to go too."

"I appreciate that, Lee. More than I can tell you."

250

Dave looked over and John read clearly in his eyes that Dave would also be prepared to quit if John wanted him to. "You don't seem at all upset. Have you got something else lined up? For all three of us, I hope!" Unanimous laughter.

"Yeah, I got something lined up, and it does involve the three of us. For starters how would you guys like to be partners in a leading firm?"

It was the kind of question that needs no answer. All professional people in investment banking strive for a partnership or directorship level. Promotions take time, though, and not everyone makes it. Besides, partners in their early thirties are rare indeed. No, the question needed no answer, so John kept talking.

"I offered Grayson a fair deal. He turned it down. The hell with him."

"So we're going to another firm, right?"

John ran his hands through his hair, as if to massage an overworked brain. He looked up and smiled at Dave. "Would you hand me that manila folder?" He pointed to the desk.

As he looked in the folder, John asked Lee to press the symbol THC on the quotation machine. John could clearly see from across the room that it read "last sale 13¼." He wrote something on the paper in the manila folder.

Dave looked at Lee, who returned his puzzled stare.

"What firm are we going to?" Dave asked.

"You'll never guess."

Lee suddenly jumped to his feet, looking at John while at the same time pointing at the quotation machine. He tried to speak, but at first the words seemed to get in the way of each other. "THC is the symbol of Thompson, Caldwell!"

John nodded.

Dave slapped his forehead. "Oh, God! Is what I'm thinking true?"

John nodded again and smiled. Then he opened the manila folder and handed the single sheet of paper to Lee.

"Would you mind taking this up to Grayson, Lee? He ought to be the first to know."

Dave jumped up to have a look at the paper whose contents he had already guessed. It read:

NOTICE OF OFFER TO
PURCHASE
ALL OF THE OUTSTANDING
COMMON STOCK
OF
THOMPSON, CALDWELL AND
CO., INC.
FOR CASH AT
$20 NET PER SHARE
BY
JOHN HADDAD
137 EAST 67TH STREET
NEW YORK, N.Y. 10021

Epilogue

CAPTAIN Bjorn Johanssen sat in his chair on the bridge of the Norwegian freighter *Femund,* squinting out at the waters of the Persian Gulf. The long and slow trip, all the way from the east coast of the United States, had kept them at sea since August. He had just changed the heading of the ship from directly west to a more northerly course, planning to pass about five miles off the coast of Qatar before turning north to the Iranian port of Bushire. The captain had ordered full speed ahead in spite of the early morning December fog. He was running late. The enormous weight of the shipment of forty of the new General Motors M-90 tanks, consigned to the Iranian Army even before the Saudi takeover attempt of General Motors, had slowed his ship from her normal cruising speed of seventeen knots down to a maximum of twelve. He would be glad when he got rid of this unwieldy cargo, and he was more than a little nervous about the possibility of being stopped on the way by the Saudi Navy's fast torpedo boats for an inspection.

In the communication room behind him Johanssen heard the radio operator's chair scrape against the deck as the man pulled himself closer to his table and began to write, his brow furrowed with concentration on the sounds coming through his earphones.

The radio operator came forward and placed the message before the captain without comment. It read: "DIVERT FE-MUND CARGO TO DHAHRAN, SAUDI ARABIA . . . REPEAT DHAHRAN, SAUDI ARABIA. DO NOT DELIVER TO BUSHIRE, IRAN. CARGO NOW PROPERTY OF SAUDI ARMY."

At the same time a teletype message was being received by the Iranian Armored Command in Teheran: "REGRET DELAY OF DELIVERY OF ORDER NUMBER 79404 DUE TO DAMAGED PRODUCTION LINE AND LATE RECEIPT OF KEY ELECTRONIC COMPONENTS. WILL ADVISE NEW ESTIMATED TIME OF ARRIVAL." It was signed by the vice-president of export sales, General Motors, Detroit.

The captain, incredulous at this last-minute diversion, called in the radio man and made him get confirmation of the instructions. The confirmation came from the Norwe-gian Line's home office within a few seconds. Johanssen shrugged his shoulders, looked at the burly seaman man-ning the wheel, and gave the order "Hard aport!"

As the bow turned slowly in toward land in the direction of Saudi Arabia, Johanssen saw two plumes of white racing across the water toward him. The Saudi Arabian Navy was taking no chances, and had sent him an escort.

Colonel Mohammed Faleh stood on the concrete pier next to the wide berth prepared to receive the *Femund*. Lined up behind him, standing at ease, forty tank crews were ranged alongside their duffel bags. They had not had a chance to unpack them because the plane returning them from six weeks of training on M-90's in Detroit had landed only half an hour before.

The ship pulled in and was made fast, and within an hour the first of the enormous battle tanks clanked slowly down the ramp from the hold and crunched onto the concrete. When all had been unloaded, a squad of painters swarmed over them, obliterating in minutes all the Iranian insignia that had been painted on in Detroit. With the fresh green and white of Saudi Arabia still glistening wet on turrets and side armor, the tanks formed up into a column and roared off to the coastal road that would take them north to renew the battle for Al Jubayl.